A RAIN OF DEATH

"What the hell happened to McCall?" asked Paul, smoothing his perfectly silver hair with one hand.

"Sudden death," Morris said.

"From what?"

"Good question."

"Did anybody ever die of a crappy disposition?"

"No. He would have been dead years ago," said Morris.

Taking it on himself, Morris motioned to the security guard and said to him quietly, so as not to cause further panic, that he should close down the bar and secure all the bottles and glasses—touching things as little as possible.

"Are you sayin' somethin' in his drink did this to him?"

"I don't know," Morris said. "But it's possible . . . they'll want to question everybody who was in the bloody room . . . that is, if we're right about how he died. Who can remember who was there? It was chaotic with people. There must have been a hundred of us. But a room hasn't been built large enough to hold everybody who despised Andrew McCall. I wonder who was desperate enough to kill him?"

Morris and Sullivan Mysteries by John Logue

Follow the Leader

Murder on the Links

The Feathery Touch of Death

A Rain of Death

A RAIN OF DEATH

John Logue

A Dell Book

Published by
Dell Publishing
a division of
Bantam Doubleday Dell Publishing Group, Inc.
1540 Broadway
New York, New York 10036

ISBN: 0-440-22397-0

Printed in the United States of America

Published simultaneously in Canada

March 1998

10 9 8 7 6 5 4 3 2 1

WCD

To Ed Miles, Furman Bisher, Jim Minter, Greg Favre, Gene Asher, Bob Christian, Terry Kay, Bill Robinson, Lee Walburn, Jerry Chatham, Kim Chapin, Tom McCollister, Steve Clark, Jack Doane, and the old days of writing sports on the *Atlanta Journal*.

CHAPTER ONE

The wind blew against the rain, but the rain was not impressed. Green, golden mountains rolled down into the Pacific Ocean, hidden far below in silence and in fog.

Julia Sullivan sat at the wheel of the rental Ford until John Morris was entirely awake.

"As near as I can get you to heaven, Morris, unless you change your idle ways."

Morris rubbed his eyes with his big fists. "Why don't you preach to the sun? He hasn't shown up here since the Spaniards packed it in."

The sun, insulted by wind and word, struck through the deep clouds, igniting the mountainside, and setting the fog afire, the entire Pacific coast seemingly consumed in flames. The sun retreated in a moment as if content with its display of unearthly powers. Rain again crashed down on the windshield, a double warning for those who would blaspheme nature in its finest hour.

Morris, properly chastised, took a deep breath to taste as well as see the mountains tumbling into the fog and sea, then admitted, "Lord, it's beautiful."

"Welcome to Big Sur," Sullivan said. "Do you think God has kept it here just for us?"

"Of course," Morris said. "He couldn't leave it with the Native Americans, they never had a chance; the Spaniards were foolish enough to pull out in 1822; the Mexicans were bullied into a fire sale in '48. That leaves us, Sullivan, you and me, to keep coming back as long as we live. Of course, God Himself avoids the Monterey Peninsula in January. If the singing and the drinking won't kill you at The Crosby, holes eight, nine, and ten will bury you alive at Pebble Beach."

"I'm glad to have all history of the Northern California coast set straight," Sullivan said, "but you haven't mentioned the actual word *golf*."

"Hush," Morris said. "The gods don't forgive true crimes against nature."

"Speaking of crimes against nature, should we stop in and say hello to your old one-night drinking buddy Henry Miller? He lives on this side of the mountain."

"Ohmygod, no!" Morris said. "He'd have us up all night listening to excerpts from *Big Sur and the Oranges of Hieronymus Bosch*. We've got to save our livers for The Crosby. The world of golf is depending on the worthy Associated Press."

"The *worthy* AP, all *accuracy* and *dependability*," Sullivan said, "as at the U.S. Open three years ago, when you signed your overnight sidebar from Oakmont, when the tournament was being played at Merion."

"It could happen to anybody," Morris said. "Even New York had to admit both clubs are in Pennsylvania. And I got the correct spelling of Lee's wife's name in the tattoo on his arm, and nobody knew Mexican beans about Trevino before he beat Jack in the bloody tournament."

"You did, indeed." Sullivan leaned over and kissed him on the lips, her soft brown hair falling around his solid face.

"You'd better crank this Ford," Morris said. "We are liable to get in trouble here on Highway One. I don't want to be a steamy chapter in Henry's next novel."

Sullivan's slim hand lingered over the car key while a thoughtful look passed into her blue eyes. Then she turned the key and cranked the car. "Better not tarry. We've got to make all our faithful stops on the peninsula before we get down to serious partying . . . not to mention casual golf among the boy players."

"About as casual," said Morris, "as the great white sharks feeding on the sea lions off Monterey Bay."

The landscape of Big Sur continued to fall away below them as if in an arrested earthquake. The fog began to thin, and they could see the Pacific Ocean detonating against huge, dark rocks like ruined castles.

Sullivan always drove while Morris stretched out his bad left leg, his perfect excuse to nap as a passenger. His knee had been shattered in the car wreck that killed Monty Sullivan the same year he won The Crosby. Monty, twenty years older than Julia, had been her pal and husband and John Morris's best drinking, singing

buddy. Before either of them met him, Monty had retired the title as the life of the PGA tour in its formative
years. Morris and Sullivan missed Monty equally but
had taken the pledge against all guilt while enjoying
each other's company, though several unspoken words
short of marriage. That Monty had also left Sullivan
downtown Denver gave her the freedom to meet Morris anywhere in the world his duties took him as the
AP's golf writer.

"One more year, and I'm hanging it up while I'm
still a young man, able to pee standing alone," Morris
was wont to say. Sullivan would raise her trim brows
and volunteer to prop him up in an emergency.

She slowed the Ford, looking for the turnoff to Point
Lobos State Reserve, which they always stopped to visit
before driving into Carmel. They passed among Monterey cypresses, which grew nowhere else in the world
and held to the sheer rock cliffs with the will of the
human race on the edge of extinction.

Morris unfolded his considerable bulk from the car,
propping himself erect with his cane, which in another
life had been Monty Sullivan's two-iron. They followed
the rocky trail into the seventeen-hundred-acre reserve,
one-half of which was perpetually under water. Morris
didn't bother to loop his binoculars strap over his head
as Julia Sullivan would be stealing it at the sight of the
first swimming sea otter. It didn't take but a minute for
one of the furry comedians to pop to the surface of the
sheltered waters off China Point, where the Pacific
Ocean exhausted itself after its long pull from the Ori-
ent. The point had got its name from the Chinese im-
migrants who had been smuggled ashore here after the

infamous Chinese Exclusion Act of 1882. Sullivan lifted his binoculars as if they were her birthright, all the while talking to the twitchy otter as though it were a California cousin.

"Look, Morris!" She handed the binoculars back to him. "Look what he's carrying on his stomach!"

Adjusting the glasses, Morris could not keep from grinning. The otter swam on its back as if the ocean were its private aquarium. It carried a dark rock on his furry belly which it was using to crack the shell of a mollusk. "A floating gourmet," Morris said, "no doubt paddling toward a vintage California Chablis."

Sullivan took back the glasses and followed a flight of cormorants headed for Bird Island off Point Lobos, where they nested by the thousands.

Had he been leaning on his cane a hundred years earlier, Morris might have been the prototype for the one-legged Long John Silver. Robert Louis Stevenson loved to hike this same path in the 1870s when courting the fair divorcée Fanny Osbourne, and very likely this isolated shore influenced his great yarn *Treasure Island*.

Morris picked his way among the rocks, following the excitable Sullivan, as Stevenson must have lusted after Fanny until he married her and lived happily ever after, but that was not a thought that bore expressing.

"What are you smiling at, John Morris?" Sullivan had stopped and was looking at him over the binoculars.

"Robert Louis Stevenson," he said.

"Now there was a writer . . . who found his true love on this peninsula." Sullivan kept looking at him as if he might well learn something from the silent rocks under his feet.

"Behind you!" Morris was pleased to alert her.

She turned to fasten her binoculars on a beautiful speckled harbor seal that lifted itself out of the chill water onto a large, flat rock to take the reluctant sun, which was nowhere to be seen.

"Good boy," Sullivan said.

"It might be a girl," said Morris.

"Entirely too handsome to be anything but a boy. All he needs is a golf club and a sunburn, and they could enter him in The Crosby."

"Oh, no," Morris said, "he would need a hangover. Which reminds me, this much nature always puts me in need of a drink."

"Done," Sullivan said, handing him his binoculars and looking once more at the tide creeping in among the aged rocks as if she had known the place since the first stroke of time.

Morris expected to hear a local mountain lion scream, probably for a drink.

Sullivan slowed before Highway 1 intersected with Carmel Valley Road, which led to the Long Valley of John Steinbeck, past wineries and cattle farms and horse farms and the new agricultural harvest: resort golf, but that was a drive for another day. She turned west toward Mission San Carlos Borromeo del Rio Carmelo, founded in 1770. It was restored to its glory in 1936 and today is known as plain Mission Carmel. Just beyond the brown dome of the mission were the Carmel River and Carmel Bay shining in the suddenly bright sunlight. Carmel was not a small city; it was a picture postcard hidden in the cypress trees. No loud neon, no fisherman's wharf, no roller coaster, no bumper cars, no live music and alcohol under the same roof. In the original one square mile of Carmel, none of the houses were permitted street numbers. "If you don't know where you're going, you probably don't belong here" seemed to have been the philosophy of James Devendorf and Frank Powers, who at the turn of the century bought the property and laid out the city that was now Carmel. In the midst of all that tranquillity, the literary set—the Sinclair boys, Lewis and Upton, Mary Hunter Austin, George Sterling, the poet Robinson Jeffers, who visited and stayed for life, not to forget Jack London—came down from San Francisco to make the place famous, or infamous if you were keeping score at the beach parties thrown by London, who only had to search his social experience to come up with his gutsy title *The Call of the Wild*. Jack would have been a welcome celebrity at The Crosby Clambake, thought Morris.

Sullivan eased the Ford through the narrow residential streets, past English cottages, even a stone cottage with a true thatched roof, tiny Old World houses where Hansel might have been searching for Gretel, Mediterranean villas, houses with roofs that rolled like waves over mysterious dormer windows, all tucked into the trees and all with tidy gardens blooming even in January. There seemed to have been a contest of architects to set down no two houses alike in the entire little postcard city.

Sullivan wound around until she stopped in front of a small frame cottage with a brown shingle roof and a garden chaotic with winter flowers. Morris tapped on his side window with his cane in salute to the moment in this house in 1929, when photographer-journalist

Jack Calvin introduced John Steinbeck to marine biologist Edward F. Ricketts, resulting in some of the amusing moments in American literature. A pity the critics never forgave Steinbeck—who'd won all the prizes for *The Grapes of Wrath*, a dark song of the Great Depression in Oklahoma and California—for writing such falling-over-funny books as *Cannery Row* and *Sweet Thursday*, with Ricketts as the immortal character Doc.

"Remember what Steinbeck said about the critics?" asked Morris. He did not have to explain that Steinbeck said it having won the Nobel Prize in literature late in life while out of favor with the American literary tastemakers. "He said, 'The critics always know what to take out, but they never know what to put in.'"

"We'll drink to that on Ocean Drive," Sullivan said, and turned the Ford in that direction. She made the swing around Carmel Point to Carmel Beach curving away to the north. Downtown Carmel was a lively sea of shoppers, drifting from art gallery to antiques shop to tony clothing emporium to a movable feast of eclectic restaurants. Most of the major languages of the world could be overheard on Ocean Drive on a tourist-flooded weekend. Sullivan lucked into a parking spot by a small inn where they always had a drink and a sandwich and watched the bay weep on the shore.

"To the critics," Morris said, raising his scotch, "may they live in anonymity."

"And to Mr. Steinbeck and to Doc," Sullivan said.

Suddenly a blast of rain and sleet blew against the large windowpane in front of their table as if the dead critics were having the last word.

"Forget the golf, I think I'll join Crosby in the hospital," Morris said. The tournament's namesake was suffering a dangerous lung infection and was likely to miss the entire Clambake.

Sullivan kept an eye open for any Crosby regulars, but even Clint Eastwood, who lived here, would have had to be on his horse for her to recognize him in the rainstorm.

True to their tradition of exploring the entire peninsula before going to ground at Pebble Beach, Sullivan cranked the Ford and headed north for the old industrial town of Monterey, which had been sacked in 1818 by the villainous pirate Hippolyte de Bouchard. His raid probably wasn't as big a hit against the peninsula as the modern-day California income tax.

Monterey's honky-tonk rowdies, its cheap bars, its whorehouses, its shantytowns of poor workers in the now-extinct sardine factories on Cannery Row were gone, all gone with the sardines, which had mysteriously disappeared from these waters in the 1950s. But the old town center of Monterey was intact, including some forty adobe buildings constructed in the nineteenth century of local clay. The Monterey Custom House, built in 1827, stood as the oldest public building in California. Colton Hall, built of local stone, hosted forty-eight delegates who wrote the California Constitution in 1849. Farmers and ranchers still came to Monterey to sell their harvest and finance next year's struggle. Fishing boats worked the Pacific from the Monterey port, site of the Naval Post-Graduate School. Sullivan wound their way down to the water, and stopped at the unpainted frame building where Edward Ricketts—Doc—operated his Pacific Biological Laboratories until a train on the Southern Pacific line hit his car and killed him in 1948, taking much of the joy out of the life and work of Steinbeck. Only a couple of abandoned relics of the old cannery factories teetered on frail wooden pilings at the edge of the bay, unmissable targets for amateur photographers and dilapidated way stations for weary seagulls. Seals and otters swam in the once again clean Monterey Bay as if time had never passed.

Sullivan swung the Ford back south into Pacific Grove, home of the younger workers of the peninsula—waiters, bartenders, greenskeepers—as well as a number of elegant Victorian cottages and inns, including the Gosby House, which had boarded travelers since 1887. Obviously missing in Pacific Grove was the grove itself. The trees gave way to God, beginning about 1875, when a serious Christian sect began holding religious retreats and cutting down the trees to pitch their tents. At Pacific Grove there was no drinking, no smoking, no dancing, no staying up late at night, no loud singing, and very soon no cypress trees. God help a man caught cardplaying.

"Morris, I don't think you would have been voted citizen of the year in the original Pacific Grove," said Sullivan.

Morris tapped the floorboard with the tip of his cane and pointed a hefty finger toward Pebble Beach.

Sullivan wheeled the Ford south, paid the three-dollar toll, and took the inland leg of the seventeen-mile drive through the Del Monte Forest. Old, barely seen mansions loomed in the pine and cypress forest deep with shadows and silent with money.

Samuel Finley Brown Morse—named after his great-uncle Samuel Finley Breese Morse (of Morse code fame)—put the ball on the tee at Pebble Beach in 1916, when it was a log cabin outpost of the once-famed Del Monte Hotel in Monterey. Morse had been hired to revitalize the old aristocratic hotel and its properties. He eased the Victorian manners at the Del Monte Hotel with a new tolerance for collarless whiskey drinking and soon became intrigued by the hotel's virgin property at Pebble Beach.

Morse inherited a set of typical development plans for the beach that would have cut down the forest and obscured the oceanfront with multiple rows of cottages. The idea appalled him. At his disposal were an untouched forest and the world's greatest ocean. What he needed to draw a crowd of swells was a four-letter word, *golf.* The first decision he made was a remarkable one: He left the greatest oceanfront property along the twisting cliffs of Carmel Bay for the golf course.

Morse commissioned two young California amateur golf champions, Jack Neville and Douglas Grant, to design the course. What the two amateurs came up with was merely Pebble Beach Golf Links, still arguably the greatest golf course in America and the only public course ever to hold the U.S. Open Championship, as it has done several times, not to mention the U.S. Amateur and in later years the PGA Championship.

Morse liked it so well that when Pebble Beach opened in 1919, he borrowed the money and bought it for $1.3 million, including seven thousand acres of forest bounded by *seven miles* of Pacific oceanfront. Now he needed willing victims to build their eighteen hundred hidden mansions. And what do the very rich love more dearly than their own money? Hanging with the famous, even notorious figures of their own time. California had plenty of the famous and the notorious in Hollywood. Morse, now the Duke of Del Monte, courted the silent movie stars until Douglas Fairbanks and the It Girl were as common to the grounds as the bent grass on the greens. Before a visiting robber baron knew it, dazzled by the company he was keeping, he found himself with a thirty-thousand-dollar lot bought from S.F.B. Morse and building a five-hundred-thousand-dollar house in the Del Monte Forest.

"Mighty quiet," Sullivan said. "Saving your voice to harmonize with Crosby if they spring him from the hospital?"

"With Phil Harris carrying the melody, so long as it's naughty enough," Morris said. Something gave him a turn, maybe the word *hospital*. "How old is Crosby?"

"Seventy?"

"Couldn't be," Morris said. "Somebody stop the years. We have to squeeze all we can out of every Clambake."

A number of amateurs had long taken on this intent as a life's challenge, to squeeze every joyful moment out of the night and the day at The Crosby. For them, the parties, the songs, the big Calcutta gambling auction, the foolishness never stopped, even under the television cameras. For the golf pros, all foolishness came to a screeching halt at the first tee of the three greatest golf courses on one peninsula: Pebble Beach, Cypress Point, and Spyglass Hill. Dr. Alister MacKenzie, who with Bobby Jones designed Augusta National, also designed Cypress Point, and it leaves no nerve untested. Robert Trent Jones designed Spyglass Hill to be his masterpiece, and so it is and of fiendish difficulty.

Morris had seen the best players of the age risk health and reputation against the ever-changing, sometimes unspeakable weather and the brute cruelty of the cliffs over the Pacific. Champions of The Crosby read like the inner circle of golf's greatest players: Mangrum, Hogan, Burke, Nelson, Demaret, Middlecoff, Casper, Venturi, Lema, Nicklaus (three times a winner and defending champion), Miller, Littler. Snead also won three times before The Crosby was moved, after 1942, from Rancho Santa Fe near San Diego. Palmer tried for a quarter of a century to win at Pebble Beach, finishing second twice, once by a bare stroke, one of the few major tournaments he never dominated.

Sullivan said into the silence: "Speaking of this year, do we stay up with the social athletes, or do we get up with the golfers?"

"What kind of question is that? We're only thirty-two, Sullivan. Granted that makes *sixty-four* if you count the days and the nights, and that's what we will do—count the days and the nights—and how can you count them, old girl, if you don't stay up to see them?"

"*Thirty-one!*" Sullivan said, pointing to her youthful bosom. "You were alive a full month before me, John Morris. I was a child bride, remember?"

"I can't remember a thing. Except that was Monty Sullivan you married. The whole wedding weekend is lost to recorded time."

"Yeah," she said, smiling, turning north along Pebble Beach Golf Links, which fell directly into the Pacific Ocean. Trunks of Monterey cypress writhed out of the earth as in a Japanese lithograph, framing the wild cliffs above the sea.

"There is no other satisfactory place on this planet to be in this first week of January in the year of Our Lord, 1974," Morris said as the fairways slid past their windows as green as a Disney fantasy.

The sun teased through the clouds, but a thin sleet began collecting on the windshield. There was no other weather to be had in one day on the peninsula, saving a deep snow, and it would not have been the first one.

"Oh, God," Sullivan said, reaching out the window to touch the sleet. "The AP will find Julia Sullivan in the hospitality suite."

"The hell you say. I have to have my beater out on the links, to stir up the animal golfers, as in *Out of Africa.*" Morris winced to think that he couldn't immediately join her in the shower or the bar or the bed. He would have to run down Nicklaus and Crosby's brother Larry, who was running the show in Bing's absence the same as he did in Bing's presence, and whatever other random victims he could find to quote in his write-through for Monday's papers. That was the AP's new hot term, *write-through.* It meant sending better stuff later than the shit you sent earlier. You hoped.

They overtook twin white horses pulling an old black carriage to the Del Monte Lodge up ahead.

"Newlyweds. Poor babies," Sullivan said, trying to catch sight of the pair in the carriage.

"Impossible. Nobody gets married here the week of

The Crosby," Morris said. "They are all lucky . . . those who don't get divorced."

The Del Monte Lodge sprawled in its separate, low-slung buildings behind No. 18 green on the most scenic and most famous finishing hole in golf. Sullivan tooted the horn at their second-story room at the south end of the lodge. As was their habit, she did not stop but drove on north around Pescadero Point to Cypress Point, where she turned back at the famous lone cypress tree, which seemed to hold together with its ageless roots the great granite cliff over the Pacific.

The Ford was pleased with itself, stopping now in front of the Del Monte Lodge among the Mercedeses and random Rolls-Royces.

" 'American poets, learn your trade,' and get your asses to your typewriters," Sullivan said, crossing herself to appease Mr. T. S. Eliot. "I'm for a shower and a drink and a nap."

"God is a woman. There's no denying it," Morris said, "leaving us chaps to get the sun into bed."

Just as he opened his car door, the wind rushed in off the ocean, blowing rainwater like a riptide over the Ford and against the white sides of the lodge, offering a loud, drenching, ominous beginning to the new week.

CHAPTER TWO

Nicklaus did not love the idea of being on the Monterey Peninsula on New Year's Day 1974. It was not the weather. It was not any of the *five weathers* they'd had that Tuesday. It was his kids. They were still out of school for the holidays, and he wanted to be home with them.

"Jack," Morris said, "give me ten minutes, and I'll raise the ticket to fly you to Florida. The rest of the field would be willing to fly you to the Outer Hebrides."

Jack was not amused. He could stare down a writer more intensely than he could stare down a six-foot side-hill putt. Morris was not intimidated.

Nicklaus admitted he itched to win The Crosby for the third consecutive year. Morris wrote, "God help the golfer who ties him. He's won the last two Crosbys on the first hole of sudden death play-offs." Jack loved playing Pebble Beach, where he'd also won the U.S. Open and U.S. Amateur, and he admired Cypress Point. He winced when he said the words *Spyglass Hill*. Crosby, the year he added Spyglass to the three-course competition, bet Jack five hundred dollars he couldn't match par on the course in his first practice round. Nicklaus, of course, ripped out a 2 under 70 and gave Bing's money to charity. Nicklaus wouldn't say it, but he'd also have liked to give Spyglass Hill to charity. Jack insisted he "had not played a round of golf in a month." He confessed he'd hit his share of practice balls. But home was where he wanted to be.

Palmer and Trevino were taking the week off. But there would be plenty of competition from Weiskopf and Crampton, runners-up to Nicklaus himself in money won on last year's PGA tour, as well as from the likes of Johnny Miller, Tom Watson, Billy Casper, Gene Littler, and friends.

The television world of course was delirious to see the Hollywood stars make happy fools of themselves in the Pro-Am competition. Morris, in his write-through, recalled Jack Lemmon's famous adventures across the peninsula in pursuit of his elusive golf ball, once causing TV commentator Jim McKay to remark, "And now here is Jack Lemmon, about to hit that all-important eighth shot." One Lemmon chip shot rolled up the hill and back down between his legs to the glee of the television audience. At least the ball was not alive. A couple of years earlier Lemmon, whose own trophies run to Academy Awards, stood on the 15th hole at Pebble Beach. This time a stray dog burst between his legs while he stood paralyzed, addressing the ball on the tee. Lemmon never looked up, finally poking a wobbly drive down the fairway. Crosby later praised him for not losing his cool when the dog ran under him. Lemmon, still in a state of arrested shock, said, "Was that a real dog?"

Morris handed over his copy to the tall, thin teletype operator who would feed it on to the Associated Press wire through the San Francisco office. "Such as it is," said Morris, shaking his head at his own composition.

Walking into the lobby of the Del Monte Lodge, he ran into the old song and dance man Ray Bolger. "Have you seen Sullivan?" Morris asked.

Bolger, himself stone sober, let his legs wobble like the Straw Man from the *Wizard of Oz*. "You better save her. She's in the Snake Pit, listening to dubious lyrics sung by Phil Harris and Jackie Melton."

"Of course," Morris said. So much for Julia Sullivan and her "nap time."

The Snake Pit was the inner sanctum of excess as practiced by the serious party hounds of The Crosby. Lights never went out in the suite in the annex of the Del Monte Lodge. A real estate developer, who owned a great quantity of Palm Springs, had set the party standards exceedingly high in the Snake Pit before succumbing to a much-needed eternal rest. Hotshot amateurs from all around California continued to keep the fireplace burning twenty-four hours a day in the suite where the bar never closed, even for tee times.

Morris stood at the door. Sullivan was sitting on the piano bench with Jackie Melton, who was playing a furious accompaniment to Phil Harris. With the noise level in the room, it was impossible to know if everyone was

applauding or if maybe there had been a tidal wave of
laughter that rolled in from the Pacific Ocean. Phil
Harris, always bigger than you imagined and with the
iron hair and broad cheeks reminiscent of an American
Indian, a glass of Jack Daniel's forever in his hand, was
leaning over and kissing Julia Sullivan on the mouth
with entirely too much concentration to suit John Morris.

Jackie Melton sat back, his hands in his small lap, a
short, plump version of his younger self, though his hair
yet spilled in blond waves of artificial youth above his
round blue eyes and pudge of a nose and pouting mouth
of an eternal cherub. Hard to realize he was two years
older than Crosby. Now Melton's small hands eased
among the piano keys, leading into an old ballad the
world had forgotten he had helped make famous. His
clear tenor voice might have sprung four decades before
from an Atwater Kent radio, the notes as youthful as his
dyed blond locks: " '. . . Just one of those things . . .
just one of those fabulous flings.' " The golden era of
Hollywood before World War II seemed to hang trembling over the piano. And then the room was again
awash in the sounds of a favored people in search of
pleasure.

Morris had once sat up until the wee hours of the
morning with Jackie, who told him without apparent
bitterness how in 1931 his own promising radio show
had given way to young Bing Crosby, who lit up the
wireless for CBS and Cremo cigars. Only baritones
Rudy Vallee and Russ Columbo could survive the
broadcast heat from Crosby, and then Columbo was

killed tragically in a handgun accident. Melton's radio
career had simply died of neglect.

Morris also knew that Melton had beaten Crosby
and Bob Hope both to Hollywood and into major motion pictures, but with the same result. Melton played
the funny, tag-along friend of the romantic lead in three
successful but forgettable musicals. He sang in all of
them and sang very well and was signed to a major contract by Paramount. After Crosby and Hope hit Hollywood and Paramount like a two-man earthquake,
Melton's star quickly dimmed. Hope loved the guy and
always found a part for Jackie in the *Road* movies with
Crosby. Crosby didn't mind who was in the movies so
long as he could get in a round of golf at Lakeside
before shooting started.

Melton gradually became an obscure personality,
making occasional guest appearances on someone else's
radio or television show. Not that he was ever down and
out. Melton never lost his surprising popularity in Europe, and at home he made shrewd real estate invest-
ments in Southern California and was damn near as rich
as Crosby and Hope. Melton was also a songwriter of
note. Of course the best song he ever wrote was made
famous by—who else?—Crosby.

Crosby loved to golf more than he loved to sing or
make movies, and Melton was a four-handicap golfer
and fellow member at the Lakeside Club in L.A. Jackie
had once been golf champion of the movie star–studded
club and would have won it several more times except
for Crosby, a two-handicapper in his youth, who won
the Lakeside title five times and once qualified for the
U.S. Amateur and the British Amateur. Jackie claimed

he never won a bet from Crosby, who would always be well into his wallet at the turn and refuse to give him more strokes, saying, "Get out the same way you got in, old pal." Jackie was rich enough not to mind and had played in the Pro-Am as Crosby's special guest since it was a two-day tournament at Rancho Santa Fe.

Morris in fact had just written that "singer, entertainer Jackie Melton, who had never missed playing in the Clambake Pro-Am since 1937, had decided to lay down his golf clubs this year at The Crosby but, happily, could still be found after hours at the piano with his impeccable style and his haunting tenor voice."

Listening to Melton's still-pure style sell the words of the song, Morris hurt for the absence of Jackie's wife, Mary, who had never lost her beauty or her place in the affection of the crowd at The Crosby until she was killed in a small plane crash. Could it have been two years ago? It seemed to Morris Mary was alive and teasing everybody in the last thirty minutes.

Morris poled his way deeper into the crowded, smoke-drenched room ragged with laughter and lost words and ice clanging into just-emptied glasses. He might have found himself in one of the old speakeasy cabarets of the 1920s that Crosby and Harris loved to remember playing . . . and loved to have left safely behind long ago. He nodded here and there to young professional golfers seeking dubious comfort in the Snake Pit, including a young man from Georgia who had the goods to go all the way, if demon rum didn't overtake him as it had many before him, and a young Texan who was his equal. The old-timers, with any chance to win The Crosby, were carefully in their rooms, nodding toward their beds.

"I say, Morris."

Morris turned awkwardly on his cane in the crowd.

Jay Martin, a young ABC publicist, offered his slim hand into Morris's large one. A California-blond young woman pouted behind Martin, barely acknowledging her introduction to Morris as "My fiancée, Trudy Standridge." Morris ignored her ignoring him. "I'd like to catch you for five minutes tomorrow, Morris," said Jay. "You'll be hanging around the press room?"

"Sooner or later," Morris said.

"I need your advice," said Martin, turning, looking back over his shoulder at the nearly vanished Trudy Standridge. "Catch you tomorrow," he said, fleeing after his fiancée.

"Poor bastard," Morris said to himself. "My advice is to run like hell into the Pacific Ocean and drown yourself."

"We all come to that, talking to ourselves—the only intelligent conversation left," said a tall, too-thin man with an impressive head of prematurely gray hair. Jacob Hyche, failed movie producer, but no slouch of a golfer. His grip was surprisingly firm for so thin a man.

"Morris, how are you . . . and who is this drowning himself in the Pacific Ocean? Sounds like another remake of A Star Is Born. And where is my favorite sex symbol, Julia Sullivan? Only she can play the broken-hearted lead to this dark drama in the Pacific."

"She's up there flirting with the young Jackie Melton," Morris said. "You playing again this year?"

"Or swimming," said Hyche. "I don't mind the rain.

I'm usually drowning in red ink." He said it with undisguised cynicism. Morris knew that all his last pictures had bombed, big time. In fact, Sullivan—who had known Hyche as a drinking buddy of Monty's—had forced Morris to sit through two of Hyche's pictures, a sort of war between the sexes, that seemed to go on forever, like awkward marriages.

"I'd better find the wife," Hyche said. "She doesn't trust me alone at The Crosby." More cynicism.

Now there was a lady a man might drown himself for, thought Morris, waving Jacob to his undeserved good fate. Elizabeth Hyche was maybe ten years older than Jacob. Still glamorous. Still more fun than Crosby and Hope and Harris in the same room. Morris knew that she was the true bankroll for most of Hyche's boring films. And that she came to The Crosby because she loved it, everything about it but the golf. She'd long since given up keeping score of Jacob's running infidelities. Why the hell did she put up with him?

"Ah, sweet mystery of life," sang Morris to himself, this time careful not to be overheard.

He picked his way, not an easy feat with his considerable bulk, careful not to put his cane down on some slender foot. He started toward Sullivan but veered naturally to the bar. Charging into the crowd ahead of him was the infamous American advertising tycoon and resident asshole Andrew Reed McCall. His suite of rooms was just down the hall from the Snake Pit. McCall held his tall glass aloft, rattling the bare ice as if he'd killed his last drink in two swallows. Now he banged the glass on the temporary bar.

The young bartender, a college-age kid with thick

glasses, was obviously a novice pressed into service by the Snake Pit regulars.

"Scotch and water and not too damn much water," McCall ordered, ignoring the clutch of men who had been waiting for a drink ahead of him.

Morris knew it was no accident that Crosby tolerated Andrew McCall. McCall's agency, under his long-dead father, had created the ads for Crosby's original radio show in 1931. Each of Crosby's forty Christmas shows, first on radio and then on television, had carried advertising from the McCall agency. Crosby bowed to nobody, but he did genuflect in the direction of Andrew Reed McCall and his electronic muscle.

Morris had long ago learned that sports vendettas were as nothing compared with the blood hatreds in the cheerful world of big-time entertainment where megamillions of dollars rode on the public's fancy for a song and a dance.

Morris had to admit McCall stood enviably trim in his fifteen-hundred-dollar Italian suit, with his long graying hair turning fashionably up from his collar and his lean face perpetually tan from flying visits to his second homes on several of the oceans of the world.

"I told you, goddammit, easy on the water!" McCall snarled, though not a full thimble of water had violated the scotch resting amid the ice in his glass.

Standing behind McCall, no little embarrassed, was his young thing of the moment, in a tight yellow dress and yellow shoes, a natural redhead of such beauty as to dazzle, even among the Hollywood wives and "friends" in the crowded suite.

"Well, hand me the glass, son; the tournament only

lasts a goddamn week," said McCall. The young man carefully handed over the double scotch and ice and touch of water as if his own life hung in the mix.

"Why don't you put an extra ice cube up his ass . . . to cool the bastard off?" The bass voice came from behind Morris.

Morris loved it.

McCall did not love it. He turned, the scotch and water trembling in his hand as if it might leap out of the glass of its own volition into the round face of Sidney Barker, the last of the big-time bandleaders in America.

Morris knew that Sidney loved only to hate McCall. Sidney's band had backed Crosby from his radio days on the *Kraft Music Hall* until he'd been lobbied off Crosby's ABC show in the 1940s in favor of a rival bandleader whose essential qualifications included having married the niece of Andrew McCall's rich father.

Nothing like a little forty-year hate fest, thought Morris, laughing aloud, hoping the two aging playboys would duke it out in the crowded room. He'd even be willing to score the bout, which had been a long time coming.

McCall, with his inflated handicap, had won the Pro-Am three times in three separate decades with three different pros as partners. McCall said grace over a half billion dollars in television advertising. Not even Crosby on a nasty day would challenge his longtime sponsor's reputation as a championship sandbagger.

Sidney's round face and slick bald head sat atop a perfectly round stomach, like two fat circles above his short legs and tiny feet. Ironically, Sidney was the really fine amateur golfer, who, despite his gathering weight, kept to a five handicap, while the svelte McCall played to a fraudulent eighteen handicap when he could go around even Spyglass Hill in eighty-five strokes.

Sidney, with his true handicap, had never won the Crosby Pro-Am. In 1973 he incurred the wrath of his professional partner of several years, Ed Waters of Orlando, by showing up drunk as the Lord on the first tee with them comfortably in the lead in the last day of the Pro-Am. Waters, a journeyman pro who watched his nickels and dimes and who needed the two grand they might have won, had dumped the repentant Sidney as a partner. Ironically, Waters came into this year's Crosby playing very well and was a threat to win it.

Morris was sure he had glimpsed the quiet, balding Waters keeping the crowded room between himself and Sidney Barker. Meanwhile Sidney was narrowing the distance between himself and the livid Andrew McCall.

Crosby often put Sidney—no one ever called him by his last name—and McCall in the same foursome just for the perverse pleasure of it. The pros couldn't wait to crack Crosby up after every round with the nasty ways the two career enemies snubbed one another. "I swear, Bing, McCall kicked Sidney's ball down the cliff on No. 10. I swear it. I saw him do it. Then he stood there laughing, pointing at the ball on the rocks, saying, 'Goddamn, jump down the goddamn cliff and play it. It would play better than that goddamn band of yours.' I thought Sidney was going to knock him off the cliff with his six-iron. I like to broke a rib laughing. Cost me a double bogey."

Bing loved it. Made the pro tell it to Hope and then to everybody who came into his suite. And he couldn't wait to say to Sidney: "I hear you had a tad of trouble on No. 10." Bing couldn't hear the resulting, raging obscenities for laughing until he cried. Ah, that was The Crosby.

McCall elected not to throw his ill-won drink in Sidney's face. He handed it to his young thing and turned toward the bandleader, murder in his gray eyes.

Sidney did not flinch. "I hope the scotch is stronger than that limp dick swing of yours!" he spit at McCall.

"Fuck you, you fat never-was!" snarled McCall.

The crowd in the room had taken that exact moment to hush, and the words boomed over the Snake Pit like a public announcement of coming attractions.

"Don't take that shit, Sidney!" hollered somebody behind him. The mindless crowd surged against the two aging antagonists, as if taunting two small boys at recess into a fistfight neither had the stomach for.

Sidney grabbed McCall by the lapel of his expensive suit and swung a round arm and solid fist with surprising result against the side of McCall's face, knocking blood and spit out of the corner of his mouth and sending him against the redhead, who spilled a bit of the scotch on the floor.

McCall stood shocked, not having been struck in the face in five decades, though America's television boardrooms were filled with men who would have crawled to the Monterey Peninsula to make it happen. Now McCall roared and kicked Sidney in the knee.

There wasn't room among the crowd for either man to retreat.

Morris loved it. He looked over the chaos in the room until he caught the smiling face of Julia Sullivan, who flashed him a V, no doubt for worthy victims. Small Jackie Melton, beside her, was dancing up on his tiptoes in a vain attempt to catch the action.

Sidney grabbed his wounded knee, and McCall grabbed him, one long arm wrapping around his head as if he would twist it off.

Sidney dropped his own empty glass, and it shattered on the floor under their feet.

Morris was now afraid that the two aged Greco-Roman wrestlers would fall on the broken glass and seriously cut themselves or that one of the women pressed excitedly around them would be tripped onto it. Much as he hated to break it up, Morris took each of the already exhausted combatants in one big hand and pulled them apart.

Sidney's hair was down in his eyes, and McCall's cheek was swelling by the moment.

"You boys kiss and make up," Morris said, releasing the two of them, confident they had had enough.

McCall straightened his shirt and ripped jacket and said very quietly, for all the world like a scene in an old RKO movie, "I'll ruin you, you son of a bitch!"

"Yeah, knot face, you do that," Sidney said, pushing his hair out of his eyes.

"That's the bell, boys, recess is over," Morris said, laughing, and the crowd laughed with him. Crosby, lying up in the hospital, would be even sicker that he had missed it all.

McCall turned to the startled redhead, snatched his glass out of her two hands, and, as if to celebrate a great victory, took a strong pull, draining the scotch and water to the ice. The glass instantly slipped from his hand

and smashed on the floor, scattering raw fragments among the already broken glass. McCall gave a strangled cry and fell against the alarmed redhead, pinned against her by the crowd, his face dead white, foam rushing out of his mouth. Then he was sliding down the bosom of the speechless young woman until his face ground into the broken glass on the floor, screams flying up around him as if the room were on fire.

CHAPTER THREE

Morris, ignoring the broken glass, was the first to kneel down to Andrew McCall. His ragged breathing choked to a stop. Morris tore open the pricey shirt and put an ear to McCall's chest. His heart was leaping madly out of sync—and then it stopped. Morris did not hesitate to blow life into his mouth, which tasted of a great and familiar bitterness, as if the man's soul were all corruption. Now he was pressing his weight rhythmically into the lean chest, to no effect.

A medical doctor, an amateur golfer Morris recognized from San Francisco, touched his shoulder and took over the rowing stimulation of the dying heart, but with no better luck. Already McCall's lips and face were blue facsimiles of the living man.

The Snake Pit had never been so quiet on the eve of The Crosby. The silent revelers huddled away from the body as if they feared death itself might rise up from the floor.

"Hold still, Morris." He was surprised to find Sullivan, squatting on her heels, picking bloody glass fragments from his knee and trousers. He reached for one of her hands to steady her balance in the sea of shattered glass.

A tall, bony security man was now urging the stunned crowd out of the room. Two sportswriters protested, the younger one telling him to "stick it where the sun dudn't shine . . . right here'n the goddamn Monterey Peninsula."

Sullivan, looking up, did not recognize the volatile young reporter, who was less than sober. He was embarrassing the older columnist behind him, their good pal, Paul Shirley, from the *San Francisco Chronicle*.

The younger man shouted at the guard, "I'm Butch Dobbs from Phoenix," as if that gave him some legal standing in California. He was very drunk, on the brink of being abusive, until Shirley physically steered him out the door. Shirley came back inside alone, whispered to the thin security man, who nodded his consent, and made his way through the broken glass to Morris, standing over the dead or dying man.

"What the hell happened to McCall?" asked Shirley, smoothing his perfectly silver hair with one hand, as was his habit when he was writing against a deadline.

"Sudden death," Morris said.

"From what?"

"Good question."

"Did anybody ever die of a crappy disposition?"

"No. He would have been dead years ago," said Morris.

"I promised the guard I'd wait outside; we'll count on the good AP as our pool reporter."

"Indeed," Morris said. He was sure a larger story lay on the floor than Paul Shirley imagined.

Sullivan put one arm around their old pal from San Francisco and walked with him to the door. She'd seen enough of Andrew McCall in life and in death.

An ambulance, engaged for the tournament, pulled up outside the lodge annex, and two medical attendants were now squatting with a portable bottle of oxygen beside the stout young doctor, who warned them to mind the broken glass. They strapped an oxygen mask over McCall's mouth and nose, but Morris was sure the man had breathed his last breath. From the absence of urgency in the doctor's movements, he shared that belief.

Morris, taking it on himself, motioned to the security guard, an old man with the name tag James Cobb; Morris said to him quietly, so as not to cause further panic, that he should close down the bar and secure all the bottles and glasses—touching things as little as possible—and see that the young bartender stuck around.

Cobb said, "Are you sayin' somethin' in his drink did this to him?"

"I don't know," Morris said, "but it's possible."

A couple of younger guys, getting their drinks refreshed, put up a bit of a fuss when Cobb laid his old hands on the tops of their glasses. The young bartender went white in the face. Cobb handled it all rather well, not adding any appreciable alarm to the others in the room, who were too fascinated with the man on the floor to pay serious attention. All of them who had drinks were busy knocking them down.

And nobody else is dying . . . that's a good sign, Morris thought, irreverently, making damn sure that Julia Sullivan did not have a glass in her hand.

Another fifteen minutes passed before the doctor and the ambulance attendants gave up the ghost.

"Better leave him as he is," said the doctor.

"It'll be a hearse you're needing, not us," said the youngest ambulance attendant.

Morris looked around to see the redhead, the young thing, peering in the door. She stepped inside, then stopped on her high heels and teetered there, as if between life and death. She chose life. And turned to flee down the hallway, the back of one hand pressed over her mouth as if to edit her own alarm.

The young doctor was winded. He stuffed his shirt over his considerable girth deeper into his size forty trousers. His concerned eyes found Morris.

"You *are* John Morris?" he said.

Morris nodded. The shattered glass under their feet shone like gemstones. Across the empty room the abandoned piano rested silent as the grave.

"You might not remember . . . my name is Sanders. Dr. Richard Sanders," he said, offering a damp hand.

"From San Francisco," said Morris. "You hit a mean tee shot, always play with the pro from Canada, James Hempfling."

"James puts up with me," Sanders said, "I think because I helped his sinus condition. In truth I once wrote the same prescription for your friend Julia Sullivan at the U.S. Open."

"I'd forgotten that," said Morris. "It didn't help. She still snores. But for God's sake, don't quote me or I'll be deader than Andrew McCall."

Morris gestured toward the doorway where Sullivan had moved to stand guard, as if the barbarians were at the gate. And those grand, unholy sportswriters of America were gathering out there with Shirley and this "Dobbs from Arizona," those of them not too deeply into the free booze to know the difference between life and death of a son of a bitch.

Sullivan lifted her hand to the doctor, whom she recognized.

"McCall was damn near dead when he hit the floor," said Morris.

The doctor nodded. "I couldn't have helped him if I'd had him in the emergency room. Too late for anything after . . ." He looked at Morris. "Did you know McCall well?"

"Well enough to know what a bastard he was," Morris said.

"I've been coming to The Crosby . . . I guess . . . five years," said the doctor. "I always wondered why Crosby put up with his rude behavior." Sanders was immediately worried that he'd spoken rashly. He opened his mouth to apologize.

"There were about one hundred million reasons Crosby put up with him," said Morris. "Ads from his agency bankrolled many a Crosby TV special. Somebody better let Larry Crosby know what happened."

"The security guard has gone for the lodge manager.

. . . You know Jack Houghton. He'll get word to Larry . . . if he can find him. No telling how many parties he'll hit tonight. You know how it is at The Crosby," the doctor said.

"I know how it is," Morris said, one arm sweeping around the abnormal silence of the Snake Pit. He turned back suddenly toward Sanders.

"It was 'too late for anything after' . . . *What?*" he said, quoting the doctor's inadvertent words. "After he drank what was in his glass." Morris answered his own question.

Dr. Sanders winced. "I can't give an impromptu diagnosis to the Associated Press . . . of the sudden death of an advertising executive." He said it more plaintively than arrogantly.

"What can you say?" asked Morris. "You'll have to say something, unless the body gets off the stretcher and walks back in here."

The doctor tortured the possibilities in his mind. "How about 'He died in a very few minutes. All efforts to revive him were unsuccessful. We'll know the cause of death after the autopsy'?"

"That's a start," Morris said. "There will be an autopsy?"

"In this state, yes. After any sudden, unexpected death."

"The bitter smell and taste." Morris winced at his own recollection of the sourness. "They put me in mind of . . . spoiled almonds."

Sanders did not conceal the ready agreement on his face. But he said, "I can't comment on that."

"No, but I can write what *I* smelled and tasted," said

Morris. "And you'd better see that this suite is sealed off. The Monterey County Sheriff's Department will want its lab to test the broken glass . . . and the bottles and glasses at the bar . . . and every possible container in the suite. One thing we know: It was not a heart attack. The bastard didn't own one."

Dr. Sanders smiled in spite of himself.

"Let me ask you a question, off the record," said Morris.

"Off the record?"

"Yes."

What the hell, Sanders seemed to think, then decided to trust him; Morris's reputation for fairness was well known among golfers. "Okay," he said.

"Was his death consistent with cyanide poisoning?"

"I don't know why, but suicide seems to be an occupational hazard of living in San Francisco," Sanders said. "I've seen seven cases of death by potassium cyanide. The bitter smell is not from the cyanide itself. It's from the cyanide's action on human tissue. Only two of the victims were still alive when I got to them. One of the two cases died in the floor with me pounding his heart . . . exactly like tonight. Same instant coma, same foaming at the mouth, same bitter smell, same cramping, same quick death. I'm betting McCall swallowed it on an empty stomach."

Sanders looked directly at Morris. "For God's sake, don't quote me until after the autopsy. . . . I could be dead wrong."

"Not to worry," said Morris, who, sure of what the autopsy would reveal, was committing every detail to memory for later use. "Victims of cyanide don't always die so quickly?"

"No. The other victim I treated while she was still alive was in a coma for forty-five minutes before she died. A lot of vomiting . . . on a full stomach. Not a pretty sight. Luckily she never regained consciousness. That isn't always the case. It can be a terrible death, with ghastly tetanic convulsions." Another thought interrupted him: "Andrew McCall didn't strike me as a man who would kill himself."

"No way," Morris said. "He had the world by the throat. And he'd never have let go . . . willingly. Unless maybe he had some terrible disease we don't know about."

"We'll know soon enough," Sanders said. "Was he married?"

"Not for years," Morris said. "He has grown children, but I'm not sure they were on speaking terms."

"I'll leave notifying the next of kin to Larry Crosby and the sheriff's department," Sanders said.

There was a commotion in the hallway.

"My *gentle* friends of the Fourth Estate," Morris said. "We'd better feed the savage beasts a bite of news. At least that it was a sudden death. And that under state law there will be an autopsy. And that circumstances are . . . *questionable*, enough that the Monterey County Sheriff's Department is being notified."

"Oh, Lord, there's no avoiding that," said Sanders, sweat still beading under his eyes.

"No," said Morris. "I'll repeat your statement to my buddies in the hallway, speaking as a pool reporter, if you like. Then you can take questions or wait until you've spoken with the sheriff's people."

"No questions," said the doctor, sweat breaking out all over his chubby face. "The sheriff will want to talk to you as well as me. You got to him first."

Morris said, "They'll want to question everybody who was in the bloody room . . . if we're right about how he died. Who can remember who was in the room? It was chaotic with people. There must have been a hundred of us. But the room hasn't been built large enough to hold everybody who despised Andrew McCall. I wonder who was desperate enough to kill him?"

The word *kill*, even spoken softly, seemed to overrun the empty room.

Morris led the dozen reporters and columnists, in various stages of intoxication, to the press room. He quickly typed out the good doctor's statement and read it aloud and then passed it around. He was hit with a squall of questions, primarily among them: What questionable circumstances provoked notifying the sheriff?

"Sudden death," Morris said. "The state of California requires the unexpected sudden death of any person to be reported to authorities." Morris had to smile to himself. "Sudden death" to this crowd meant losing the silly game in overtime.

"Give me five minutes to knock out my own observations," Morris said, "not to confuse them with the doctor's. I'll pass it around before putting it on the wire."

"Who the hell are you? I'm Butch Dobbs, an' th' *Phoenix Herald* ain't quotin' no fat-ass reporters." It was not a sober complaint, and it was being made to a man of large bulk and surprisingly little fat.

Morris walked over to Dobbs, who came up almost to his chin. "I'm with the Associated Press. The *Phoenix Herald* is a client. I'm in a hurry to serve that client. But I have time to kick your drunken ass."

"Go it, Morris, we'll wait!" came a voice from the group, followed by much laughter.

Dobbs burned in the laughter, but he was not deep enough into the bottle to raise a finger against the large, wide man looking down into his drunkenness.

Morris rapped out his AP lead in five minutes on the money, including in it his own observations. He passed two copies around the group, which had swelled to seventeen writers, the latecomers a little shakier in their knees from the free booze flowing over the peninsula.

"Morris, your description of what happened to McCall is consistent with cyanide poisoning," said Paul Shirley, in no way surprised.

"I'm no medical examiner," said Morris. "I can only write what I saw and smelled and tasted." The word *tasted* made him and the entire roomful of writers flinch.

Morris's TTS operator had turned in for the night. He called the AP office in San Francisco and dictated his lead. The other writers—the sulking Dobbs among them—rushed to their own phones to show their managing editors what swell and sober reporters they were, beating the AP wire to the punch. God help those writers who hadn't got the word and were still partying. Their papers would be rattling the phones in their rooms until the wee hours to find out what the hell was going on at The Crosby.

* * *

Morris made his way back to the Snake Pit.

Sullivan hovered near the door. "How did it go?" she asked.

"Not bad. Most of the boys were sober enough to type. What's happening?"

"The sheriff's patrol deputy is here." She nodded toward the door. "You behave, Morris. I wouldn't want to have to make a citizen's arrest."

Morris frowned to understand what she meant. Best not to ask. He'd know soon enough. He stepped through the door. A figure in a rain jacket was bending over the very dead Andrew McCall.

When it straightened, it was a she. Morris turned to look at Sullivan, who raised a small fist ever so slightly.

Dr. Sanders had been only too happy to turn events over to a higher authority: "John Morris, meet Sheriff's Patrol Deputy Patricia Jordan. John is with the Associated Press," he explained.

Under her rain hat, which she had not taken time to remove, Deputy Jordan was startlingly young. A few short tufts of auburn hair leaked from under her hat. She looked up at Morris as if he could explain the body lying on the floor.

Morris took her very slim hand in his own large one, careful to hold it just a moment longer than necessary, sure of Sullivan's wicked stare behind him.

"Did you come from Salinas?" Morris asked, knowing the county seat to be some thirty-five miles away in the valley of John Steinbeck country and, in fact, being on friendly terms with Sheriff Tommy Whitlock, who played to a respectable eleven handicap but who declined to tee it up in The Crosby though he'd often been invited. Better the Monterey County voters saw him with his pistol on his hip, standing between civilization and anarchy.

"No," Deputy Jordan said, dominating her nervousness, "I'm from the substation in Monterey. I'm here to take the details. I thought there'd been an accident—" She bit off the last sentence, as if she hadn't meant to say it aloud. Her calm voice went exceedingly well with her fair looks, which could hold their own in Northern California, without a hint of makeup. Her eyes were wide and hazel above a strong mouth, purposefully set. Her nose might have been bent ever so slightly in a girlhood accident. She was a patrol deputy from central casting who had stumbled into a very real death. What else could you expect at The Crosby?

She repeated her question before Morris caught it. "You were the first to reach him?"

"Yes." He added a nod, all cooperation. He dared not look at Sullivan, who would be laughing, he knew, at his awkwardness, like that of a young boy on his first date.

"I understand you instructed the bartender to close the bar," she said.

Morris nodded again.

"Why?"

Morris told her what he'd smelled and tasted before the doctor took charge. "Just a precaution," Morris said. "I'm no expert on potassium cyanide."

"It was good thinking," she said, her wide hazel eyes measuring him.

Morris did not deny it.

"Tell me what happened. From the moment you stepped in the room." A pad and pencil appeared in her hands, as suddenly as if she had drawn her weapon, which hung above her hip, sensuously. She was a young woman made for trousers.

Morris described the Snake Pit as he remembered it at 7:35 P.M., Pacific coast time. There was Jackie Melton at the piano, with Sullivan worshiping after his music, and Phil Harris belting out his theme song through the obligatory cigarette smoke, and the favored people, chaotic with pleasure, in the crowded room; his bumping into young publicist Jay Martin and his (reluctant) fiancée, then bumping into movie producer Jacob Hyche, looking (reluctantly) for his wife. Morris included both *reluctants* sure the investigation would ultimately lead to a charge of murder. At that time, every action, every intonation would be fair game for the young sheriff's deputy, though she would doubtlessly give way to a superior officer before the night was over. Pity that, Morris thought. He sneaked a look at Sullivan, who was grinning at his pleasure and discomfort in the presence of Deputy Jordan.

Morris described, in as tight detail as he could recollect, McCall's thrusting of his glass to the young man behind the bar and McCall's impatience with him for adding too much water, though he'd barely hit the scotch with a thimbleful.

"You're sure it was scotch and water," said the deputy, pausing with her pencil.

"I'm sure he *said* scotch and that it came out of a *scotch bottle*—Johnnie Walker Black Label—and it *looked* like water," Morris said. "I'm a scotch drinker myself, but I didn't get to the bar, thank God."

"Where did . . . McCall"—she remembered his name—"get the glass?"

"I don't know. He had it in his hand when he pushed ahead of two, three guys already at the bar."

"Did you recognize them?"

"Two of them." He described the lean, hard-muscled young golf pro from Georgia, Jake Hill, who had been standing at the bar when McCall reached past him with his empty glass. Jake was a throwback, the last of the onetime caddies who made it on the tour. He'd come from the mountains of north Georgia, a rough-and-ready sort of character, the youngest son of a bootlegger in jail for life. Jake would bet any man on the tour almost any amount in a practice round. He didn't choke, and he didn't often lose.

Morris was sure the slightly older guy at the bar had been Ed Waters, the journeyman pro from Orlando. He explained how Ed had dumped Sidney as his longtime Pro-Am partner after Sidney, God bless him, had shown up drunk last year for the final round when they were in contention. He explained how the two-thousand-dollar Pro-Am prize meant a lot to Ed, who was never a headliner. Morris did not recognize the young man standing between Jake and Ed when McCall banged his glass ahead of them at the bar; the tilt of the young man seemed familiar, but Morris had not actually seen his face.

The deputy listened, then nodded for him to continue.

Good Lord, Morris had almost forgotten the redhead, McCall's young thing of the moment. How could he forget that action? He described her, down to the double cross-strap yellow high-heel pumps she wore. The deputy smiled in spite of herself at the exactness of his recollection. It would not do for Sullivan to catch him rattling off all that specific detail of what another woman was wearing.

"McCall handed her his glass before the fisticuffs," Morris said. "Afterward he snatched it back and killed the drink—if you'll excuse the expression—in consecutive gulps." Morris shook his head. He had no idea who the redhead was. He'd last seen her disappearing down the hallway toward McCall's longtime suite in the annex.

Morris couldn't help grinning as he described the catfight between McCall and the old bandleader Sidney Barker. "I scored it a one-round TKO for Sidney," he said, "but I don't think the right to the head killed McCall."

The deputy was dead serious. "Were they enemies?"

The formality of the question tickled Morris. "Nothing serious," he said, allowing a smile to break through. "They'd only been hating each other forty years. It was a professional thing. You'll have to ask Sidney." And where had Sidney gone? Morris could not remember seeing him again after McCall slid down the front of the redhead to the floor.

Morris thought, *Sidney will miss him in a crazy way. It's comforting to have some one person to despise all your life. Especially a true asshole like McCall. He'll leave a perverted vacuum in Sidney's life. Who can Crosby kid him about in the years to come?* Morris had no idea how few years there were to come for Crosby himself.

Morris thought: While McCall was standing in the crowd and making his way to the bar, and while he was at the bar, and while the bartender filled his glass, and while the redhead was holding his glass during the ruckus, any number of people might have slipped something in it. Or even swapped glasses. Morris had no idea if the empty glass had been out of McCall's hands before he went to the bar, and he hadn't been watching the young bartender that carefully because of the people jammed in front of him.

Morris explained to the sheriff's deputy exactly what he had been thinking. She took down his words in her own made-up shorthand, which Morris caught a glimpse of and preferred to his own.

"You don't doubt he swallowed poison," she said, lowering her pen and pad.

"No," said Morris, "I can *say* it, but I won't *write* it until after the autopsy. The good AP frowns on speculation."

Deputy Jordan smiled, and she had a smile to light up the Monterey Peninsula. She asked him to show her to the nearest telephone.

Morris pointed it out between the bar and the piano. He was certain she was ringing her superiors at the Monterey Substation. *Pity*, he thought again.

The deputy's conversation was brief. She returned to the prone body, her notebook folded away in her jacket pocket.

"Would you like me to round up the young bartender?" Morris asked.

She shook her head no. "Homicide will take over
. . . Sheriff's Inspector Stanley Gooden." There was
no inflection in her voice, but in giving his official title,
she unconsciously pronounced her disappointment and
maybe her distaste for Inspector Gooden.

"If you will just wait in the main lobby." She touched
Morris's arm with one finger. "Thank you for your
help," she said.

Morris raised his own finger. "They'll need you
around here. You ask all the right questions." It won
him an all-points smile.

Morris poled his way through the straggling, come-
lately reporters and the famous and curious in the hallway.

"What's up, Morris?" asked the *Detroit News*, a
columnist and an old friend.

"Nothing I didn't put on the wire," Morris said.
"You'll have to ask the sheriff's inspector, who's due
any minute."

Morris dropped a quick description of the death of
Andrew McCall to a singer and to a producer and to
"Dirty Harry" himself, Clint Eastwood, who lived in
the Del Monte Forest, and who swung a serious golf
stick, and who looked in plenty trim enough shape to
take care of the guy who took care of Andrew McCall.
Morris was careful not to say McCall had been murdered.

Sullivan was waiting for Morris in the lobby of the
lodge, where more curious and famous faces had gathered. Two waiters were taking drink orders. Morris put
in for a scotch and water— "Make that bourbon," he
amended.

"Since when did you start drinking bourbon?" Sullivan asked.

"Since somebody put potassium cyanide in the scotch," Morris said.

Sullivan looked at the half-empty glass of scotch in her own hand with alarm.

"Don't worry. If you're still standing, it's safe to finish anything in your glass. Swallow cyanide now, and it kills you a little while ago."

"Are you sure that's what happened to McCall?"

"I'm sure. Dr. Richard Sanders is sure. The deputy, Patricia Jordan, I think, is sure. But the autopsy may show he died of embarrassment . . . after taking a right to the face from an old bandleader."

"You seemed pretty cozy with the deputy," Sullivan said.

"We're tight," Morris said with fake solemnity.

"There's room on the floor for another body," Sullivan said, lifting her glass more as a challenge than a toast.

Morris held up both hands in surrender, just in time to accept his bourbon and water. "Here's to a little casual murder among friends," he said, tipping his glass against Sullivan's.

Morris told her everything he'd told the deputy.

"When did you first notice McCall?" he asked.

"I saw the redhead first," she said.

"Always scouting out the competition."

She admitted it with a smile. "There was something about her body language. She was with Andrew McCall. But she was apart from him, in a way you can see and can't describe."

"All of us guys have been there."

"Poor baby," Sullivan said. "She's some number, the redhead. Must be twenty-one if she's a day. She posed in her skintight yellow dress in the doorway, as if waiting for Hollywood to discover her. I looked to see who was with her. No surprise: seventy-year-old Andrew Reed McCall. I'm only surprised he didn't die of a heart attack when she squeezed into the yellow dress."

"He would have been in more danger when she wiggled out of it," Morris said, careful not to comment on the detail of the yellow shoes. "Think a minute . . . was McCall carrying a glass when you first saw him?"

She considered it. "Yes! He was. Remember, he raised it over his shoulder to avoid some drunk stumbling toward the door. He shouted something after the drunk, but who could hear a shout in that room?"

"Was it empty, the glass?"

She thought about it. "I don't know. It must have had something in it. He lifted it to protect it from the drunk."

Morris appreciated the logic. "Did the redhead have a glass?" Morris tortured his own recollection but could not picture a glass in her hand before the fight—and he remembered her down to her double cross-strap yellow shoes.

"I don't think so. No," Sullivan said, shaking her head. "I remember her sleeveless arms . . . and empty hands . . . on a chilly night."

Now Morris remembered them also but was careful not to look too appreciative. "How long had you been in the Snake Pit when they came in?"

"Maybe an hour."

"Thought you were headed for a nap?"

"Thought about it," she said, "but who can sing and drink in her sleep?"

"Good point. McCall and the redhead weren't in the room when you first got there?"

"No." She didn't hesitate. "There were just a few of the regulars. Then the Pit filled up in a hurry. Truly, what did you make of the deputy?"

"She asks all the right questions," Morris said. "That's three-fourths of the game . . . the same as pitching in baseball. Do you remember Dr. Sanders?"

"Sure. He's from San Francisco. He once gave me a prescription for my sinuses."

Morris, God forbid, did not mention her snoring that year during the U.S. Open. He said, "Off the record—*way* off the record—Sanders told me McCall's death was the near duplicate of a suicide he witnessed in San Francisco. He said McCall likely drank the stuff on an empty stomach, it acted so quickly on his system. You can die a lot nastier death from potassium cyanide than McCall did. And his was nasty enough."

Remembering, Sullivan squeezed her eyes shut. "You are right, Morris. There was such chaos in the room . . . anyone could have slipped something in his glass or even exchanged glasses. You'd have to say the young bartender doesn't look like a killer."

"No. He looks like a sophomore in accounting. I expect he's feeling the heat about now. We'll see what Sheriff's Inspector Stanley Gooden can sweat out of him."

"Who?"

Morris explained that Deputy Jordan had—it seemed

to him, *reluctantly*—called her Monterey substation, and Stanley Gooden, sheriff's investigator, was on the way with his homicide team.

"I bet he doesn't look as good in his trousers," Sullivan said wistfully.

Morris was not about to touch that line, not even with a smile.

Two drinks later the inspector sent for Morris. Morris was sure he'd already questioned Sidney Barker and Dr. Sanders and the young bartender, all of whom had passed through the lobby of the lodge without speaking. Probably they had been warned not to approach him until the inspector had finished with him.

Sullivan was right. In his trousers Inspector Stanley Gooden looked like a sackful of doorknobs. He was as wide and low as a John Deere tractor. Maybe forty years old. Rainwater clung to his blouse as if he'd waddled for the lodge door without a rain jacket. He stood with his heavy chin stuck out as though the body on the floor were a personal affront. There was an unnatural sheen of sweat under his round eyes.

"You're John Morris," the inspector said, as if to identify Morris to himself. He didn't offer to shake hands.

Already Morris didn't like him or the horse he rode in on. Morris looked toward Deputy Jordan, standing well away from Inspector Gooden. Careful to keep any hint of emotion from her own face, she met his eyes. Morris smiled for them both.

He also smiled at the county photographer, carefully shooting the remains of Andrew McCall, as if he were lying as he'd fallen and hadn't been racked and pummeled in an unsuccessful attempt to breathe life back into his body. The photographer was also making a record of the shattered glass on the floor. Two scene-of-the-crime technicians then began lifting the glass with their gloved hands into plastic bags, careful to mark each bag. It would be a problem separating the fragments of Sidney's broken glass from the fragments of McCall's broken glass. Presumably Sidney's would be minus any residue of potassium cyanide, or Sidney was condemned to live forever. A fingerprint technician had already dusted the bottles and glasses at the bar. There was going to be a madhouse of latent fingerprints in the room.

"You got here at seven thirty-five P.M.," the inspector said, looking at his notes, no doubt taken from Deputy Jordan and from his interviews with Sidney, Dr. Sanders, and the bartender. "What happened?"

Morris described what he'd seen and done without the least animation. He found himself unconsciously abbreviating his narrative, leaving out the various subtleties he'd related to the sheriff's deputy. No hint of the "reluctance" in Jay Martin's fiancée's eyes or in Jacob Hyche's voice as he spoke of his absent wife. Just the facts, ma'am. There appeared a hint of a smile on Deputy Jordan's impassive face at the leanness of his narrative.

"You saw McCall's glass in the bartender's hands." The inspector said it as an accusation.

"I saw *a* glass in McCall's hand as he pushed his way to the bar. I *heard* McCall jam *a* glass on the bar. He was standing in the way. I didn't actually *see* the glass hit the bar. I saw the bartender's hands hold *a* glass, which he filled, *presumably* with scotch and a bit of water. The scotch came out of a Johnnie Walker Black Label bottle. The water came out of a pitcher. I *heard* the bartender set the glass back down on the bar. I did *not* see McCall *pick it up*. I saw *a* full glass in his hand as he turned from the bar."

Inspector Gooden lifted his pen from his pad and stared at Morris through the thick, unnatural sweat on his heavy face. "Do you doubt that McCall picked up the same glass he set down in front of the bartender, the glass the bartender filled and set back down?" the inspector asked with every skepticism.

"I did not doubt it at the time," Morris said. "I can only vouch for what I *saw* and *heard*."

"You think the bartender might be an amateur magician?" Doubt leaked from every word.

"Amateurs sprout among all professions: magicians, bartenders . . . inspectors." Morris threw in the latter without so much as a blush. "The young man certainly appeared to be an amateur bartender."

Inspector Gooden might not have been able to spit as far as his outthrust jaw. Deputy Jordan was lucky. He was too angry at Morris to turn and see the huge smile on her face.

"You don't know what you saw, but you don't hesitate to declare this to be murder," Gooden said, every word a challenge.

"The room was chaotic," Morris said, with maddening thoughtfulness. "My eyes took in a lot that did not register on my memory. The same with the clash of conversation and music. But those individual movements I did see . . . and those separate words I did hear, I *do remember*. And yes, I believe Andrew McCall was murdered. Or he chose a dramatic exit from life. Which puts the ball in your court, Inspector. If I can help you further in any way, please let me know. I'm staying here at the lodge. The other reporters and I would like to speak with you when you finish here. Will that be all for now for me?"

Morris looked down at him from the height of a large man whose written words went to every major newspaper and radio and television station in California and America and many cities around the world.

The inspector was too furious to swallow and chewed on his own spit. "How well did you know Andrew McCall?"

Morris resisted the urge to say, "Not so well as I know Sheriff Tommy Whitlock." He said, "I've only seen him here at this tournament for the last five years. I've spoken to him. Quoted him twice when his team won the Pro-Am." He did not say that McCall's malignant ego was larger than his bankroll.

"Did he ever take exception to anything you wrote?" Gooden asked. It was a good question the deputy hadn't thought to ask.

"Yes. Last year. I described him as 'an aging advertising executive with a friendly eighteen handicap.' 'Friendly,' of course, was a euphemism for 'fraudulent.' "

"What did he say?"

"He said I could 'kiss his ass.' I told him that wouldn't be necessary. There seemed to be a long line of gutless wonders waiting to do the job around the clock."

"What did he do?"

"He complained to Crosby."

"What did Crosby do?" Gooden was too intent now to take notes.

"He laughed. He said he'd been kissing it himself for forty years. He told me to forget it and have a drink on him. He couldn't wait to quote what I'd told McCall . . . to Sidney Barker and his other pals."

"Barker hated McCall," the inspector said.

"I'm sure Sidney answered that question for himself. I know they weren't pen pals."

The inspector made him describe again the brief skirmish between Barker and McCall. Morris did, using only nouns, verbs, objects, periods. With no hint of humor.

"Was the redhead McCall's mistress?"

Morris had to smile at the antique word *mistress* here in pagan Hollywood country. "You'll have to ask her. I don't think she was his executive secretary." He thought about it. "Hell, she may have been."

"Were you glad to see him die?" Gooden asked cold-bloodedly, as if to catch him in some way off-balance.

"No. I don't favor train wrecks, either, or earthquakes, or poverty of imagination, even among the lesser government officials." Morris looked directly into Gooden's round eyes.

The inspector was livid. "I want the written name of every person you *remember* seeing in this room tonight. I want it tonight."

Gooden looked again at his notepad. "You know the

woman . . . Julia Sullivan." He said her name as if there were faint hope for any woman who had sunk so low as to be on friendly terms with him. "I want to speak with her next. That'll be all—*for now*," the inspector said.

Morris started to give him a British salute, palm out. But thought better of it. He waited until the inspector turned his head and winked at Deputy Jordan, who looked down at the floor to keep from smiling.

"You're up, Sullivan," Morris said when he got back to the lobby, which had grown fuller and louder.

"What's he like, the inspector?" she asked.

"A lovely man," Morris said, no hint of the ironic in his voice.

Sullivan knew better than to trust him, looking back once and shaking her fist at him.

Oh-oh, Morris could tell across a crowded room when Julia Sullivan was angry. Her eyes narrowed so that you couldn't believe she could see to walk.

"*A lovely man* . . . my anatomy!" she said.

"You mean he was less than cordial? I'm shocked."

"*You*, Morris, put the ferret up his trousers."

"I'm sure you were a calming influence on the inspector."

Her blue eyes were small craft warnings. "He asked if you and I were 'intimate.' I asked him what he meant, 'intimate.' He said, 'Did we share the same room?' I asked him, very politely, if he was fucking the sheriff's deputy."

Morris was not amused.

"I know. I went a bridge too far," Sullivan said. "I apologized immediately to Deputy Jordan, who didn't say a word, and I liked her immediately. I think she was having a hard time not smiling."

"What was his response?"

"He said we could 'continue the interview at the Monterey substation.' I said I didn't mind if we continued it 'in Tommy Whitlock's living room.' "

Morris *was* amused. Sullivan knew the sheriff even better than he did. He'd been an old drinking friend of Monty's. Hadn't everybody in California and America?

"The inspector didn't flinch. I'll give him that," Sullivan said. "But he got off the 'intimate,' and I told him what I'd seen and heard, mostly from the piano bench and then near you after the fight started and McCall fell to the floor. I remembered to tell him that McCall held a glass in his hand when he entered the room. He made me repeat that twice. He made me tell him how I was certain of that . . . *twice more*. This boy is no Hercule Poirot, no little gray cells whirling about in his cranium, but you have to say he's a fat bulldog, won't let go of any bite of information. I wouldn't want him after me."

"If I'd killed Andrew McCall, I'd pay to have the bastard after me," Morris said, "but I'd fear the sheriff's deputy."

"I bet you would," Sullivan said, laughing. Then frowned. "Now I've got to make a list of everyone I remember seeing in the bloody room. The inspector doesn't seem to realize it's known as the Snake Pit for the teeming thousands drinking their hardest."

"The boy detective will stumble on that history any minute. I've got to make the same list," Morris said, pulling out a pen and pad. Between them, feeding off each other's memory, they came up with the names of twenty-seven people they'd recognized in the Snake Pit, the large number surprising them both.

"These names ought to keep the bastard busy," Morris said, holding up the two lists, about half the names overlapping.

Lodge manager Jack Houghton had finally located Larry Crosby, who stepped out of the rain and into the lodge, immaculate in his black horn-rim glasses and dark suit and rep tie. A cigarette burned perpetually in his fingers, but there was a rare frown on Larry's face as he thanked Jack for finding him.

Morris could almost read Jack's lips as he explained what he knew of what had happened to Andrew McCall. Then Jack, his unsinkable enthusiasm flagging under the stress, was pointing Larry to Morris himself, who lifted a hand in salute.

"What happened, Morris?" asked Larry, having made his way across the crowded lobby.

Morris gave him the longhand version, including the careful opinion, shared by Dr. Sanders, that it was murder almost surely.

"Bloody hell. And Bing laid up in the hospital," said Larry, biting his lip with concern.

"How's he doing?" Morris asked.

"Not so well. He's likely to have surgery on his lung. That's not for—"

"Publication." Morris agreed. "No sweat. The tournament has troubles enough at the moment."

"McCall was not one of Bing's favorites," admitted

Larry, "but he ran a successful advertising agency. And he sponsored many of Bing's shows over the years. He was not a pleasant man. But you'd have to say he supported the tournament."

Morris cut to the reality. "The peninsula, not to say the Snake Pit, wouldn't hold the Americans who despised Andrew McCall. It apparently held one American who killed him."

Larry could only shake his head with regret. "I'll see this Inspector Stanley Gooden. Then I want to speak with Sheriff Tommy Whitlock, if I can reach him. Then I'll go to the hospital. I'd better tell Bing myself."

"You might hustle back for the press conference," Morris said. "The inspector will have to say something, even if it's only 'no comment.'" Morris handed him a copy of his own AP release from earlier in the evening.

Crosby read it, nodding his head to the inevitable. "The fat's in the fire. Best to get it all out in the open. We have one day before the tournament starts. Do you imagine they can catch his killer by Thursday?"

Morris considered it. "Possibly. But I wouldn't count on it. A person who can poison a man in a crowded room will take some catching." He did not add that whoever they were looking for was bold and violent and reckless. What if the redhead had taken a sip of the scotch during the silly fight? The amateur bartender might have accidentally swapped glasses in the confusion. Damn! What if he had? What if the drink was meant for someone else at the bar, or someone else in the room, even the redhead herself? What if it was meant for *anyone* in the room? That would make it a terrorist act. None of those possibilities had occurred to him. He bet they hadn't occurred to the inspector. He wouldn't bet against the wiser sheriff's deputy. When Morris looked up, Larry Crosby was gone.

CHAPTER FOUR

The impromptu press conference did not go well. Sheriff's Inspector Stanley Gooden found himself on the other end of the interrogation. He didn't like it. He avoided any reference to the word *murder*. Andrew McCall might have died of old age. "Was the bastard poisoned?" asked the *Phoenix Herald* in his "gentlemanly" manner. Was the bartender a suspect? Had he been arrested? Were any suspects being detained? Questions flew from all corners of America by its resident golf writers, accustomed to competition more murderous than simple murder.

The sheriff's inspector only shook his head, no comment; he'd have to wait for the postmortem to know how the man died. He did admit the Snake Pit was locked and off-limits for the immediate future, bringing a few groans from the more rough-and-ready partyers among the reporters. Gooden declared the press conference closed. He marched out of the lodge, a threat to trip over his outthrust jaw.

Morris enjoyed every step of his discomfort.

Sullivan, in the hallway, had offered a cup of hot coffee to Patrol Deputy Patricia Jordan.

"You saved my life," the deputy said.

"Too bad I couldn't have done the same for Andrew McCall."

"I think your friend John Morris and Dr. Sanders did all that could have been done. He seems a capable fellow, Morris."

"He is. But let's not speak of it too widely. He's vain enough already. You know these Georgia boys."

"I don't. I've spent my entire life in California," said Jordan, her smile as bright as the sun on the desert. "But I enjoy following golf. And I've read John Morris's stories. I think he's very good."

"And so he is. But he doesn't think so. He hates everything he writes. That's one reason I put up with him," Sullivan said.

"Tell me . . . was Andrew McCall despised by everybody?"

"I don't know about the redhead. The rest of America couldn't stand the sight of him. He used everybody, even Crosby. He cheated at golf. It's a wonder he hadn't been killed years ago. By the way, who is the redhead?" Sullivan asked.

The deputy considered the question. Then she said, "You're a friend of Tommy Whitlock's. You mentioned his name."

"Not very proper of me," Sullivan said. "I meant to intimidate the aggressive Inspector Gooden, probing into my personal 'intimacies.' "

Jordan smiled her understanding.

"Morris scolded me for asking him such a fake, vulgar question, involving you, an innocent witness. I'm as embarrassed as I am sorry."

"No problem." Jordan's smile was in no way forced.

Sullivan could not imagine the striking patrol deputy, with her soft auburn hair, lusting after the dumpy, ill-tempered sheriff's investigator. "Tommy was one of my late husband's best pals," she said. "Morris and I always have a drink or two with him at The Crosby."

"Mr. Whitlock . . . is a very capable sheriff," the deputy said, seemingly unaware she had already called him Tommy, "and a good politician. He knows everybody, but I think he's careful who he makes real friends with. Still, I can only tell you facts about the case that will be on the public record. The redhead's name is Tana Daly. An actress. An *apprentice* actress. From Chicago. She now lives in L.A."

"She's standing at the end of a long line of *actresses* who've kept company with Andrew McCall."

"One minute she seems terrified," Jordan said, veering from her own factual resolve; "the next minute she's careful we spell her name correctly. I have an idea she would be a willing interview."

Sullivan put the thought in her memory bank. "I've never seen her at The Crosby before."

"No. She said she just met McCall . . . a few weeks ago. She had a small role in a television movie of the week for CBS."

"Sponsored by . . . I can guess," Sullivan said.

"Yes, one of McCall's clients."

"Isn't life a coincidence? Did she know where McCall got the glass he brought into the Snake Pit?" Sullivan could not slide the question past Deputy Jordan.

"I can't tell you that. I can only tell you it's baffling. I'll report to . . . Sheriff Whitlock . . . everything I know. Inspector Gooden will do the same. I imagine the sheriff will want as much help as possible from you and John Morris. You both know the golfers, the whole crowd so well."

"Too well. We're part of the crowd. Don't forget that," Sullivan warned, absolutely certain that Tommy Whitlock, for several years a divorced man, was more than a boss to Patricia Jordan. In fact, she would lay heavy odds on it, but then John Morris had long ago learned never to bet against her on anything, least of all those questions involving romantic entanglements.

Sullivan asked, "Will you stay on the case? Seems to me it would really help. You were on the scene so quickly, you saw everybody in shock, with their guards down."

"Not likely." Jordan shook her head with no little remorse. "I respond to calls to take the initial details. When there's been a suspicious death, homicide takes over. But sometimes . . ." The deputy left it at that.

The door to the press room began to open. Sullivan said, "I'd better let you go. I think the press conference is breaking up. I doubt Inspector Gooden will be in the best of humor."

Deputy Jordan had a smile to break your heart—not that the sheriff's inspector could be said to have one.

* * *

No bed ever felt so warm and welcoming, with the rain and maybe sleet beating against the lodge window.

"How did our boy Gooden respond to cross-examination?" Sullivan asked.

"Not well. He'd rather be on the working end of the nasty questions," Morris said. "He answered, 'No comment,' to everything he was asked, including 'will the tournament be canceled?' Of course his 'no comment' spawned many AM leads: 'The Crosby Pro-Am might be canceled because of suspected murder.' That'll play until Bing and Larry put the quietus on it for the afternoon follow-ups. Of course the good, reliable AP did not raise the false question in its dispatch."

"So the boys will tee it off even if somebody offed McCall?"

"Of course. It's true, his pro playing partner will miss his fake eighteen handicap."

"You're terrible, Morris."

"Every chance I get."

"I had a friendly visit with Sheriff's Patrol Deputy Patricia Jordan."

"The hell you say?"

Sullivan folded her arms below the rise of her bosom, as if that was it.

Morris captured her, arms, bosom, and all. "Come on, what did she say?"

"She told me the redhead's name is Tana Daly, from L.A., by way of Chicago. She's an apprentice actress. Appeared in a CBS movie of the week, sponsored by one of you-know-whose clients."

"An apprentice actress," Morris said. "Some apprenticeship. There used to be a less glamorous name for it."

"The deputy speculated she would be a good interview."

"I'll try her out."

Sullivan gave him a slow stare.

"A journalist has to get close to his source."

"A journalist might wind up close to the victim," Sullivan said.

Morris held up both hands in serious surrender. "Did you ask the deputy—"

"Yes," Sullivan said, reading him like an AP advance. "She wouldn't tell me where McCall got the glass he brought into the Snake Pit. She did say where he got it was 'baffling.' She said she would be reporting everything she found out to 'Tommy . . . Sheriff Whitlock.' And that he might well be interested in our help, our knowing the golf crowd so well. Morris, I bet you—"

"Oh, hell, no. I'm not betting with you," said Morris, rolling over to his side of the bed. "I'd rather take my chances at the dice tables in Vegas. At least some poor sucker wins there once in a blue moon."

Sullivan ignored him. "I'll bet you a dinner in Carmel that Tommy Whitlock and Patricia Jordan are more than sheriff and deputy."

"You think?" Morris raised up on one elbow. He hoped so. She was special. And Tommy deserved it. His vain wife had left him several years ago for a richer man.

"I don't *think*. It's a bet."

"You're on. The old expense account can stand a dinner for two in Carmel—if we eat fish and chips."

"Oh, no. Steak and vintage wine."

"How do you *know* they are a twosome?"

"Just the way she inadvertently said, 'Tommy Whitlock,' and then, awkwardly, 'Mr. Whitlock,' as if he were a character in nineteenth-century Monterey."

"Too bad we can't have the murderer speak four words. The bastard would be under lock and key."

Sullivan's first pillow missed him.

She switched off the light in the one lamp, leaving them in a separate darkness. "It's pretty cold over here, and I can hear the rain on the window."

"It's warm over here, and the rain sounds wonderful."

"I think I'll leave over here."

"Good thinking," Morris said.

Morris left for breakfast with Sullivan's head still conveniently under a pillow.

First person he ran into in the hallway was Larry Crosby. Who'd already read the morning paper and the speculation the Pro-Am might be called off and was angry with Inspector Stanley Gooden.

"You'd better get in line," Morris said. "How is Bing?"

"Worse. He's out of it. But he's aware enough to make it plain we are not to stop the tournament, come high water or murder."

Morris knocked out a quick lead, quoting Bing Crosby that the Pro-Am was on, in spite of the weather and the murder.

* * *

Morris made it to the dining room, and who was sitting at a table by himself? Sidney Barker, the one and only bandleader.

Morris pulled out a chair without asking. "Did you get any sleep?"

"Why, hell, yes," Sidney said. "I haven't been to bed that early since The Crosby was canceled for World War Two."

"Hell of a thing, Sidney. McCall dying on the floor."

Sidney paused with a strip of bacon between his thumb and his finger and waved it once like a baton before popping it into his small mouth. "Some exit. Somebody hated the bastard worse than I did." He thought about that. "No. If you hadn't stopped the fight, I was going to beat the son of a bitch to death."

"It's true you hung a nice right hand on him, Sidney." Morris hushed to order eggs and bacon and the whole nine yards. "But you are going to miss having him around. So will Bing. So will all of us. I mean, even in Hollywood it's tough to find a one hundred percent lead-plated asshole to bitch about."

Sidney laughed in spite of himself.

"What did the inspector ask you?"

"Speaking of assholes." Sidney sipped on his coffee. "But I liked the deputy patrol officer."

"What's not to like?"

"She's a pro. Asks the tough questions but in a professional way. I didn't hold back," Sidney said. "I told her McCall was a lying, cheating bastard, who was very nearly killed twice in the same night. I told her we had hated each other since the forties, when he kicked me and my band off Bing's radio show, looking out for his goddamned daddy's niece's goddamned husband, who was tone-deaf. Go and find his goddamned band. The army wouldn't take 'em. Go and find one golfer who won't swear the son of a bitch McCall was the biggest cheat who ever teed it up in the rough. I told the deputy I didn't deny a damn thing. But I couldn't see the bar and what went into McCall's damn glass."

"Your man Ed Waters was standing at the bar. Have you spoken to him?"

"No. Ed avoids me like I have a social disease. I hate it. Ed's a good man, a solid playing pro. What the hell, Morris, I got to thinking about the old days last year, and I had a few too many before the last round of the Pro-Am. I offered to pay him what we might have won. He was insulted."

"He'll get over it. He went on to have a lucrative year. What did you tell the inspector?" Morris asked.

"As little as possible. I told him to check with the deputy."

"I know he loved that."

"He threatened to haul me down to the sheriff's of-fice. I told him the same things I told the deputy in one-half as many words."

Morris laughed. "He's a beauty, the inspector. That's exactly what I found myself doing. I told him what I'd seen and heard, the same as I told Deputy Jordan, but I left out anything I thought or sensed. Who hated him enough to kill him, Sidney?"

"You don't doubt he was poisoned?"

"No." Morris shook his head. His bacon was crisp and wonderful.

"No tellin' who killed him," Sidney said. "I hope they never catch him."

"Do you know the redhead?"

"Never saw her before. She must be desperate to make a living."

"I understand she's an actress," Morris said.

Sidney rolled his eyes.

"Did he have one true friend, Andrew McCall?"

Sidney thought about it. "I never met him, if he did. Those people on the payroll kissed his ass. Crosby even kissed his ass. I never did. Cost me plenty in the forties."

"Do you remember his wife?"

"Sure. Sarah. She was from Cleveland. A singer, actually, and a damn good one. She never deserved McCall. She died years ago. Long after she left him. She kept the kids. I don't think his two grown sons even spoke to him."

"One thing you can say for the bastard," Morris said, "he could run a big-time advertising agency."

Sidney nodded it was true. "Says something for the business."

"Had you done any work with McCall lately?" Morris asked.

Sidney looked up somewhat uneasily. "I should have told the deputy. McCall's agency recently took over the General Electric account. Or part of it. He killed the campaign they were using, with my music in the background. Cost me a few bucks. The son of a bitch."

"You didn't mention it to the inspector either?"

"No."

"Better do that, Sidney. The cops don't like surprises. Even small ones."

"I'll call the deputy. Her name was Jordan?"

"Patricia Jordan, from the Monterey substation. I hope she's still on the case. But the inspector won't like hearing it from her."

"Piss on the inspector," Sidney said, getting up, throwing his napkin on his plate. "I'd better call before I hit some practice balls. I ain't gettin' on the course in this weather until I have to. I'm too damn old."

"Not that old, Sidney. You still pack a good right hand."

Sidney, round and low, stood up, grinning like a man pleased with himself.

Morris finished the bacon and eggs and was working on a second cup of coffee.

"The man I'm looking for. May I sit down?" asked Jay Martin, the ABC publicist and fiancé to the unhappy Trudy Standridge. Jay had that translucent prep school complexion that left him looking younger than his years, and he couldn't be thirty. Nothing a writer could ask of ABC that Jay couldn't get. Sometimes he seemed too helpful, like a too-willing lapdog.

"By all means, sit," Morris said. "How's the fiancée?"

"That's what I want to talk to you about, Morris. I mean, I've got a problem. ABC is moving me to New York. Trudy's a California girl. She wants no part of New York. You got any suggestions for jobs here on the Coast? ABC's been good to me. But New York is out."

"Did you talk to Roone?" Morris asked, as in Roone Arledge, head of ABC sports.

"Yeah. Roone said, 'Kid, the action's in New York,' and hung up."

"Roone should know. Did he give any specific reason for transferring you? The network does plenty of business on the West Coast."

Martin busied himself with his cup of coffee, shaking his head.

"Maybe you'd better talk some more with Trudy. The move to New York doesn't have to be forever. ABC is a tough act to follow. It's not your local five-thousand-watt setup. You've done good work for them, old man. I'd think twice before leaving ABC."

Martin continued to shake his head. "It's no go. She won't change planes in New York, except to go to Europe on our honeymoon—*if* we get married at all."

Morris almost said, "Buy the lady a one-way ticket," but caught himself. "There's plenty of work out here on the Coast. I doubt you'll need my help. But I'll put in a good word where I can." Morris said, "Were you still in the Snake Pit when McCall died?"

Martin looked down into his coffee as if avoiding the memory. He nodded yes.

"Did you see the boys fight?"

Now Martin smiled. "Some fight. I think they would have called it, even in Vegas."

"You were pretty close to the bar when the two of us spoke. Did you see if the bartender filled the same glass McCall set down?"

Martin seemed to turn away from the question.

"Think back."

Martin looked down until his eyes were almost closed. "I could see the bartender. He was pouring scotch, I believe. I couldn't see the bar itself. I don't know what glass the bartender picked up. You're certain McCall was murdered, Morris?"

"Oh, yes."

Martin seemed dislocated by the direct answer.

"Did you happen to see McCall enter the room . . . with the redhead?" Morris asked.

"I came in behind them."

"Did he have a glass in his hand?"

Martin closed one eye in thought. "Yes. It was almost empty. He made immediately for the bar."

"Was the redhead carrying a glass?"

"No." He smiled, if painfully. "I think I looked at her too closely. Trudy gave me an elbow in the ribs." It seemed to please him to remember her anger. Then he was frowning again.

"I expect you've worked with McCall's advertising clients," Morris said.

Martin nodded, volunteering nothing.

"How did the bastard keep such powerful clients?"

"He drove a nasty bargain with the networks. He never paid top dollar for a minute of prime time. Don't think he didn't let his clients know it. I'm glad that's not my end of the business."

"Did he meddle in the publicity end of things?" Morris asked.

"When he could. Nothing pleased Andrew McCall." Martin tapped his spoon on his cup for emphasis. "I'd better go. I've got visiting firemen to entertain. Keep me in mind."

"I'll do it," Morris said. "One thing."

Martin paused, as if for last-minute instructions he didn't look forward to.

"Did the deputy or the inspector question you?"

Martin's prep school complexion faded even paler. "No, thank goodness," he said.

Morris nodded him off, not saying, "Don't worry, young friend, they'll catch up with you . . . probably before the day is over."

Morris hoisted his umbrella and poled his way with his cane to the Pebble Beach practice tee. A few desperate souls were beating balls off the soppy grass. They included wealthy amateurs suddenly terrified, with good reason, of the three formidable courses sure to savage their egos with wind and mud and rain and sheer cliffs they might want to dive off to escape the laughter of a national television audience.

An invitation to The Crosby Pro-Am was more to be desired by an amateur golfer than a free pass from the Internal Revenue Service. No invitation went out, unless signed by Bing himself. Fame, money, and power did not hurt your chances of being invited. But none of the three could buy you an invitation if Crosby wasn't humming your tune. Given a letter from a young man who'd caddied in the tournament and would love to play in it, Crosby wrote him, "You're invited." One of Crosby's longtime friends and Pro-Am regular was the crack amateur Johnny Swanson, who lived in San Francisco and ran a bowling alley.

Certain corporate giants were Crosby institutions. The Sheraton's Ed Crowley was playing in his twenty-fifth consecutive tournament. He'd won the Pro-Am twice with Cary Middlecoff and was teamed with him when Middlecoff shot an unmatchable closing 68 in a violent rainstorm to win the 1956 Crosby.

Crowley, now sixty-eight himself, was lashing practice balls, stepping into his shots as vigorously as he had a quarter of a century ago, though his hair was now streaked with white.

Morris edged over to him. "You're going to play forever, Ed."

"Oh, no, Morris." Crowley spun an acceptable five-iron into the rain. "One more year. And that's it. If I don't drown before the week is over."

"You'll be playing as long as Crosby doesn't run out of stamps for invitations."

"One more year," Crowley insisted, and in truth he lived up to that promise. He was not so pleased with a four-iron, which scudded off the wet grass. "Any further word on what happened to McCall?" he asked.

Morris shook his head.

"Not a lovely man," said Crowley, "but you hate to see your own generation go down . . . especially that way."

"Indeed," said Morris, passing a short salute. Crowley was lucky. He hadn't been in the Snake Pit to see Mr. Death on the loose.

Morris moved on, stopping to watch two kids smash balls, the pair of them looking like skinny young twin California blond giraffes in their unfortunate bell-bottom trousers: Johnny Miller and his amateur partner, Locke de Bretteville, a recent University of California graduate. Miller was razzing him about his grip.

"Just catch this one," said de Bretteville, launching a serious drive into the wet sky. Miller, the new rising young talent to challenge Nicklaus, laughed at the drive and cracked a rifle shot of his own that flew de Bretteville's ball, vanishing out of sight into the mist. But it was Miller's seeing-eye irons that lashed every ball to the flag stick that separated him from the PGA crowd.

"Morris," Miller said.

It had been a struggle to break him from saying, "*Mr.* Morris," since he burst on the tour, winning the U.S. Open last year at rugged Oakmont, with a record-breaking 63 on the last day.

"De Bretteville helping you with your game?" Morris asked.

"He thinks he is."

"I'll have him straightened out before Thursday," de Bretteville said.

Miller's face grew serious. "I didn't really know the man, Morris," he said. He didn't have to say which man. "I can't believe somebody killed a golfer here at The Crosby."

"Believe it," Morris said.

"Any chance they'll cancel the tournament?"

"Not a chance. Crosby promised Nicklaus his third straight championship," Morris said, needling Miller.

Miller crinkled up his eyes at that. "Best not to get into a sudden-death play-off at Pebble Beach with Mr. Nicklaus," he admitted.

Morris moved along to watch the young Tom Kite, from Austin, Texas, lay pipe with his driver, successive balls traveling so straight they might have landed in the same dimple marks. Kite, even under his rain hat, was having trouble keeping his glasses free of fog and spray. He could not know that one day, years from now, he would subdue Pebble Beach in wind as fierce as the devil himself to win the U.S. Open championship.

The Old Sarge, Orville Moody, repeated his effortless swings, careless of the rain and the memory of the three-putt on the 72d green that threw him into a play-off with the all-mighty Nicklaus and cost him The Crosby title last year. Moody had tried every known variety of putter, but nothing could cure his frightful "yips" on the greens. He'd won only once as a professional, hitting the ball so purely at the Champions course in Houston in 1969 that no one in the U.S. Open field could overtake him, even on the relatively benign greens. Moody sent another immaculate shot into the falling mist. Nothing. Not fate. Not the yips. Not the rain itself could wash away the name Orville Moody from the Open trophy.

Young Hale Irwin, as thin as a one-iron, looked neither left nor right, as he willed shot after shot in the tenacious manner that later won him three U.S. Opens. For the moment he labored in a certain mechanical anonymity, but that changed before 1974 passed into time, with the playing of the Open at Winged Foot.

Morris paused to watch the action of the young rookie Gary McCord, from Riverside, California. With his plump face and long sideburns, McCord looked as if he belonged on the old TV cowboy show *Bonanza*. The kid had finally escaped the minitour circuit and earned his PGA card. Morris liked his irreverent sense of humor.

"You mean the AP is out in the rain?" McCord said. "They must have padlocked the bar."

"*McCord?*" Morris said. "Wasn't that a failed automobile?"

McCord misfired a purposeful shank, a very difficult thing to do. "Can the AP cure that?" he asked.

"No, but we can identify it: 'Heavyset Gary McCord showed up at The Crosby carrying the weight of his usual game,'" Morris dictated.

McCord cracked up. Then he walked over and asked quietly, "Are the police looking for a killer? Here at the tournament?"

"If they aren't, they will be shortly," Morris said.

"Let's hope they find him in a hurry."

"Yes," said Morris, who wouldn't bet on it.

Ahead on the tee was the lean, muscular, herky-jerky figure of Jake Hill, with his short-short abbreviated backswing reminiscent of a Georgia player of an earlier age, Doug Sanders. Guys on tour laughed to themselves that Jake'd grown up so far back in the Georgia mountains he'd never had enough level ground to make a full turn on the ball. They didn't laugh about it in front of Jake. He'd as soon challenge them to a round at one thousand dollars a hole—even two years ago, when he was a rookie and broke as a Georgia dirt farmer.

Jake lashed a low, nasty ball that bored under the wind off the Pacific and had enough spin to stop on a church steeple.

"All those high rainbows are gonna get you killed in this wind," Morris said, knowing Jake didn't take to anybody speaking to him while he practiced. Or while he changed shoes. Or while he ate. Or while he breathed in air and breathed out carbon dioxide.

Jake turned his dark, deep-set eyes, under darker brows on Morris. "You givin' lessons? You're the bastard didn't think I oughta've been rookie of the year."

"That's me. And you didn't 'oughta've been,' " Morris said. "But you weren't shabby. Remember, the other kid finished ahead of you on the money ladder."

"Yeah? I beat him twenty-three times last year." Those results were obviously in the front of his memory bank.

"Then I would have voted you rookie of the year . . . *last year*," Morris said, smiling to see the "Angry Young Man" of any year.

Jake himself showed a crooked smile you rarely saw. He'd made a half million dollars in the last two years and hadn't bothered to have his teeth fixed.

"Jake, you were at the bar last night," Morris said. "Did you know the young man—well, not that young— standing there between you and Ed Waters?"

"No." Jake, uninterested, shook his head.

"Did the bartender fill the same glass that Andrew McCall put down?"

Jake turned back to the mound of practice balls and lashed a white streak, bare inches off the wet grass, as if to parody his own style.

Morris figured he wasn't going to answer him and turned on his cane, which sank in the wet ground.

"Yeah," said Jake over his shoulder. "The same goddamn glass. I know. The dumb bartender was about to mix it up with mine."

"Be thankful for large mercies," Morris said.

"You think the sumbitching bartender killed 'im?" Now Jake was looking directly at him from under his rain hat.

"No," Morris said. "I doubt he had any idea who McCall was. Did you know him?"

Jake stood poised over his pile of practice balls, as if searching for a chosen one to beat into submission. "I knew him. I liked him." He didn't offer any explanation.

"Why?" Morris asked, amazed to find someone who actually liked Andrew McCall.

Jake turned back to his labor, his jaw set against par and to hell with murder.

Well, ready or not, he would be talking to the inspector soon enough.

Stepping onto the practice tee, carrying one club, a six-iron, was the good-time tenor Jackie Melton, sans rain suit. He held one golf ball in his pudgy hand.

"I thought you had retired to the piano," Morris said.

Jackie smiled his cherubic smile. "Wanted to hit one more here . . . for old times' sake." He dropped the ball. Took a stylish practice swing. And then lifted an effortless six-iron that belied his seventy-two years. He watched it as if seeing his youth descend from the wet sky and held the pose long after the ball was on the ground.

"Come on inside before you show up these young hotshots," Morris said. "I'm good for the Bloody Marys."

Jackie walked with him back to the lodge, his six-iron over his shoulder like a spent fishing pole.

"To the good times to come," Morris said, touching his glass to Jackie's.

"I enjoyed Julia Sullivan last night on the piano bench," Jackie said, brushing the rain from his artificially blond hair. "She can't sing a note; she loves life; she reminds me of my Mary." The rain might have clouded his blue eyes.

"To Mary," Morris said, touching glasses again. "You'd have to say God is in lucky company."

Jackie was not ashamed to dab his eyes with his napkin.

Morris reached for a bit of cheer on a rainy day. "What was it like, The Crosby, in the early days?"

Jackie tilted the Bloody Mary as if to strengthen his memory. "Damn wonderful. Bing had a little ranch down in San Diego County. Kept him near a racetrack he was backing, Del Mar. I raced a big Thoroughbred, Long-Gone, who won the first stakes race at Del Mar. It was a better payday than the three movies I made." Jackie laughed and lifted his glass to signal a refill.

"In those days I could play a little golf," he said. "Bing hit it big time. I have no doubt he could've made it with the pros. Of course he would have made about two hundred million dollars less than he did singing a minor-league baritone." Jackie laughed, pleased to be needling Crosby and talking about the old times.

"Bing invited some local pros, and a few top guys off the PGA tour, to come down in 1937 and tee it up in a Pro-Am. He invited his show business buddies and a bunch of the best amateurs in California. Entry fee was *three dollars*, if you can believe that. Among the pros, I know, were Lloyd Mangrum, and Johnny Revolta, and

Henry Picard, and Denny Shute, and Paul Runyan, and
Dutch Harrison, and . . . let's see . . . Leonard
Dodson. I think Olin Dutra and Willie Goggin. God,
those are names lost to time. Lawson Little, who'd won
the U.S. Amateur twice and the British Amateur, tried
to enter as a pro before he joined the PGA. Caused a
big stink. But he didn't get there anyway.

"It rained like the end of the world. Does that sound
familiar?" asked Jackie, looking out at the rain pounding on the window. "We were playing the nifty little
course at Rancho Santa Fe. Or trying to play a two-
round tournament. Finally, we got in one round on
Sunday. Sam Snead of course won the pro title. He won
it twice more before the Japs bombed Pearl Harbor.

"This 1937 Snead had hair up under that hat. Even
had a widow's peak," said Jackie. "I bet he still has the
seven hundred and sixty-two dollars and thirty-two
cents he won. Shot a 36-32—68. In all that rain and
mud. Never had a bogey. Sam could play. He can still
play. He and a guy, George Lewis, won the Pro-Am,
only Bing called it the Amateur-Pro in those days, he
having *top billing* as an amateur, of course," Jackie said,
with no little cynicism.

"Remember the songwriter Harold Arlen?" Jackie
broke into a gutsy tenor. " 'Every trick of hers you're on
to.' " Harold and Tony Joy finished third in the Pro-
Am. Hey, my partner—a local pro—and I had to be led
home, with a bunch of others, by the highway patrol
just about daybreak, and we got up and finished in the
top five. I don't know how well we might have done if
we had been alive." Jackie laughed, forgetting the
Bloody Mary in his hand, loving those long-gone days.

He looked up as if taking his cue from a conductor. "Bing, you see, threw a big barbecue for everybody at his house near the golf course. I don't why it got to be called The Clambake. He didn't barbecue any clams. I guess because the Pacific Ocean was hanging around close by to the west. I guess it still is, Morris. If the rain hasn't flooded it out.

"Now we had a few people at the barbecue who had been known to sing and dance and tell a few lies: Fred Astaire, Zeppo Marx, Edgar Kennedy, Guy Kibbee, Andy Clyde. Hope wasn't there for the first one. Didn't take him long to get there. He and Bing were buddies in those days and big rivals. Bob could play a little golf, but Bing could spot him a couple a side. We all played the same course. We mostly stayed at the Del Mar Hotel. It's where I met Mary Lindsey, hostess in the lounge at the Del Mar Hotel." Jackie lifted the Bloody Mary to keep his chin from trembling.

"After the war Bing moved the Pro-Am here to the Monterey Peninsula. He still runs it like a private party. Nobody ever dreamed it would be the big show it's become on national television. I guess Bing quit playing in the late fifties. He couldn't stand not being on the tube himself as guest announcer. And he didn't want people seeing him hit it like an old man. Me? I'm through myself." Jackie killed the rest of the drink and set the glass down as if his song were sung.

"What was your reaction last night to what happened to McCall?" asked Morris.

"It was sad. Not his death. His bloody life," Melton said. "A sorry man, McCall."

Morris nodded his agreement. "Jackie, could you see the bar in all that crowd?"

"Not from the piano bench. I couldn't see much when I stood up. You know me, Mr. Five Foot Five."

"You're not shocked somebody wanted to kill him?"

"A small bandstand could hold those people who knew him who *didn't want to kill him*," said Jackie.

"Somebody chose a dangerous method. He, or she, could have killed the redhead just as easily. Or anybody whose glass became confused with McCall's."

"I suppose the killer didn't give a damn, just took his chances. How did he put the poison in the glass, Morris?"

"*That* is the question. It'll keep the sheriff's department up nights. Have they spoken with you?"

"No. I don't know why they should," Jackie said. "I didn't speak to the man all night, and I never intended to speak to him ever, if I could help it."

"You two have a recent run-in?" Morris asked.

"No. But who doesn't hate a sandbagger? A cheat. An egomaniac, who made life miserable for his wife, Sarah, a lovely woman, once a favorite of my Mary's. And a vindictive bastard who used his power to bully everybody, including Crosby, who never had the guts to stand up to him. And those were his good points." Jackie ran his fingers slowly, rhythmically over the tabletop as if making a sad riff on the piano.

Sullivan lost the towel running from the shower to the telephone.

"That you, Sullivan?"

"It's me all right. And only me," she said. "This

wouldn't be the local sheriff?" She was sure she recognized his voice.

"Himself," admitted Tommy Whitlock, sounding as much as he could like Gary Cooper in *High Noon*. "I suppose John Morris is out harassing the golf population."

"At least."

"Good. I'd rather talk with you. If you'll come down to Jack Houghton's office, I'll buy the coffee."

"I better put my towel back on," Sullivan said.

"Oh, hell, no. This is the Monterey Peninsula, California, the Age of Aquarius, by all means come as you are," the sheriff said.

"I wouldn't want to scare the help," Sullivan said. "Tommy, we're all worried to death."

"For good reason. I'll keep the coffee hot."

Sullivan, in her dark trousers and turtleneck sweater, opened the door to the lodge manager's office.

Tommy Whitlock stood up in his boots. He was tall, as tall as John Morris, but altogether leaner. It was good that he had lost some of his hair, or he would have been entirely too handsome to be sheriff. He gave her an absolute hug.

"You look wonderful . . . too beautiful to be hanging around with the Associated Press," Tommy said. "Have to say I'm disappointed. I was counting on you wrapped in a house towel."

"Trust me. Arresting me for indecent exposure would be a misdemeanor," Sullivan said. "Lead me to the coffee."

Rain of course blew against the floor-to-ceiling window.

"To the sheriff of Monterey County," Sullivan said, raising her cup.

"Until the next election," he said, raising his own.

"So the man was murdered?" Sullivan said.

"Oh, yes. Potassium cyanide. My pathologist was up all night. He said if McCall hadn't been poisoned, the bastard might have lived to be a hundred."

"That's a depressing thought. I can't believe I said that," said Sullivan.

"The question of *who* killed him isn't as puzzling as *how* it was done," Whitlock said. He indeed had the long, lean face of a movie cowboy. But Sullivan knew he'd graduated at the top of his class at Stanford, boots and all.

She said, "Only one-half of the population of the peninsula was in the Snake Pit when it happened. Morris and I, between us, remembered twenty-seven people who were there."

"I know. I've read Inspector Gooden's report." Whitlock's expression offered no opinion of the inspector.

"How about Deputy Jordan's report?"

"I've read it too."

"I bet it was thorough," Sullivan said, no hint of a smile on her face.

"It was."

"Are you going to keep her on the case?"

The sheriff crossed one boot over his knee. "What are you trying to say, Sullivan?"

"The inspector can use all the help he can get. It's a

high-profile case. And God knows, a complicated one."
Sullivan couldn't help the tiny smile tugging at her lips.

The sheriff sat looking at her with his gray eyes.

"Morris and I thought she was meticulous . . . and insightful." She did not say, "She looked damn good in her trousers," but it was written in her eyes.

"Don't go jumping to conclusions," Whitlock said.

"Not me."

"The hell you're not." He put his boot back on the floor, an act of surrender. "You must understand, Julia, she works for me." It had to be serious for him to call her Julia. "She likes her job. She's good at it. I like my job. I'm not bad at it. It puts me in an awkward position. And I've already proven I'm not much good at the man-woman thing."

"I don't think you could get reelected on that platform," Sullivan said. "Who would believe it? Not me. I liked her a lot. We both did."

"I'm not surprised." He lifted the coffeepot to refill her cup. "But that will keep for another time."

"Only if you two promise to invite us for a drink—before or after this is over."

"A promise. Now tell me everything you and John Morris know," the sheriff said.

Sullivan began her story at her sitting on the piano bench with Jackie Melton. She included everything she saw and heard, and everything Morris had told her of what he had seen and heard, including his Mexican standoff with Inspector Gooden.

The sheriff could not help flinching at that encounter. "Gooden is a thorough investigator. His strength is not as a diplomat."

Sullivan arched her eyebrows in agreement.

"So you two didn't talk with the kid bartender?" said Whitlock.

"No."

"Listen, both of you can help me. I know quite a number of these people at The Crosby. You two know them all."

"We're strong on killer personalities," Sullivan said.

Whitlock shook his head. "You're incorrigible, Sullivan. I can't believe I need help this badly. The bartender's name is Dudley Greene. Never bartended before. But what could you expect of a Berkeley man? He came down to make a few bucks toward his tuition. He had no idea who Andrew McCall was. He had no idea what McCall meant, 'Not too damn much water' in his scotch. But he's very sure that's what McCall said and then got upset about. The kid swears he barely wet the ice in the glass. Dudley admitted he broke the seal on the bottle of Johnnie Walker Black Label when he opened the bar.

"Pretty fancy scotch for the Snake Pit. In fact, all the other scotch behind the bar was much cheaper stuff. Jack Houghton's trying to find out who bought it. Of course there was no cyanide in the scotch. Or the whole Pit would be full of bodies," said the sheriff.

"Including my own . . . twice over," Sullivan said.

"The kid said he drew the water in the pitcher himself. About an hour earlier, when he came in to set up the bar for the night. It was a cash bar. He'd already made two hundred dollars in tips. Not a cent from McCall, of course. But I don't guess that was reason enough to kill him?"

"It would be in Manhattan," Sullivan said.

"Of course, no poison in the pitcher," Whitlock said, shaking his head again. "The kid couldn't remember who was drinking what. He barely knew the vodka bottle when he picked it up. He must have been sweating bullets to fill the orders. Dudley has agreed to take a lie detector test. He doesn't want a lawyer."

"In California you get a lawyer to be baptized."

"They'll baptize you all right," said Whitlock; "they'll drown you in red ink. Just try getting a divorce here, even if your wife leaves you." He was embarrassed to have said it.

"The second best thing that ever happened to you, Tommy," Sullivan said. "I think we've already met the best thing."

Even the high sheriff could blush.

"The redhead. The actress. What's her story?" Sullivan asked.

"Her professional name is Tana Daly."

"Daly . . . if not nightly," Sullivan said.

The sheriff ignored her. "Her real name is Dora Hudgins from Chicago. She's twenty-two. McCall met her at a party in New York, premiering a CBS movie of the week."

"And she's the flavor of the week."

"It seems. One of his advertising clients was a sponsor of the movie. A suspense movie."

"Don't tell me. The victim was poisoned."

"No. Our girl, Daly, killed with a screwdriver."

Sullivan wrapped her arms around herself. "Terrific. Just what America needs, a nonviolent narrative."

"She drove up from L.A.," Whitlock said. "And she's staying in McCall's suite."

"How long's she known him?"

"Three weeks."

"Well, that's a marriage in L.A.," Sullivan said. She bit her lip as Tommy winced. "Sorry about that."

Tommy only shook his head a third time. "She told me, cold-bloodedly, that coming here was 'a career decision.' You'd have to say McCall wasn't leading her on. She's already signed for a bigger part in another TV movie . . . with another McCall sponsor."

"The romantic lead, no doubt."

"The victim."

"Don't tell me, killed Valentine's Day with a crowbar."

"No, strangled."

"At least a hands-on crime," Sullivan said.

The sheriff ran his hand over his receding hairline. "I hope you never go in for crime, Sullivan. I don't think the pathologists of California are ready for you."

"So where did our boy McCall get his drinking glass?" Sullivan asked.

"From his suite. A plain water glass. Tana says she took it out of the plastic wrapping. She said McCall poured his own first scotch and water. Glenlivet, single-malt scotch. Top-of-the-line stuff. We've tested it. We've tested every bottle in the suite. We've taken the suite apart. His and her luggage apart. No particle of potassium cyanide anywhere. You wouldn't believe the nightclothes in her luggage," he said, as an afterthought.

"Try me."

"I'm too old to describe it."

"Morris is right. If she is the one who wanted him dead, she should have waited until bedtime. How much can an aged heart stand?"

"Let's not get personal."

The sheriff, she knew, was barely in his forties. "I wonder . . . after the bartender filled his glass, did McCall drink from it *before* the fight?"

"Good question. Tana Daly isn't sure. She doesn't think so. The glass was almost full when he handed it to her. Then she was jostled from every side. Anyone might have dropped something in the glass. She only recognized a few famous faces. She had no idea who might have been crowding against her. The fight so upset her, she almost took a sip of the scotch. She turned pale remembering it. But she's sworn off booze. Trying to keep her weight down. *She says.* She must not weigh a hundred and ten pounds."

"Tommy. I left the piano bench during the commotion between McCall and Sidney. I was standing pretty close when the fight started. I'm sure Tana spilled a bit of scotch on the floor when he first handed her the glass. She looked down to be sure it didn't hit her yellow dress. I don't think she was concerned if Andrew McCall got his nose relocated. If there was cyanide already in the glass, it might still be in that spot on the floor."

"Damn. I just gave Houghton permission to have the Snake Pit cleaned up. I thought we'd finished with it." He snatched up the phone. It was too late. The cleaning women had mopped and cleaned the floor.

He said, "That's how sheriffs get careless and get

voted out of office. If there were still traces of cyanide in the spot you remember, it would be impossible to know if they were spilled or if McCall spit them up."

Sullivan set down her cup. "I think I've had enough coffee."

"Just as a precaution, we're checking every bottle of booze in the lodge that has been brought out of storage," said Whitlock, "even those that appear unopened."

"You'll have a mess if you also check the soda and tonic water," Sullivan said.

"We're checking it."

"Isn't that a bit extreme?"

"Yeah. And so would be the death of Clint Eastwood."

"You've got a point there. But who would want to kill Clint Eastwood?"

"I can only say I'm glad he wasn't holding Andrew McCall's glass during the fight. Clint might have taken a sip. Clint might have downed it all. Clint doesn't have to worry about his waistline," said the sheriff.

There was a rap on the door. John Morris stepped inside. "If there's something going on, I hope to hell I'm interrupting."

"Bad timing, Morris," Sullivan said.

"So they voted you back in office," Morris said, shaking the sheriff's hand.

"But what have I done for them lately?" said Whitlock.

Morris poured himself a cup of coffee and set about describing what he'd learned that morning. Sidney Barker was supposed to have called Deputy Jordan and told her that McCall had recently killed a General Electric ad, featuring Sidney's music. Costing him "a few bucks." The sheriff made a note of it. Sidney had been honest. He hoped they never caught the guy who'd killed McCall. Jay Martin had entered the pit behind McCall and the redhead, and he was sure McCall was carrying a near-empty glass.

Sullivan dropped the redhead's name on him, followed by a silent warning with her trigger finger. She told him how Miss Daly had unwrapped the glass in their suite and McCall had poured his own first scotch and water of the night.

Morris said Jay Martin had not seen which glass the bartender filled before setting it back in front of McCall. "But," said Morris, "the young Georgia golfer Jake Hill was standing at the bar and saw the bartender fill McCall's glass, after almost confusing it with his own."

Whitlock knew Jake Hill as a rising young professional but hadn't met him. He made a note to have him looked up.

"Jake said he knew Andrew McCall and *liked* him," Morris said. "I swear that's a virgin opinion. I never heard it said aloud before by anybody."

"Why, for God's sake, did he like him?" Whitlock asked.

"I don't know. Jake turned back to hitting practice balls. He'd already said a week's supply of words. But tell me something more suspicious than a grown man liking Andrew McCall," Morris said. "I understand from Larry Crosby that Bing's not going to stop the tournament even if somebody offs Larry."

"Oh, hell, no," said Whitlock.

"Before I forget it," said Morris, "I still don't know who the youngish man was standing between Jake and Ed Waters at the bar. Jake said he didn't know him. I haven't run into Ed this morning. Do you know Ed?"

The sheriff nodded.

"The back of the guy's head looked familiar. But I didn't see his face."

The sheriff made a note to look up Ed.

"Anything we can do to help, we will," Morris said, tapping Julia Sullivan on the back of her hand.

"Yeah, I should have you two on the payroll already," Whitlock said. "I hear you and my inspector didn't— what do you southern plowboys say?—didn't gee and haw."

"I think he'd rather have a hernia than put up with me," Morris said.

"He's not Miss Congeniality," said the sheriff, "but he's a thorough investigator."

"I'm sure," Morris said, in no way sure.

"Okay, I'm also keeping Deputy Jordan on the case," said Whitlock. "You two get out of here. I've got work to do."

"Better you than me," Morris said. "I only have to knock out a few hundred words for my dear readers and viewers, all of whom move their lips, even when they're listening."

The sheriff waved them out of the room.

Morris thought, *It will take a brave man to drink the next scotch and water in the Snake Pit.*

* * *

Many brave men and women—celebrities as thick as seashells—gathered in the night to hear Bob Hope fill in at The Clambake for his old friend and *Road* show rival Bing Crosby. Hope was in vintage form: "I used to advertise Pepsodent. Now all the people who heard me are using Polydent."

Murder never seemed so far away.

CHAPTER FIVE

"No wonder Sadie Thompson took up with that preacher in Pago Pago. Somerset Maugham got it right. It wasn't the devil; it was the rain that made her do it," Sullivan said.

Morris steadied the large umbrella over them both. "You mean, if it keeps raining, I'd better look out for any Pentecostal preachers?"

"This isn't Georgia, Morris. I don't think they have them on the Monterey Peninsula."

"This is California. They have everything here," Morris said, "except sunshine." The mud threatened to pull the shoes off their feet, and the rain whipped under the umbrella.

Gary Player's wedge lifted a mud ball the size of a soccer ball. The small, muscular South African tossed his club to his caddie, and said, "That's it, mate. I've teed it up on all the continents. Don't mean to try the oceans."

The Wednesday practice round was a washout.

"You know I'm soaked and freezing, Morris, when I choose a cup of coffee over a free brandy," said Sullivan, too drenched to sit down in the crowded hospitality suite. "My hair's wet; my blouse is ruined; my under-clothes are soaked."

"I never realized golf affected you so intimately," Morris said, luxuriating in the warmth of the brandy.

"I'm drinking the wrong liquid," Sullivan said, putting down the coffee and asking for a brandy.

Morris turned to a tap on his shoulder.

"I'm been looking for you," said Ed Waters, his round face and receding hairline and pudgy torso revealing nothing of the professional athlete. Ed, long fixed in his habits, was half again more formal than his fellow golfers. "Did you speak to the lady deputy about me?"

"I did. You owe me one. Did you ever see a more beautiful sheriff's deputy?"

"I have to say no. But I don't fancy being a witness in a murder investigation." Ed, a quiet bachelor in his late thirties, had played the PGA tour for fifteen years in near obscurity. In his best years his winnings were in the low six figures. But major advertisers ignored him. He didn't bother to have an agent, which was a mistake, Morris thought.

"Better to be a witness than the victim," Morris said. "What did you tell her?"

"That I didn't know, or see really, the fellow at the bar last night standing between myself and Jake Hill."

"Had you ever seen him before?"

"I don't honestly know. I wasn't paying him any attention. Maybe Jake knew him."

Morris didn't say he'd spoken with Jake, and Jake said he didn't know him. "Did you help the deputy at all?"

"I doubt it." Waters swung his coffee in his cup. "I did see this man McCall arguing with Sidney Barker when I got here Sunday."

"What about?"

"I'm not sure. I was checking in and trying to look out for my bags and my clubs. I don't trust anybody with my clubs since they were stolen in the lobby of my hotel in L.A. and I never got them back. I still haven't found another driver I can trust."

"Snead said if you ever find a driver you like, sleep with it. He's had the same one, I know, for thirty-five years. So what were they arguing about?" asked Morris.

"All I caught was something about General Electric. I wasn't surprised to see Sidney strike him in the Snake Pit. I thought he might attack him in the lobby of the lodge."

"What did McCall say?"

"He was less than friendly. He kept saying—" Waters paused, then said quietly, " 'Fuck you and your music, Sidney.' I'm sorry about that, Sullivan."

"Not to worry. It's a grand Middle Dutch expression." She smiled at Waters's discomfort.

"I left them there, still arguing," he said.

"Did you see the redhead?" Morris asked.

"Yes. Quite a looker."

"Careful how you pronounce that," Morris said.

Waters was embarrassed enough to blush, yet on the golf course, where no quality of mercy existed, Ed Waters, with limited talent, was a fierce enough competitor to survive for fifteen years. Beneath that soft exterior was an iron rod of resolution.

Waters said, "The young woman was standing quite a distance away in the lobby, as if she didn't claim to know either Sidney or McCall."

Morris suddenly changed the subject. "Last night did you see the bartender fill McCall's glass?"

Waters slowly shook his head. "I'm not sure it was the same glass McCall put down. The young bartender was about to pour my vodka. I wasn't too pleased when McCall, standing behind me, shoved his glass past mine and Jake's. I thought the bartender, who was inexperienced and very nervous, confused this man's glass with Jake's. I started to say something. But then I thought, *Well, Jake's standing right here; he's not saying anything.*"

"Did you tell the deputy this?"

"Yes. But the way she questioned me about it, I'm afraid I contradicted Jake. I'm not looking for trouble with Jake. He's got a hot enough temper. He doesn't need any heat from me. Jake hits his ball, finds it, and hits it again. Never opens his mouth. Suits me. It certainly worked for Hogan. Do you know what Jake told the deputy, Morris?"

"I don't believe she's talked to him." Morris was careful not to say he had. And that Jake was sure the bartender had *not* confused the glasses. In all the noise and chaos in the Snake Pit, Jake might have been very mistaken . . . and could have been very dead. Then again, it was likely the poison never hit the glass until McCall stepped away from the bar. *What connection did Jake have with McCall, if any?* Morris wondered. *What on earth made Jake like the man? Or pretend he liked him?*

Morris asked, "Did the other guy standing at the bar speak to you or to Jake?"

"Not to me. I didn't really see him. Maybe he spoke to Jake. Listen, Morris. Don't go stirring up Jake on my account." Waters was not faking his concern.

"When it comes to murder, Ed, privacy goes out the window. On a happier, soppier subject, how do you like the muddy track?"

"It doesn't work for me," Waters said. "I don't have the distance. I can't fly the ball like Nicklaus. Who can? I get no roll in the mud. I'm standing in the fairway at Pebble Beach on No. 8, with maybe a one-iron in my hands and little hope of putting the ball on the green. And there's every possibility I'll send it down the cliff into the ocean. Nicklaus calls it the greatest second shot in golf. I suppose it is . . . for him. For me in the best of conditions it's difficult; in the rain and mud it's terrifying. I don't know why I come here. I've never won enough to pay expenses. I just don't like being in Orlando when the game is here in California."

"Did you know Andrew McCall?"

"Not really. I'm too small-time to know the advertising wheels," Waters said. "And that suits me. I catch a few top ten finishes, pay my way, invest a bit in the stock market, see the world on my own terms, and the world doesn't know I exist. How can you improve on that for a life?"

Morris found it unrelentingly sad, a solemnly aging bachelor golfer with no home, no family, no slice of fame, just a golfing bedouin wandering the fairways of the world without so much as a tent of his own as refuge. Morris figured to use it as his rainy day lead: "Golf's Quiet American Goes His Lonely Way." It was either that or quote Nicklaus until they both ran out of nouns and verbs.

The sun never made it up on Thursday morning.

"Hard to beat a shower and dry clothes on a rainy day," Sullivan said. "Especially when you have company in the shower."

Morris sat on the bed. "Was that you in the shower?"

"What? Did you have an out-of-body experience?"

"An encounter of the first kind," Morris said. "I'll buy you a bowl of chowder."

"You're on." She patted him on the shoulder as if he were among her favorite possessions.

Morris was pleased not to be dressing alone in the smallish room with the rain blowing against the window, lost in a storm on the Monterey Peninsula. He was in luck that Julia Sullivan could meet him anywhere in the world she chose. And that she often chose to do it. There were times when she was home in Colorado, and he was stalking some golf course he'd memorized in other years and was reaching for words he hadn't used to capture out of time a moment of the game that played incessantly on, that he felt as abandoned as the bachelor Ed Waters, whom the world did not know was alive.

"What are you thinking?" Sullivan asked, he sat so still on the edge of the rumpled bed.

"I'm thinking I'm glad you're not in Colarodo."

"What's Colorado?" she said, putting one arm at a time around his neck.

"Careful, or we'll never see that bowl of chowder."

But then, what kitchen ever ran out of chowder?

The phone rang at an inappropriate moment. Larry Crosby said today's first round was rained out. And it didn't look good for Friday. Morris called in a bulletin to San Francisco. Then hung up the phone. "Now, what was that I was saying about never seeing a bowl of chowder?"

"What was that you were saying?" Sullivan said.

The warm smells from the dining room drew Sullivan like a long shot bet on an underbacked Thoroughbred. Morris poled his way with his cane, barely keeping up the pace behind her. Inspector Stanley Gooden entered the dining room from an opposite door and waddled for the same empty table as Sullivan until he saw her and veered off without so much as a nod of the head.

"I don't think we are the favorite of the home team inspector," Sullivan said, watching Gooden fit his considerable girth into an innocent chair.

"He's afraid we'll tell Tommy Whitlock on him," Morris said.

"Whatever else he is, he's not dumb," Sullivan said.

"I wouldn't go that far." Morris watched Gooden lift the menu as if it were a written key to the kingdom.

"You're not a fan of the inspector?"

"I have confidence in the sheriff's deputy," Morris said.

"Don't forget she belongs to the sheriff."

"I knew an old colonel who said, 'The high ground belongs to whoever can take it and hold it.' "

"Is this colonel still living?"

"Actually, no."

"Think about that, Morris."

A young waitress appeared, pad in hand.

"In honor of The Clambake, I'll have the clam chowder," Sullivan said.

"I'll have the same," Morris said.

" 'Is it true what they say about Dixie? Does the sun really shine all the time?' " came a singsong voice behind Morris. No less than Phil Harris, in person.

"Morris. Lay it on the AP wire. The late Maurie Luxford is long gone. Buried at sea. Thirty years of rain on the job was enough. Bing's going for more experience . . . bringing in Noah as the new starter, announcer, and tournament chairman."

"It'll float," Morris said. "And we've already rounded up all the lesser creatures, even have a Snake Pit."

The words *Snake Pit* leaked all the fun out of the air.

"I just saw Bing," Harris said. "The boy's down an' feelin' lower than that . . . about this murder. What does our man, the high sheriff, know?"

"Not enough," Morris said. "The Pit was full of suspects—if you count everybody who didn't love Andrew McCall. Has Inspector Gooden spoken to you?" Morris's eyes moved toward the dumpy inspector, alone at his table.

"Yeah. I told him I was helpin' with the singin' and

the smokin' and the drinkin'. Like always. Didn't see McCall till he went to Fist City with Sidney. Now there was a match made for Madison Square Garden. Then our boy was lyin' on his back dyin'. Like every pug I ever laid a dollar on. Oh, hell, I didn't hate McCall. His people backed me years ago on television. The boy just needed a personality transplant. Morris, why would somebody kill him this late in his life?"

"That's a terrific question. Maybe an old hatred boiled over and couldn't be contained. Could be he made a new enemy of a more dangerous variety." Morris did not say, "Maybe the dose of poison was meant for somebody else or, more terrifying, for *anybody* else."

Harris lifted Sullivan's hand and kissed it. "Don't mind if I don't speak, bandstand buddy. You're so beautiful I can't pucker my mouth to whistle."

"Whatever you're drinking, Morris will have two of them."

"I saw who you were kissing Tuesday night," Morris warned him. "You keep those lips at arm's length."

Harris laid an elaborate kiss directly on the lips of Julia Sullivan, who made no effort to escape.

"Yes," she said when she could breathe out carbon dioxide.

"You're lookin' at a man born with short arms disease," Harris said.

Morris could only laugh. Who could get the best of Phil Harris?

"If you hadn't heard," Harris said, "the first round is down the toilet. A man could drown on the low greens."

"I got the word," Morris said. Then asked, "Just how sick is Bing?"

"Not for publication—our boy's in bad shape," Harris said. "Pleurisy. And the drugs ain't helpin'. The cutters may move in and open him up. I'm shaking in my trousers. If the bloody rain ever stops, I've got to be Bing up on the TV tower with Chris Schenkel."

"I'm sure you're terrified," Morris said.

"Don't know if the nation can stand that much ham in one weekend," admitted Harris. "Gotta go. If Time comes lookin' for me, tell 'im, sorry, I had an appointment."

"Here's hoping it's west of Samarra," Sullivan said as Harris made his way through the room, kissing hands and spreading happy nonsense.

Deputy Patricia Jordan seemed to be waiting for them outside the dining room. She was careful not to be seen by the inspector, who was worshiping over his large offering of eggs and ham and pancakes.

"Could I speak with you two for a minute?" Jordan asked, her auburn hair shining free of her hat.

"Sure," Morris said.

She led them to a tiny two-chair office that might have originally been a broom closet.

"Welcome to field operations," said the deputy.

Morris perched on the edge of the small desk. "It's good they kept you on the case."

"The inspector isn't thrilled," she said, her smile igniting the tiny room. "My job is to do what he tells me to do. But I can't just sit here doing nothing. He hasn't said I couldn't speak with you two. Tell me what you've heard since Julia and I spoke Tuesday night."

It made Morris smile to hear Sullivan identified by her first name. He said, "We went over all we could remember yesterday with the sheriff. Have you spoken with him?"

The deputy's face burned to match her hair. "Not about you two."

Morris told her of his long talk with Sidney Barker, and his visit with publicist Jay Martin, and his encounter with the young Georgia pro Jake Hill, and his trip down memory lane with Jackie Melton.

Morris thought of something he hadn't mentioned to the sheriff. "Sidney said that McCall was estranged from his two grown sons. Their mother, who divorced McCall, is long dead. I don't know where the sons live. Or if they ever come to The Crosby."

Jordan made a note to check on the sons. "Jay Martin was sure that the redhead, Miss Daly, unlike McCall, did not carry a glass into the Snake Pit?" she said.

Morris nodded.

"Miss Daly told me the Glenlivet scotch was an anonymous gift, sent to their suite," said the deputy. "She didn't mention that in her interview with the inspector. Lodge manager Jack Houghton has been trying to trace who sent the scotch. The bottle was gift-wrapped and left with a card at the front desk. No one saw who left it. We found the card with the address. McCall's name was hand-printed in block letters. It had the number of his suite."

"Not likely a gift from a stranger, although McCall

has holed up in the same suite for years," said Morris. "I suppose there was no trace of cyanide in the scotch."

She shook her head no.

"Whoever sent the pricey single-malt scotch could count on McCall's pouring himself a drink of it," Sullivan said. "He loved his scotch. But what was the danger in that?"

"Maybe the redhead was hired to poison his drink," Morris said. "And couldn't get up the nerve when they were alone. And then slipped it in his glass during all the commotion. Then again, maybe it was a dramatic gesture, the killer wanting to send him into the next world in the style to which he was accustomed."

"We speak here of a sophisticated assassin."

"Maybe."

"The inspector is questioning Tana Daly again this morning," Jordan said. "I wish I could be there."

"You look her up, Sullivan," said Morris. "You have a way with your own species."

"We are not a separate species."

"Couldn't prove it by me."

"Then again," Sullivan said, smiling at the deputy, "maybe we are. A higher species, of course."

The deputy was not touching that, except with her own priceless smile.

"I got the impression," Morris said, changing the subject, "that McCall stuck his heavy hand in ABC's publicity machine. I don't know how that might have affected Jay Martin. He is looking for another job on the West Coast. He says his fiancée has no intention of leaving California. I believe him." Morris could not control the sympathy in his expression.

"You think his best course of romantic action is to beat it to New York tonight, if not sooner," Sullivan said.

"Remember what Churchill replied when confronted by an angry woman who swore if she were married to him, she would put poison in his drink. He said, 'Madam, if I were married to you, I would drink it.' Young Mr. Martin might heed Mr. Churchill, though I'm sure Sir Winston said it more memorably than that."

Sullivan and the deputy, faithless to their gender, could not help giggling.

"I'm afraid that story falls awfully close to our crime," said the deputy, recovering her balance. She consulted her notes. "I'm sure Inspector Gooden will be questioning . . . Jake Hill, the golfer. Morris, do you think he had business dealings with Andrew McCall?"

"I don't know. Maybe it's like Jake to admire a misanthrope like McCall. Jake is a tough hombre. Raised in the Georgia mountains, a throwback, son of a bootlegger serving time in the penitentiary, a kid who learned the game of golf as a caddie. Never went to college. A pro who taught himself, who plays a lot better than he swings. A guy with the killer instinct . . . on the golf course. I wouldn't say in the Snake Pit."

"How do you explain Hill's seeing McCall pick up his own glass. And Ed Waters . . . standing right there at the bar . . . seeing McCall pick up *Hill's* glass?" asked Jordan.

"I can't," Morris said. "The hand is faster than the eye among magicians. But even a man in a hurry picks up a full glass of scotch and water with some deliberation. What did the bartender say?"

"When the inspector questioned him, Tuesday night, he of course didn't know what the two golfers saw . . . or said they saw. The bartender, Dudley Greene, simply said he poured the scotch in McCall's glass and McCall barked at him for adding too much water, though he added very little. The young man admits he was confused all night. He'd never tended bar before. He didn't mention confusing, or almost confusing, McCall's glass with Jake Hill's. And I best leave it to you two to look him up."

"We'll do it, but we won't let him pour us a drink," Sullivan said.

"Oh, did Sidney Barker call you yesterday?" Morris asked the deputy.

"He did. He said he forgot to say that Andrew McCall had canceled the GE ad on television, featuring his music. And that it cost him a 'few dollars.' Turns out the 'few dollars' amounted to *twenty-five thousand dollars*."

"In truth," Morris said, "that's petty cash for Sidney. He's good for maybe a hundred million. But rich men have killed for less. You passed the word to Inspector Gooden?"

"Oh, yes. He was not happy to get it from me. He called Barker in and grilled him for his 'forgetfulness.' The inspector hasn't yet questioned the pro Ed Waters. I'll have to find a diplomatic way of tipping him off that Mr. Waters heard Barker and McCall arguing about the GE ad in the lobby of the lodge."

"We'll look up the redhead and the bartender," Morris said.

"*I'll* look up the redhead," Sullivan said. "You have a long-standing, *and sitting*, relationship with the bartenders of America."

"True," Morris said.

It wasn't hard. Morris knocked on the door of the room Dudley Greene was sharing with three other college kids and found him alone, obviously still asleep.

The room was an unnatural disaster. Clothes in piles and hanging off the corners of doors.

Greene, whose baby fat complexion gave him the look of a high school senior, apologized with a helpless sweep of his hand. He was still wearing the jeans and turtleneck shirt of the night before. The jeans had ridden up his leg, and the shirt had wound its way around his ample torso. He gave up trying to untangle them, as if resigned to his dark fate at Pebble Beach.

Greene said he was a senior in the school of communications at Berkeley and had recognized Morris's name immediately.

"I'm just down trying to knock out a few dollars for my tuition," he said. "I had no idea I'd wind up tending bar. I thought I'd be working out on the golf course, selling Cokes and hot dogs."

"They'd do better selling life preservers," Morris said. He cut to the moment. "Dudley, think carefully. Is it possible you mixed up Andrew McCall's glass Tuesday night with the glass of the golfer Jake Hill. I believe Jake was standing at the left of the bar. Dark hair, dark eyes, rather lean. Also drinking scotch."

Greene closed his eyes, trying to picture the scene in the Snake Pit. "I—" he began, and stopped. "I had a scotch order and a vodka order. I wasn't sure which came first. There was a lot of noise and confusion. I started to pick up the vodka glass—from the round-faced guy, a golfer too, I think, to judge by his sun-burned face. Then I reached for the glass of the scotch drinker, who I thought might have been there first, the young, dark-haired guy, on my right. Jake Hill, I expect."

Morris nodded, careful not to speak.

Greene closed his eyes again. "I was just lifting Hill's glass when this older guy shoved his own glass against my arm. I let go of the first glass and almost turned it over . . . and juggled with the second glass with the guy shouting in my face, 'Scotch and not much water.' And I picked up his glass . . . or maybe *a* glass . . ." He closed his eyes again. "I put in a double scotch, at least. Added a small bit of water, no more ice, and the guy bitched about the water. And I put the glass down, and he picked it up. I couldn't for the life of me know exactly which glass I filled. The young guy, the golfer, waited for his own scotch and didn't say anything about getting the wrong glass. Do you think the wrong guy got the poison? There was no—"

Morris shook his head. "No cyanide in the bottle of scotch or the water pitcher. Or half the room would be dead. No way to know who the cyanide was meant for . . . except it wound up in McCall's glass. Unless *you* were asked to drop something someone had given you into one of the glasses."

Greene blushed as only a short, plump guy could blush, his entire face flaming red.

"No sort of gag that turned out tragic?" Morris waited.

"I swear to God, no," Greene said, raising his hand as if under oath.

A thought occurred to Morris. "Did the dark-haired pro Jake Hill bring his own glass to the bar? Or were you filling a fresh, clean one for him?"

Greene thought about it. "It was a fresh glass. I guess it was his first drink of the night."

"Had *you* washed the glasses?"

Greene shook his head. "I got them from the kitchen. I had no sink, no way to wash them. The kitchen sent in clean glasses when I ran low."

"Did you check each glass to be sure it was, in fact, clean. No dark smudges?"

The kid filled his cheeks with air and blew it out like a small bellows. "I was supposed to. And I started out checking them. But it quickly got to be panic city, mixing drinks and making change."

Morris wondered if the rim of a glass could be dusted with cyanide and not look so grungy that even a bartender in a hurry wouldn't use it. It was a question for forensics.

"Anything else unusual happen to you since you got here?"

"Only that I wound up tending bar at all," Greene said.

"How is it that the bar had this one bottle of Johnnie Walker Black Label scotch? Pretty pricey stuff for a cash bar."

"I don't know. The bottles were stacked and locked under the bar when I first got here Sunday morning.

There was even a bottle, I guess it was a bottle, it felt like one, gift-wrapped and in a paper sack, with a note stuck to the sack to deliver it to the front desk." The kid said it as if it had been preying on his mind.

"Was it locked under the bar?" Morris's eyes gave away nothing.

"No. It was on the bar itself."

"Did you deliver it to the front desk?"

"Yes."

"What did you do with the note?"

"I left it stuck on the paper bag."

"Did you see the card inside the bag?"

Greene hesitated, unable to dominate the flush of his face. "Yes."

A card with McCall's name on it had turned up in his wastebasket, along with a paper bag. But no hand-printed instructions. "Was that the first time you knew of the name Andrew McCall?"

"Yes," the kid said, fearful he might have committed some incriminating act of omission.

"Did you tell the deputy or the inspector about this?"

The kid opened his mouth to breathe in air. He shook his head no.

"Why not?"

"I . . . didn't know the man. I didn't know who he was. I didn't know what he looked like. I didn't recognize him—"

"You are a senior in the school of communications and you never heard of the McCall agency—the fifth-largest advertising agency in the country?"

Greene, his mouth still open, nodded that he had

heard of the agency. "I didn't think about this . . . McCall . . . being that McCall," he said weakly.

Morris did not doubt him. "There was nothing wrong with the bottle of Glenlivet scotch delivered to McCall's room," he assured him. "The puzzle is who sent it. Do you remember the handwriting on the note stuck to the bag?"

Greene thought about it. "The instructions were printed in block letters and Scotch-taped to the bag," he said. "I'm sure of it. I looked for a name . . . of who might have left it. I wanted to be able to tell him I delivered the bottle to the front desk . . . in the event I was asked. I never was."

Morris asked quickly, "Did McCall drink from the glass immediately after you filled it?"

"Yes," the kid said, without hesitation, contradicting Tana Daly. "He took a quick sip. I imagine to see if I'd added too much water. I saw him do it. Then I was back to work, filling drink orders."

"Did you tell the inspector that?"

Greene shook his plump head. "No. He didn't ask me that."

It was only the kid's word. But Morris did not doubt him. "You'd better get dressed and find Inspector Gooden, or Deputy Jordan, and tell one of them about delivering the bottle of scotch to the front desk. And explain how you saw McCall take a quick sip of his drink after you poured it. Expect to be quizzed very closely about that. And you can bet they will question others who were around the bar. Let me caution you: Be sure of what you saw."

Greene was all enthusiasm. "I'm sure. I saw him lift

the glass and take a quick drink. He turned away. He
didn't look back at me. He didn't complain again about
the water in the drink." Greene now understood how
important the simple sip was to him. It eliminated the
possibility of his being even an innocent accomplice to
the murder.

Sullivan knocked on McCall's suite, with no result.
She checked the dining room. The lobby. Looked out
the front door. It was still blowing and raining. She
hung around the crowded lobby, and within the hour
the redhead walked up to the front desk to check for
messages. Sullivan stepped close enough to hear that
she had none. Tana Daly carried no umbrella and was
not wet. Wherever she had come from, it had been inside the lodge.

Sullivan introduced herself. The redhead was apprehensive. "I hang out with John Morris, the big guy with
Associated Press, who gave first aid to Andrew McCall."

Miss Daly remembered Morris and remembered seeing her. She was still apprehensive.

"Share a cup of tea with me," Sullivan said. "I think I
may have information that will interest you."

Tana was still nervous. But curious. "What kind of
information?"

Sullivan led her to a far table in the now-uncrowded
dining room. With a gentle smile on her face, she said,
"There's a theory you were hired to drop poison in
McCall's drink . . . in your suite. But with the two of
you there alone, you lost your nerve. You recovered it in
the Snake Pit, with everyone watching the brawl. And
good-bye, Andrew McCall."

Daly stood up out of her chair, her eyes wide with real or invented indignation, revealing green-tinted contact lenses. "That's insane! I never!" Tears flowed into her artificially green eyes.

"Easy." Sullivan guided her back into her seat. "It's just a theory. I'm sure the sheriff's people have others." She implied that this particular theory belonged to the law and not to John Morris.

Tana's hands and arms trembled, as did her lower lip. It might have been the big closing scene in the television movie.

Sullivan said, "How did you come to know McCall?"

Daly was relieved to be asked so ordinary a question. She slipped into her Hollywood persona, sitting up very straight, her shoulders back, tossing her hair, as artificially blond as her eyes were green. "I was cast in the suspense movie *The Lady Dies at Dawn.*" She said it as if it had been a major Warner Brothers production, co-starring Robert Redford. She did not say she was the lady who succumbed . . . by screwdriver.

"CBS hosted a party in New York for the cast. Andrew was invited. One of his clients was a major sponsor of the movie. We met. He asked me to dinner at '21.' He wouldn't take no for an answer."

Sullivan smiled, doubting that "no" had been offered as an answer.

"I have a few weeks before my next movie," Daly said as though contracts were piling up in her mail. "Andrew invited me here to Bing's tournament." She said "Bing" as if he were one of the lesser players in her next drama. "I came. Simple as that."

"He was a powerful man, McCall," Sullivan said.

"Yes," Daly said. "He was not unattractive. He was old, older than you might imagine. Seventy-four. He talked a good game. He was no sexual athlete." She said it with no embarrassment. "You got it right. He had power. He was good for my career. It's true he was stubborn. He picked public squabbles that were embarrassing. He was not unkind to me." She touched a heavy gold chain that hung around her slender neck as though to remind herself of his generosity.

"You are a lucky young woman you did not take a sip of his drink during the fight," Sullivan said.

Daly's very pale complexion sank paler. "Thank God it wasn't vodka. I don't drink scotch. I'm trying not to drink anything. I watch my diet."

"I can see you have a terrible problem. How can you bear being a perfect six?"

"Four," she said, running one slender hand down a slim hip.

"Did McCall take any phone calls before you two left for the Snake Pit?" Sullivan asked.

"He lived on the telephone," Daly said. "Usually cursing somebody. He never cursed me," she said, maybe protesting a shade too much.

"It's an ill wind that blows nobody good." Sullivan gritted her teeth as she reworded the quote. "I'm sure you will get a great deal of publicity from this murder."

Daly did her best not to be outrageously enthusiastic. "A photographer came by this morning . . . for *Time* magazine. That's why the heels." She lifted a perfect size five shoe at the end of a perfect leg. "Twice last night a flash went off directly in my face. I don't know who he was shooting for. It was just lucky I was standing there." She realized her growing enthusiasm was in poor taste and managed not to smile.

Sullivan asked, "Where did the photographer for *Time* shoot you this morning?"

"In the entrance to the lodge. He wanted me looking out at the rain. He wanted what early-morning light there was. There wasn't much."

So where had she been the rest of the morning? She hadn't been in her suite for at least an hour, maybe much longer. Sullivan, with the gentle smile back on her face, asked, "Who else were you with this morning?"

"What do you mean?" Daly lifted her chin in defiance. Her hands were in a knot, more of apprehension than defiance.

"I was looking for you. You weren't in your suite. Let me advise you of one thing, woman to woman," said Sullivan. "If you have a personal relationship with someone else in the lodge, do tell the sheriff's people before they find it out for themselves." Sullivan made sure there was no glass of water on the table that Tana Daly might dash in her face, à la the movies, from which she seemed to draw her vision of reality.

The actress's pale complexion lost any visible coloring. She was not angry. She was fearful. "Why do you say that?" she whispered, as if their lives were being projected on the silver screen.

"Your body language when you were with McCall. You were in the Snake Pit with him, but your physical person was in another place." Sullivan did not have the good grace to blush over her elaborate interpretation.

"To show so much, without saying anything, must be a great asset for an actress."

Daly touched her pale hair, as if in acknowledgment of a powerful talent. "If Andrew had found out, he would have ruined me," she whispered again, as though the room were full of ears and not empty chairs. "He was impotent." She said it as if this were a serious crime. "Sunday I met this young golfer he was sponsoring. That means paying his way on the tour." Daly explained it to Sullivan as though the tour were a complex venture she could not be expected to understand.

"He wanted to buy out his contract with Andrew. He doesn't need Andrew. He's made huge amounts of money. They cursed each other something terrible. I can tell you, he took no shit off Andrew." A lot of voice training lost its power . . . the way the vulgar word, *shit*, fitted in her mouth. She might have been young Dora Hudgins, stepping out in Chicago.

"The young man called me within two hours. With Andrew *sleeping in the room beside me*. I met him the next morning. He has a rough edge about him, a dangerous air. Maybe he jumped off a boxcar, like William Holden in *Picnic*." She hushed with her mouth still open, realizing that she was running on into Sullivan's silence.

"Jake Hill."

Tana Daly looked at Sullivan as if she had extrasensory perception. "How? What do you know?"

"I simply saw the way you looked at him two nights ago in the Snake Pit," Sullivan lied, with a small, fraudulent smile on her face.

"Oh." Daly accepted the explanation as true evidence of her physical powers to dominate a man, a room, a nation rather than the obvious guess that it was. Modern professional golfers, off the course, were about as dangerous as fish in an aquarium. As Morris insisted, Jake was a throwback. Oh, there had been barracudas in Monty Sullivan's time. He had loved telling her about them, and he had loved being one of them.

"You were with Jake this morning," Sullivan said, "with" being an operative euphemism.

"Yes." Tana lifted her chin, a movement deliberately reminiscent of Kim Novak in *Picnic*.

Sullivan could see that the way she colored her hair, and styled it, and the slinky clothes she wore all affected the aura of Hollywood's onetime Golden Girl. She wondered if her suite included a bell, book, and candle.

"Jake's teaching me about golf," Daly said, as if it were an Eastern religion. "He has a deep passion for it."

I'll bet he does, thought Sullivan. She said, "Did you speak to Jake Tuesday night, before or after the brawl?"

Tana waited, a pause no doubt adopted from Novak in *Vertigo*. She said, in a voice growing more whispery by the sentence, "No. But he spoke to me."

Sullivan waited, imagining herself in *Kiss Me Stupid*.

"Jake growled at me"—Tana bit her lip—"I was frightened that Andrew had heard him"—she bit her lip again—"he growled, 'Hey, you, move it in that yellow dress.'" Daly beamed at the memory, as if David Bowie had leered at her in *Just a Gigolo*.

"Did Andrew hear him?"

She shook her head. "I don't know. Just then Sidney started the fight. I never spoke to Andrew again." She said it wistfully, but with an absence of passion.

"Did anyone jostle you, distract you during the fight?" Sullivan asked.

"Goddamn right." Again Tana was all Chicago. "I spilled good scotch on the floor. Damn near got it on my dress." Now there was true passion in her voice.

"Who bumped against you?" Sullivan asked.

"Every damn body," she said. "I don't know how I held on to the glass. I was shouting for Sidney to deck the son of a bitch." She caught herself. She said, "Things were *chaotic*," having picked up the word, very probably, from the spoken accounts on television.

"Where was Jake?"

"Behind me. I know. He pinched me," she said with undisguised pride.

"Did McCall discuss any of his business with you?" Sullivan asked.

"I could hear him on the telephone. He lived on the telephone. You could hear him across the street on the telephone."

"Did any one deal appear to be worrying him?"

"Nothing worried Andrew. He didn't have ulcers. He gave 'em." Daly laughed. She had the surprisingly genuine laugh of a young girl. Nothing about it reminded you of Kim Novak. "I heard him say that once about ulcers. But I never knew whom he was talking to." The "whom" sounded as out of place as Hollywood in Chicago.

"He and Sidney Barker had a running feud," Sullivan said.

"Yes. I thought they were going to duke it out in the lobby of the lodge. Andrew canceled some TV ad that used Sidney's music. If you can call it music. It's out of the Dark Ages. Andrew didn't care for big band music. He was all rock and roll. Until you turned out the lights," Daly said uncharitably.

"Can you place the name, or the face, of any other person, besides Jake, who touched you or bumped into you while you were holding McCall's glass?" Sullivan kept asking a variation of the same question.

Tana gazed into the distance, Novak in *The Amorous Adventures of Moll Flanders.* "The wimpy little guy with ABC . . . with the iron-pants fiancée . . . Jay somebody . . . Andrew stepped on him like a bug . . . ran him out of California. . . . He was pushed into me. . . . I guess a cat sneezed on him. That's when I spilled the scotch."

"Tell me about it," Sullivan said, rasping the words like Lauren Bacall in *To Have and Have Not.*

CHAPTER SIX

They both talked at the same time until they were laughing and then giggling. Julia Sullivan was dead sure she had never before heard John Morris giggle. It broke her up. She fell out of control again, laughing.

"Our young actress isn't *that* funny." Morris suspected she was laughing at him.

That wouldn't do. Sullivan imitated a trumpet flourish into her balled fist. Then announced: "Greta Garbo and John Barrymore in *Grand Hotel*. Vivien Leigh and Laurence Olivier in *That Hamilton Woman*. Lana Turner and John Garfield in *The Postman Always Rings Twice*. Kim Novak and William Holden in *Picnic*. And now Metro-Goldwyn-Mayer brings you: Tana Daly and Jake Hill in *I Can Get It for You Retail* or, in its California translation, *Poison, My Lovely*."

"I like it," Morris said. "Bring on the Golden Globe

Awards. Who was it that said, 'I've underestimated the sex life of everybody I've ever known'?"

"Maybe it was you."

"Not me. What do I know? I was born in Atlanta. I thought Jake Hill saw the world down a tree-lined fairway."

"I'm not touching that," Sullivan said.

"Called her with the big shot bastard sleeping in the bed beside her. Now that's balls," Morris said.

"Let's not talk physiology."

"I would be surprised if Jake could count his external organs, much less identify them. Obviously he is aware of their uses."

"Obviously."

"She was with Jake *this morning*?"

"Yes."

"Certainly a preferred way of *mourning*. Does the Monterey Peninsula's intrepid inspector know about this?" Morris asked.

"I advised Tana to speak to Deputy Jordan. That it would be easier to tell her."

"Yes, but the inspector will want his own pound of flesh."

"He may have met his match. This Tana is a tough broad," Sullivan said.

"I believe it. How will you mourn me, Sullivan?"

"I couldn't imagine a liaison with some young golfer before the following . . . *afternoon*," she said, jumping off the couch to escape him, taking his cane and affecting his limp around the small bedroom.

"Tell me again what Jake *growled* at her in the Snake Pit."

" 'Hey, you, move it in that yellow dress,' " quoted Sullivan.

"That's wonderful. I will steal that. I will use that somewhere, somehow. I hope not in a profile of Jake Hill as a jealous murderer. Then he pinched her?"

"She seemed especially proud of that, as if he were Italian and they in Italy." Sullivan grew serious. "She insisted McCall was impotent. That he was all 'rock and roll. Until you turned out the lights.' "

"This kid isn't an actress. She's a bloody script-writer," Morris said, filing away her description of McCall to steal, for his own use.

Sullivan said, "Tana Daly lives in a screenplay. Even in mid-sentence she sees herself projected thirty feet high, her voice whispering over a darkened theater."

"Damned if I'll bet against her career. Unless she ends up doing twenty-five to life in the state peniten-tiary for unjustifiable homicide."

"Oh, I almost forgot. Tana said that during the fight in the Snake Pit, Jay Martin was pushed into her, maybe by a cat sneeze, causing her to spill the scotch on the floor. She called him 'wimpy . . . with the iron-pants fiancée.' "

Morris laughed with honest appreciation. "That's it. I'm hanging it up as a failed writer. I'm coming back as this girl's agent." He said, seriously, "We'd better be sure our deputy knows about that."

"*Our* deputy? You mean the sheriff's deputy."

Morris acknowledged that painful reality. "I wonder if McCall is the guy who put the arm on ABC to run Jay out of California? If so, why?"

"Tana Daly said McCall lived to curse on the telephone. No doubt he cursed ABC as often as anybody. With his list of advertising clients, he could swing a big hammer."

"We'll see what Deputy Jordan can pry out of young Jay Martin."

Sullivan remembered something else. "Oh, yes. Daly confirmed Ed Waters's description of the cuss fight between Sidney and McCall in the lodge lobby."

"Odd that Sidney never mentioned it to me," said Morris. "No reason for him to deny it. He admits he was pissed with McCall for pulling the ad with his music. But I wonder if we know just how angry he truly was?"

"Tell me, Morris, how could two golfers, who depend on their acute eyesight, disagree on which glass one of them lifted, and drank out of, right in front of them both?"

"Beats me. I lost many a bet in a bar. I never lost my own glass." Morris advanced the "loony idea" that one portion of the rim of McCall's glass might have been dusted with cyanide before the scotch was poured into it. "But that would have been an act of random murder. Unless the bartender was involved and was saving the glass for McCall."

"You say the bartender swore to you he saw McCall take a quick sip of the scotch immediately after he picked it up."

"Yes. It's possible he sipped from a side of the glass that hadn't been dusted. That seems improbable. But so is murder. What the hell do I know about potassium cyanide poisoning?"

Morris proceeded to answer his own question. "It

doesn't take much potassium cyanide to do the job. Alan Turing, who invented the idea of the computer, killed himself by taking a bite of an apple dipped in cyanide. Hermann Göring bit down on a glass vial of cyanide small enough to be smuggled into prison inside a brass bullet and cheated the executioner. As little as *one gram* of the stuff can do you in."

"How much is a gram?"

"It equals fifteen-point-four, three, two grains," Morris said, making no reference to the dictionary he had himself consulted. "Consider that there are four hundred and thirty-seven–point–five grains in *one ounce*. A gram isn't very much, my lady."

"You're showing off," Sullivan said, lifting his cane like a sword and threatening to run him through.

"Who else tells you these things?" said Morris. "I've got to knock out five hundred rainy-day words. You call on the sheriff's deputy. Tell her what we've been up to. Then I want some true scotch, some dinner, some sleep, and some, by God, golf."

"All the staples of life . . . with one or two exceptions." Sullivan smiled at him until he laughed.

"Is this the time for 'some sleep'?" Sullivan asked, a couple of hours later, with the lights out and the covers up to her chin.

"Not yet," Morris said. "How did it go with the sheriff's deputy?"

"Swimmingly. For me. The poor thing is caught between the inspector and the killer, a deputy on a hot tin roof. I think she has less to fear from the killer."

"Is she going to look up Tana Daly's lover boy, Jake Hill?"

"Yes. Inspector Gooden be damned. She's going to find out if he had any business dealings with Andrew McCall. And there's Ed Waters, who's sure McCall took the fatal drink from Jake's glass."

"How about Jay Martin? He was near enough to the poisoned glass to jostle scotch on the floor."

"She's going to rattle his cage. Find out if McCall did stick his nose in ABC's publicity efforts and if he did lobby to have Martin transferred from California. Whatever she learns, the inspector is sure to resent it."

"Hadn't he better watch his own backside? She is the sheriff's deputy . . . professionally and personally."

"She hopes the inspector doesn't know about the 'personally,' " Sullivan said.

"As my old uncle used to say, 'Spit in one hand and hope in the other and see which fills up faster.' "

"That's a lovely image here in the dark."

"My uncle was an unseemly man. But he had a beautiful sister."

"Your mother was as beautiful as her photographs?"

"Oh, yes."

"Funny how genes can skip a generation."

It's not so hard to be trapped when you are already under the covers up to your neck.

The sun didn't actually come up. But light, not rain, leaked through the clouds, and The Crosby Pro-Am was on for Friday morning.

Phil Harris and the trumpet man Harry James had survived The Clambake but had clearly forgotten that morning did follow the night. Morris learned they'd taken one look out their windows at the muddy, wind-blown peninsula and, with Crosby safely in the hospital, crawled back into their separate beds and withdrawn from the tournament.

Morris waited as Gary Player stepped off the practice putting green at Pebble Beach. Player looked up at the rain-bloated sky and the snow standing on the Carmel Moutains, and said, "I don't think we'll get this round in either."

"Maybe it's rained itself out," Morris said. "It's only been falling for twelve straight hours."

"When I was here in '63, it snowed," Player said. "But life is not all sweet things." His sweet fifteen-year-old daughter, Jennifer, was excited to be in California, not for the golf but for the chance to meet the television star David Cassidy.

"She's got pictures of him all over the walls of her room," said Player. Ah, The Crosby, with celebrities as thick on the ground as leaves of grass—with apologies to Walt Whitman.

The diminutive Player found his way to the first tee. Even swaddled in a sweater and rain jacket, he made a trim figure. No other professional golfer of the time lifted light weights and pushed himself through the conditioning drills that were to keep Player fit well into his sixties. By the 1990s all the pro golfers had adopted conditioning regimens, and the PGA tour included a mobile workout center complete with wellness experts.

Player told Morris he was braving the weather for Jennifer and for two other reasons. He'd played golf with Crosby in England, and Bing had asked him to come over. Who could deny Bing? As Art Rosenbaum of San Francisco had written, "Crosby started this tournament because he found golfers amiable types. He enjoyed the delightful needling, the subtlety in taming the little white ball, and the grandeur of everything outdoors." Not to mention raising a glass or two to the good times.

More than once Crosby had said he got the biggest kick out of the golf tournament of any other one thing he'd done with his life. When you consider his music, his Academy Award, and all those *Road* movies with Dorothy Lamour, sometimes in a sarong, that's saying a bit. The three million dollars the tournament had raised for the Crosby Youth Fund made a true difference to charities on the Monterey Peninsula and had financed loans to students attending more than a hundred small colleges around the country. Crosby, remembering his own college days at Gonzaga, was a sucker to help a kid go to school.

Player had also promised his young amateur partner John Dreyfus if he'd lose thirty pounds, he'd play the 1974 Crosby with him. Dreyfus, better known for his family's famous investment fund, had dropped the thirty pounds and was down to a svelte 170.

"Let's go, mate," Player said. He stepped into the wind and mud and held his own, shooting an acceptable 1 under par 71 at Pebble Beach.

"I couldn't find the rule for embedded shoes," he said to Morris, dropping a mud-ruined pair on the locker-room floor.

Rain drifted across the course in midmorning, and

then the sun came out, and the winds blew until the wind-chill fell into the high thirties.

"You ready for some golf?" Morris asked.

"I'm ready for some brunch," Sullivan said. "Then we'll let our stomachs settle, and then we'll send out a proxy in our place."

"Oh, no. Brunch and then golf. What's a little weather and pneumonia among us competitors?"

Jim Murray of the *Los Angeles Times* had written, "Seven thousand guys fight to get an invitation to an oxygen tent and a fever chart. They can get the same sensation by standing in a bucket of ice, turning on a 10,000-horsepower fan in their faces and hiring someone to spray them with a fire hose and shoot sand in their eyes." And that was on a fair-weather day at The Crosby.

"Morris, tell me when we're having fun," Sullivan shouted over the howling wind into his frostbitten ear.

They'd caught a lift to Cypress Point at the edge of the Del Monte Forest. Morris claimed to have it in his contract that he would never have to walk Spyglass Hill, which seemed eternally uphill. It was Robert Trent Jones's self-proclaimed masterpiece, and for Morris's part, he could worship it all to himself. But even Morris agreed that God would forgive Trent Jones for the first five holes, which played magnificently among the Pacific dunes, putting one very much in mind of Scottish links and the great Pine Valley course in New Jersey.

Sullivan and Morris huddled behind the large green at the treacherous 16th hole at Cypress Point. The gallery was bundled into every imaginable poncho, parker, pea jacket, flak jacket, rain jacket, ski suit, wet suit, aviator's cap, knee boots, Eskimo mukluk. They might have been prepared to join Mao Zedong on his Long March of 1934–35. The Long March was hardly more deadly than the 16th hole at Cypress Point.

Cypress Point, like Pebble Beach, is a true masterpiece. Sandy Tatum, distinguished USGA officer, once called it "the Sistine Chapel of golf." If so, the par-3, 222-yard 16th, played over an inlet of the Pacific Ocean, is the signature hole of designer-artist Alister MacKenzie. The Scotsman MacKenzie completed the course in 1928, a bare three years before he and Bobby Jones collaborated to design Augusta National, home of The Masters.

Cypress Point sprawls to the west from the Spanish-style clubhouse, insinuating itself through the dunes to the ocean, its 15th, 16th, and 17th holes crossing small, beautiful, seductively wild arms of the Pacific.

No hole in world golf can compare in beauty and terror with the par-3 16th. The player tees his ball on a high precipice, as at the edge of the earth, and aims it over the surf pounding against the rocks below, 222 yards to a green that seems as faint as a brushstroke on a bare spit of land, with the ocean on three sides. The golfer looks, and often seems, as helpless as a sailor in a rowboat cast in the midst of the sea.

A mere ocean can hardly contain the catastrophes that have flown off the tee at the 16th hole. Masters champion and Ryder Cup stalwart Jack Burke saw under-par rounds drowned in the sea at the 16th, five consecutive years. The redoubtable Raymond Floyd, his U.S. Open and Masters championships still in the future, could not imagine that also in his future were three consecutive tee shots into the Pacific on this same No. 16. Only a massive act of will was to keep him from leaping in after them.

But fate saved its greatest cruelty for Porky Oliver, who had won The Crosby in 1940. In 1953 he came to the 16th at Cypress Point in contention for a second championship. He teed it up into a withering fifty-mile-an-hour blast of wind. The ocean claimed his first *five* shots. His sixth landed among the devilish ice plants that consume those balls played safely left and short of the green. By the time he had hacked his way onto the green and into the hole, Porky had used up *sixteen* strokes. Friends with the gallows humor of undertakers left a message for him in the clubhouse: "Call long-distance operator number sixteen." Porky was not amused.

Bing Crosby himself put the Pacific Ocean in its place. Long a Cypress Point member with his old side-kick Bob Hope, Crosby was playing in a fivesome one misty fall afternoon in 1947. His cronies and sworn witnesses were Harrison Goodwin, Jack Morse, Dan Searle, and the club pro of forty-one years, Henry Puget. Crosby, who loved to smoke a pipe and smile at the world going by, teed up his ball and went after it with his driver. It carried the 222 yards to the green and rolled directly into the hole. Some movies Crosby made didn't attract as much international attention as that one, grand, unimaginable stroke. It was doubtful he would swap the moment for the Academy Award he won for *Going My Way*.

"Look," Sullivan shouted into the wind and cold.

The lovable Jack Lemmon was on the 16th tee with fellow actor James Garner, who knew his way around a golf course.

Lemmon stalked the tee box as if it were a stage and he'd forgotten his lines.

"Surely he'll lay up in this gale," Morris said, focusing his binoculars on the small, brave figure across chasm and ocean. "By God, he's pulled out a driver."

The wind inexplicably reversed its direction and was suddenly behind him as Lemmon unleashed a magnificent drive that sailed and sailed and sailed over the green and rolled desperately down onto the rocks.

"Poor baby," Sullivan said.

"Yes, Jack is down to his last few million friends . . . and dollars," Morris said. For all his dramatic success, Lemmon failed into the 1990s to help his Pro-Am team make the final cut at The Crosby.

Garner, fittingly for a man from *The Rockford Files*, lashed his own tee shot to the fringe of the green and two-putted for a par 3 that many of the professionals in contention would have paid a thousand dollars to own.

"Where's the other Jack?" asked Sullivan.

"You mean the actor-golfer Nicklaus?" said Morris. "The marshal with the walkie-talkie said he's already passed this way. Wasn't too happy with the mud and his two over par score."

On the 16th tee appeared the figure of Johnny Miller, praying mantis thin, even concealed in sweaters. He had grown up testing the wind and rain and limitations of gravity over these unforgiving peninsula courses.

Miller, with his very upright swing, sent the ball to the heart of the green. His look-alike amateur partner,

Locke de Bretteville, followed suit, and they swept through the hole in their bell-bottom trousers that looked wonderfully ridiculous in photographs twenty years later.

Miller winked at Sullivan, who blew him a kiss. He parred in to post an intimidating 68, fourth-best round of the muddy, blustery day.

A murmur of expectation swept over Cypress Point and settled around the 16th green as the little-known rookie Gary McCord reached the tee. He'd strung together seven consecutive birdies, through the 13th hole, and had dug out another birdie on No. 2 from the bottomless mud that threatened to swallow his fellow competitors. When Thursday's round was wiped out by rain, McCord had been standing on this same 16th tee, *worse off by twenty-one shots.*

Sideburns blowing in the wind but anchored by his considerable self, McCord put a very solid swing on the ball that cut through the air as if there were no ocean to be overcome.

Momentarily subverted by the confidence of youth, McCord failed to get down in par. He spotted John Morris as he stepped off the green. "I can't believe it," he said, "the AP out in the wind and mud. Must be trying to impress the beautiful women." He lifted his hat to Sullivan, who saluted him.

"Who the hell is keeping your score?" Morris asked. "Or didn't they teach you boys how to add all the way up to four, five, and six at Riverside High?"

McCord winked at Sullivan and stepped quickly to the 17th tee as if this professional golf were a simple matter. He went on to post a 65 for a two-shot lead on the field. Oh, but then there was the matter of tomorrow and tomorrow and tomorrow.

Later, when Morris dropped by the locker room, Nicklaus, smoldering over his putting and his own 74, said, "Gary who?" He'd never met the young man with the acerbic wit.

"He just got his PGA card this fall," Morris said. "Better watch him, he's pretty quick on the draw with a quip."

"A 65," marveled Nicklaus. "That's a hell of a round. He keeps that up, it won't be Gary who by Sunday."

McCord was not the only rookie setting fire to the rain-drenched grass. Barney Thompson, another survivor of the minitours, had scored a remarkable 67 at Spyglass Hill, to tie for second place with Lanny Wadkins, who'd dominated Cypress Point.

In the absence of Lee Trevino, Tijuana-born Vic Regalado was "low Mexican" at 69, tying Dave Eichelberger. Young Hale Irwin, Sarge Orville Moody, Jake Hill, David Glenz, Jerry Boyd, Allen Miller, Bobby Nichols, and Rick Rhoads were in with enviable 70s. And Player, Lee Elder, Kermit Zarley, Grier Jones, and Bob Rosburg were among thirteen players hanging around with more than respectable 71s. Included among them was Ed Waters. Perhaps he would make expenses at The Crosby this year for the first time.

Rosburg, a PGA champion, scored a funky 39-32 at Cypress Point, which plays to a par of 37-35-72. His amateur partner, John Brodie, more famous as the San Francisco 49er quarterback, scored four natural birdies to help the team by ten shots for a net 61, good for the first-day lead in the Pro-Am division of the tournament.

* * *

Morris swung by the hospitality suite for a quick hit of scotch to take away the chill.

"Actually walking out on the bloody course . . . you're breaking the code, Morris, giving the profession a sissy reputation. You're supposed to be in here with your peers, knocking down the hard stuff." Paul Shirley of the *San Francisco Chronicle* lifted a glass of welcome cheer.

"Hello, peer," Morris said, lifting his own glass. "Now and then I backslide, have to see an actual golf ball struck in anger."

"Can the kid keep it up?" asked Shirley, his silver hair perfectly in place as it had been for two decades.

"Of course not. But he doesn't know that, does he? But then it can happen to him. Like it happened to Palmer on the 17th at Pebble Beach . . . in 1964. Remember? There he was trying to hit the ball out of the rocks and the shallow water, with a stray dog looking on. It took seventeen minutes of television time for him to shoot a 9. He said golf has never been the same for him. Since he learned you could take a 9 on national television on a par-3 hole."

"Ah, intimations of mortality," Shirley said. "They come to us all. Speaking of mortality, what's new on your murder investigation?"

"It's new that it's *my* investigation," Morris said. "There must be somebody on the Monterey Peninsula who is not a suspect. There are leads leading in every direction. I can tell you this. I'm writing it. The bartender saw McCall take a quick sip of his scotch immediately after it was poured in his glass. So the poison had to come into play just before, or during, his scuffle with Sidney. Or he would have been instantly dead. *If we can believe the bartender.*"

"Do you believe him?"

"I do. He seems an entirely harmless fellow, too naive to lie. Of course many's the murderer who grew up an Eagle Scout and loved his faithful dog."

"With all the new security in the lodge, you'd think our sitting president were playing in the Pro-Am," Shirley said.

"Bing invited him. He damn near came. That would have been a scene in the Snake Pit," Morris said. He blew on each fist. "I can feel my fingers again. I better run tap out a few immortal words while I still remember who's leading the golf tournament and who it actually was who was murdered."

His daily double finished in ninety-two minutes, Morris stepped out of the press room, looking for his brown-haired buddy. He ran directly into the heavy, angry, unfortunate chin of Sheriff's Inspector Stanley Gooden.

Morris feared the inspector was going to unhinge his jaw and bite him.

"I'm telling you . . . for your own personal benefit . . . keep your nose out of my investigation—and the goddamn nose of your woman friend. This Jake Hill has hired a big shot lawyer before I've had a chance to ask him the first question. Now what am I going to get out of him? I warn you. I won't hesitate to cite you for obstructing a criminal investigation."

The inspector's voice, coming out of his wide, low-slung torso, was rugged enough to equal his warning, but he lost a lot in intimidation by having to crane his short neck and look *up* into Morris's smiling face.

Smiling he was, but not in amusement. "Tell you what, Inspector. My job is to ask questions. Of anybody I choose. They often answer me. I often publish their answers. Sometimes I quote those answers to investigating officers *I respect.* If I hadn't asked those questions, you wouldn't know Jake Hill was alive."

Morris took one step nearer the inspector, whose jowls quivered with rage. "I speak here of a little thing called the First Amendment. If you don't like it, you might want to start your own country. As for my 'woman friend,' she comes under the same amendment, as do about two hundred and thirty million Americans. You might put that knowledge in your hip pocket so it will be in touch with your larger, outer self."

Inspector Gooden trembled like a Los Angeles overpass at rush hour, too furious to summon up the words to answer.

"I ask you, for the record," Morris said, pulling out his notepad, "when do you anticipate an arrest of the killer of Andrew McCall? Have you identified a leading suspect? What persons present at his death had provable reasons for hating McCall? When and how was the poison put in his glass? Are other participants, and guests, at the Pro-Am being adequately warned and protected?"

"No goddamn comment," said the inspector. "But anybody on my staff jerking around with you amateurs will answer to me."

"I'll quote you exactly," Morris said, turning back to

knock out a brief insert to his just-finished lead on the murder investigation. The boys in New York could do as they saw fit with the "goddamn."

The inspector was nowhere in sight when Morris again stepped out of the press room.

Julia Sullivan was drying her hair. Morris loved to see her turn her head this way and that, rubbing the towel furiously here and there, stamping out the dampness. Then blow-drying it with the same passionate rotation. She might have been a Pekingese preparing herself for the Westminster Dog Show. Not a metaphor to kick around aloud.

"What are you smiling about, John Morris?" Sullivan switched off the blow dryer.

"I like to see you dry your hair."

She looked at him suspiciously. "Maybe so. But I know that smile." She dropped the towel she was wearing and stepped into something just slightly heavier than air. "I also know *that* smile," she said.

He did not deny it.

"Jump in the shower. We're invited for sandwiches and drinks with the sheriff. And his deputy. We can't be late. They're only taking a short break from the investigation. He wants to know what we know."

"He already does."

"He wants to hear it again."

"In the city or the country cops are the same," Morris said. "They have to have their own names repeated ten times a day to be sure the right cops go home to the right wives."

"He doesn't have a wife."

"He's not hurting for a deputy," Morris said. "But I don't envy him Inspector Stanley Gooden. A nasty, dangerous man. Dangerous because he's weak. The weak will get you killed in all the occupations . . . especially sheriff." He told her of his encounter with the angry inspector.

"You're such a diplomat, Morris."

He took a low bow. "Tommy and Deputy Jordan better watch this guy. I wouldn't trust him in the dark with the lights on. Okay, okay, I'm as good as in the shower. I don't know why we don't all just stand out in the rain with a bar of soap."

Sullivan laughed at the image of a large, naked Morris standing out in front of the lodge in the rain. "We don't want to scare the sea otters out of the ocean," she said, unable to stop laughing.

Sullivan guided the Ford among the Mercedeses and BMWs rushing to the next tony party on the peninsula. She loved to make the loop around Carmel Point. It was beautiful even in the gathering dark. With the windows down and your foot off the accelerator, you could hear the ocean rushing against the steep rocks.

"How does an honest sheriff afford to live in Carmel?" Morris asked.

"He doesn't live in one of these seaside mansions," Sullivan said, turning inland. "He did before his rich wife took off for a richer man—a Frenchman at that. We can't be too hard on her, Morris. Downtown Paris is not a terrible address."

"I can't believe you said that. I'll know where to call collect when you take up with a rich Frenchman."

"Not me. I can't leave my mountain in Colorado."

"I know," Morris said.

"Not that I've been asked to leave it." She looked at him with feigned expectations.

"You're sure you know the house," Morris said hurriedly.

Sullivan laughed at his discomfort. "Yep. Here it is."

Morris was startled. He had been expecting something like a hunting lodge, appropriate for the sheriff of Sherwood Forest or maybe Robin Hood himself. This was a pale yellow stucco forest cottage with a curved shingle roof and a stone chimney and a flower box of red and yellow pansies. It looked like the home place of the grandmother of Little Red Riding Hood. Well, that was a bloody enough scene for a sheriff.

"His grandmother left it to him," Sullivan said, reading his tangled mind as always. She was out of the car and knocking on the door as Morris poled himself up the low front steps.

Tommy Whitlock looked as if he'd slept in his sheriff's uniform. Morris had to smile at the thought with Deputy Patricia Jordan lifting a hand of welcome behind him. To Sullivan's disappointment, her uniform was immaculate.

"Come in," Tommy said. "The scotch is poured. We two are just having the one. And back to the lodge. Don't kill another golfer in my county, Morris. It's a bitch."

"I'll try to restrain myself," Morris said. He did not say, "I'm more likely to kill an inspector."

Tommy planted a serious kiss on Sullivan, who did not hesitate to hug the deputy. They held on to each other like sisters in some sorority.

Morris only got a handshake. He cut straight to the point. "I hear Jake Hill hired himself a lawyer."

Jordan handed him a scotch and water. She touched the glass before he lifted it. "Don't worry, the drink's safe, I've given Tommy a taste." She took Tommy's arm as if to reassure herself he was very much alive. There was no formal "Mr. Whitlock" in her hazel eyes, which shone under her auburn hair.

"Yes," said Tommy, "lawyer's name is Walker. Red Walker. A big noise from San Francisco. Kill the mayor, and he'd plea-bargain for six days in a halfway house. Jake didn't have to look far. Walker is his partner in the Pro-Am."

"Indeed," Morris said. "I know him. I mean, I know his face. Swings a pretty mean stick. Have you talked to Jake?"

"As he must have told you, Inspector Gooden questioned him. Or did his best to. Hill called immediately for Red Walker, who advised him before he answered each question. Typically, when asked his father's *name*, Jake turned to Walker, who said, 'No way is my client answering immaterial questions.'"

"This Walker's not dumb," Morris said. "The next question would have been why is his old man in the penitentiary."

"He's in for life, for *poisoning* a bootleg rival's moonshine. Two customers died in Atlanta, and several others damn near died," Whitlock said.

"I knew the old man was in for murder. I thought he shot somebody. So he used poison? Maybe it's genetic. We Georgia boys all have impeccable backgrounds," said Morris. He shifted thoughts. "Tana Daly said that

McCall sponsored Jake on the tour. Did he confirm that?"

"Walker offered a legal argument about it. He obviously wanted to get it on the record that Jake had legally broken the sponsorship."

"But McCall did sponsor him his rookie and sophomore years," Morris said. "A shrewd guy, McCall, to pick him out. Jake was no college hotshot, with agents falling all over him. He played hardscrabble amateur golf around Georgia. The kind where a lot of money backs the hometown boy, who Jake then drowns in his own sweat."

"Walker won't let Jake tell the terms of the sponsorship," Tommy said. "Not without a bloody warrant. I get the feeling McCall had a sweet deal when Jake came out of the chute, winning a quarter of a million dollars his rookie year."

"As if McCall needed another few dollars. It was the power game he loved. So, Patricia," said Morris, "if Jake was dissolving the sponsorship, why does he say he 'likes' Andrew McCall?"

"He said McCall was 'a rough, tough son of a bitch.' That it 'was the only way to be and survive in the golf world.' "

"Did Jake deny knowing the redhead?" Morris asked.

"No," said the sheriff. "Walker would only let him say he met her here at the tournament. He spent some time with her before the murder and again this morning. He enjoyed her company. Jake refused to comment when asked if they were in fact lovers."

Deputy Jordan busied herself with a tray of sandwiches at the word *lovers*.

Tommy said, "He denied pinching her in the Snake Pit. Said it must have been somebody else."

"Maybe it was Ms. Daly's imagination," Morris said. "Or maybe it happened to Kim Novak or Marilyn Monroe in the movies. This lady thinks the world happened in a motion-picture theater."

Morris accepted a sandwich and another go at the scotch. "I've got a designated driver," he said. "Patricia—okay if I call you Patricia when you're filling my glass with scotch?"

Her smile made the national debt seem okay.

"What did you find out about McCall and Jay Martin?"

"Martin tried to avoid the question," Jordan said. "But he finally admitted, with some passion, that McCall 'cut his legs out from under him.' McCall claimed he failed to return a phone call. Martin said he never got the message. One of McCall's clients wanted a lift on the ABC plane. He didn't get it. So McCall dialed New York and had Martin booted out of California. As you know, it may cost him his fiancée."

"Somewhere along the way our boy Andrew made the wrong enemy," Morris said.

"We are checking every pro and every amateur in the golf tournament," said Whitlock. "And we are checking every guest of the lodge. We want to know their relationship with McCall. And I believe we have put together a fairly definitive list of who was in the Snake Pit when he died. Of course we can't check the forty thousand people here to see the tournament."

Morris nodded. "Back to Jay Martin, did he remember bumping against Tana Daly in the Snake Pit?"

"He denied it," said Jordan, shaking her head. "He saw her, of course. But said he never got that close to her."

"This actress must have a world-class imagination . . . to go with her wicked sense of language," Morris said. "She's pinched in her yellow dress and 'misidentifies' who pinched her. She's bumped into and 'misidentifies' who caused her to spill the scotch. Why would she make it up? Why would these guys risk lying?"

"Who wants to be caught standing next to Mr. Death when he knocks?" Sullivan said. "Opportunity to commit murder carries a lot of weight with a jury."

"True," Morris said.

"By the way, neither of McCall's two sons is on the peninsula this week," said Jordan. "They both have second homes here, but they always leave during The Crosby. I get the idea they preferred not to run into their father."

"Did you catch up with Ed Waters?" Morris asked.

"Yes. He was extremely nervous. He didn't want to call Jake Hill a liar. He made that plain enough. He said he could have been wrong. That maybe Jake picked up his own glass. At the time it happened, he admitted he thought Andrew McCall got Jake's glass and Jake got his. Waters kept saying he was just here to play golf. He didn't want to get in any controversy."

"And he's playing unusually well," Morris said, "not like a man with a load of guilt. What do you think he saw?"

"I think Ed Waters is a meticulous sort of guy," Jordan said. "I think he saw Jake Hill pick up the wrong glass. I can't see that it really matters—if the bartender is correct. And he swore again he saw McCall take a quick sip of his scotch as soon as he lifted the glass, and McCall lived to fight Sidney Barker."

Morris didn't advance his idea that one portion of the rim of the glass might have been dusted with cyanide before the scotch was poured into it, that it might have been a glass waiting to kill anybody. And that McCall might have just happened to take his first sip out of the undusted curve of the glass. It was an absurd idea bordering on the impossible.

"Oh," Jordan said, "Jack Houghton has given up on finding out who left the bottle of scotch for McCall at the front desk. *Nobody* on his staff saw the bartender leave it. The bartender stuck to the story he told Morris: that he found the bottle of Glenlivet on the bar, with instructions to leave it at the front desk for Andrew McCall. Any hand-printed instructions taped to the paper bag have disappeared."

"Again, what does it matter?" asked Sullivan. "It was wonderful scotch."

"It matters," Morris said. He had no idea why. "How did Inspector Gooden take your digging up this information?"

"He gritted his teeth and asked tough questions. Good questions," she admitted. "I was careful not to use your name or Julia's."

"Good thinking," Morris said, enjoying Sullivan's first name being said again aloud.

"Enough about murder. For the next five minutes,"

Sullivan said, "I want to hear how the high sheriff and the sheriff's deputy became lovers."

Tommy Whitlock said, "Where's my lawyer when I need him?" He put a long arm around Patricia Jordan, who seemed to fit exactly inside it.

"I'm the villain," Jordan said. "Tommy couldn't see past the license plate of the last stolen vehicle."

"He missed the auburn hair, the smile that reaches from Old Monterey to Pebble Beach, not to mention the person in the trousers . . . sure, we believe that," Sullivan said.

"We had an opening for a deputy. She was far and away the best-qualified candidate. I talked to her two minutes. I hired her. That was it," Tommy said. "She's good at her job."

"*That* we do believe," Morris said.

"So . . . what happened?" Sullivan was always one for the big moment in any romance.

"I had a flat tire," Jordan said.

"A real one?" Sullivan raised her elegant, skeptical eyebrows.

"I also knew I had 'misplaced' the jack in the trunk. But I lied to the sheriff," Jordan said, laughing instead of blushing.

Whitlock seemed truly surprised. "I can't believe you did that," he said. "You might have gotten an emergency call." He removed his long arm.

"What was I supposed to do?" asked Jordan. "The most personal conversation we'd had in my two years on the job lasted one minute. You said I had a raise coming. And I'd earned it."

"That at least was an honest statement," Whitlock said.

"It was hard for me. I mean, the way I felt. I love my job. It seems to come naturally to me." She did blush. "Of course I have a huge amount to learn."

She pulled his long arm back around her shoulder. The sheriff offered minimum resistance. "I liked almost everything about him. The way he questioned a scared kid caught with his first stolen car. The way he kicked in the door of a cocaine hustler in Monterey and had everybody facedown on the floor without taking his gun out of his holster. If you want terrible, try telling a mother her son has been killed in a farm accident; I couldn't see out of the car for crying; the boy was only seventeen; Tommy stayed with his mother for two hours. And he always has time for Mrs. Edwina Partridge, who calls to report her husband missing, and he's been dead, killed in the war, since 1942. I liked the way he signs his name: straightforward, upright letters, no bullshit."

"Enough of this third-person witnessing," Tommy said, but pleased to hear it. He couldn't resist. "*Almost?* What don't you like about me?"

"You're my boss. You're the sheriff. We've talked about it a dozen times. What happens to my job? More important, what happens to yours in the next election? What will the voters think? What happens to us?"

"You'd make a great local police officer, and you know it," Tommy said, holding her tightly as if afraid she would vanish from under his arm.

"Show me a voter who doesn't love a love match," Sullivan said.

Morris could see her, arranging their lives into the next century.

Tommy Whitlock checked his watch.

Morris almost said, "While you're worrying, worry about Inspector Stanley Gooden. He'd love to stir up trouble." But he kept his mouth shut. He should have opened it.

"Time to go. We've got a killer to catch," Whitlock said.

Morris also didn't say, "It wouldn't be the worst thing that ever happened . . . if whoever killed the bastard just faded away into time." He kept his mouth shut. He was glad he did.

The phone rang in the kitchen. Tommy Whitlock screwed up his long face with the receiver to his ear, like a cowboy hearing that his best horse had died of colic.

Deputy Jordan opened her mouth and did not speak, expecting something unfortunate.

She did not expect to hear the sheriff say, "Sidney Barker. Dead. Poisoned in his room. Welcome to The Crosby."

CHAPTER SEVEN

Sullivan tucked the rental Ford right behind the sheriff's big, speeding Chevrolet Caprice, its lights flashing on its roof as if it were in pain.

"Morris, I ran into Sidney in the lobby this afternoon, just after we came in from the golf course like drowned rats. You were in the locker room stirring up quotes. Sidney invited us to drop by his suite tonight for after-dinner drinks."

"How did he seem?" Morris asked.

"Fine. Lively. Laughing at how wet I was. Sweet Sidney, why would anybody kill him?"

"He wasn't all sweetness and light when he slugged McCall."

"No," admitted Sullivan. "But he was so pleased that he had played his round before it started to rain so hard and that he played well. He was especially happy that he and the young pro from Florida, Jerry Boyd, were in position to make the Pro-Am cut. At least five other couples invited us to stop by their suites or houses for drinks. I made notes of each invitation. You know The Crosby, 'a movable feast.' I didn't have my Day-Timer when I saw Sidney. His invitation slipped my mind."

"Of course it did. You were matchmaking. How did they leave you out of the cast of *Hello, Dolly!*? Did Sidney mention any particular time?"

"No." Sullivan shook her head. "Just for after-dinner drinks."

"He didn't mention Andrew McCall? Or anything about his death?"

"No. I'm sure of that. Though I'm such a scatterbrain."

"Hardly. We'd better tell the sheriff or the inspector," Morris said. "Don't think the inspector isn't looking at us anyway. We knew the two victims as well as most. At least as golfers and Crosby regulars. The inspector would rather hang it on us than be elected attorney general of California."

"Then his life would be complete—if only we had done it." Suddenly Julia Sullivan took her eyes off the sheriff's Chevrolet speeding ahead of them. She lost most of the warm texture in her voice. "Morris, do you think Sidney might have killed himself? Having killed Andrew McCall?"

"It occurred to me he might have staged the fight to cover up dropping the poison in McCall's glass. Sidney was the aggressor in the argument, shouting first at McCall. That's one reason I kept thinking it might be bet-

ter if the killer faded into time. I almost said that a
minute before the phone rang at Tommy's house."

The sheriff wheeled to a stop, leaving the driver's
door swinging open on the Chevrolet. Sullivan left the
Ford at an acute angle in front of the Del Monte Lodge.

The ambulance already purred at the lodge entrance
in the drizzling rain. Even the forensic team was here.
Morris recognized its four-wheel-drive vehicle. Unfortunate timing for the sheriff and the sheriff's deputy,
arriving this late to the murder scene in the same vehicle.

Morris and Sullivan quick-stepped behind Whitlock
and Jordan, who were propelled by hotel security
through the lobby, past indignant reporters and cameramen, and down the ground-floor hallway and up the
stairs to suite 224. Morris ignored the shouts from his
fellow reporters.

Sidney Barker had held court in the same suite since
the first year Crosby moved the tournament to the
Monterey Peninsula. Morris and Sullivan and, when he
was alive, Monty Sullivan had lifted many a glass in the
suite and sung many a verse of many a ballad, many of
which Sidney had written.

Sheriff's deputies were thicker in the hallway than
reporters, golfers, agents, and manufacturers' reps in
the lobby. Inspector Stanley Gooden stood in the door
to suite 224 with his arms folded over his considerable
gut, as if justice itself were being delayed by the elected
sheriff and his "good-time" girlfriend. All of Gooden's
unspoken insinuations were obvious in his hostile eyes
and pinched mouth.

The inspector spotted Morris and Sullivan trailing

after the sheriff and reached for the open door to the suite to shut it, but Tommy Whitlock stopped in the doorway.

"What happened?" Whitlock asked.

"The maid came in to turn down his bed," Gooden said, angry that John Morris was near enough to hear him. "He was lying just as he is on the floor."

Morris could see Sidney's short, dumpy figure curled on the floor, all the music fled from it into a last silence. It appeared he had just poured himself a drink. The top was still off the bottle of half-empty scotch on the bar.

Inspector Gooden again urged the sheriff deeper into the suite so that he could close the door behind him. Tommy stood his ground, motionless in his boots.

"Forensics picked up his glass," Gooden said. "They felt sure the drink was laced with cyanide. You can still smell it on the dead man's lips."

Morris flinched to hear an old friend referred to as "the dead man." Americans who had never met Sidney Barker had known his music and his portly, energetic figure on the bandstand for two generations. Modern viewers knew him as the bandleader on America's most popular late-night talk show. And even professionals among the golfers admired his golf swing, a swing that had stood up as long as his music.

Morris hated knowing that the sour almond smell of potassium cyanide came not from the substance itself but from its terrible action on human tissue. From the anguish on Sidney's face and from the way his hands were clutching his short throat, he had died badly. And perhaps alone . . . or alone with his killer. Forensics would have something to say about that.

The forensic team had dusted the suite for latent prints until it looked as if a small powder bomb had gone off inside. There would be dozens, if not scores, of prints and faint hope of separating and identifying them. But latent prints were part of the game the law played, and once in a long while they proved decisive in a prosecution.

"How long has he been dead?" the sheriff asked.

"His watch broke when he fell against the edge of the coffee table," Gooden said, anxious to show off his attention to detail. "The watch hands are fixed at five-thirty. He was seen in the lobby at five P.M. The maids found him in the room at six-ten P.M."

Morris wondered why the sheriff had not been called at home for a hour and forty minutes.

Tommy looked at his watch and looked back at Inspector Gooden, who could see the same question on the sheriff's face.

"I called your office," Gooden said. "I left word there. I rounded up forensics, and the medical examiner, and the photographer." He made it sound as if he were the lone man in the sheriff's department standing between anarchy and civilization on the Monterey Peninsula.

Whitlock ignored his explanation. "Did the maids see anyone entering or leaving his suite?"

"Not that they admit." The inspector said it as if there were a California-wide conspiracy among the maids.

Morris realized that none of the reporters and television cameramen stuck in the lobby had managed to sneak past security and up the hallway. Well, the Associated Press would again be their intrepid pool reporter.

"Anything unusual in the suite?" the sheriff asked.

"Yes." Gooden lowered his voice, but Morris could make it out in the silence of the suite.

Whitlock waited for his answer.

"He'd written the room number of a lodge guest on the pad by the telephone."

The sheriff waited for him to continue.

"Aubry Hicks," Gooden said, almost whispering the name. "No one answers the number."

"Let me see," the sheriff said. He walked deeper into the room, Deputy Jordan following after him, listening and not speaking. Gooden quickly closed the door behind them.

Morris ran the name Aubry Hicks through his memory. He could almost place it, he felt the tug of Sullivan's hand on his arm.

"God bless Sidney, he was a sweet man," she said.

"He was all melody," Morris said. "If you knew his music, you knew Sidney. He loved to be up on the bandstand, he loved people, especially crazy golfers, but in his own life he was a very private guy. Who hadn't thought of braining Andrew McCall? But who would want to kill Sidney Barker?"

"It doesn't make sense," Sullivan said. "What motive could drive you to kill two such opposite men?"

"Let's see: money, sex, power, jealousy, money, revenge, insanity, fear, money." Morris had the vague idea it was a sentence he had rehearsed.

"Sidney wasn't as rich as McCall. But if he was broke, you couldn't prove it by the way he lived."

"Sidney controlled music rights worth millions," Morris said. "*Variety* did a piece on him a few years ago."

"What are you doing reading *Variety*?"

"Who knows? When I hang it up with the AP, I may go into show business."

Sullivan laughed out loud, before catching herself. The idea of Morris in front of an audience with his barroom baritone broke her up, even in the presence of Mr. Death.

"Maybe somebody owed both guys a bunch," Morris said.

Sullivan opened her mouth to speak but put one hand over her lips.

Morris continued. "I can't see McCall lending 'a bunch' to anybody. Sidney was more likely to give money away to an old friend. I doubt a stranger killed them, Sullivan. There were dozens of people, but most of them regulars, in the Snake Pit. And how does a stranger introduce cyanide to Sidney's private suite?"

Sullivan shook her head that she had no idea. When she could speak, she said, "Is it possible Sidney wanted us to find him dead?" For the first time that night she had tears in her eyes.

Morris thought back to his own last conversation with Sidney Barker. "It's possible. Sidney said to me at breakfast, 'I hope they never catch him.' He could have been speaking of himself as murderer. You can make a case for it . . . and worry about it, as I did . . . but in the end it's hard to believe. Sidney never seemed to me a self-destructive man. Some of his best tunes were his

saddest tunes, but always there was a vitality about him
and his music."

"Then why kill so sweet a man as Sidney?"

"The ultimate question," Morris said. "Still, I see
him most clearly as victim. One who admittedly wished
that McCall's killer might never be caught. Careful
what we ask the fates for, Sullivan."

"Indeed."

"Another thing Sidney said at breakfast, about the
way McCall died: 'Some exit,' he said. 'Somebody hated
the bastard worse than I did.' I don't think he ever
imagined he would go the same ugly way as Andrew
McCall. Sidney, the very private man, would hate having Inspector Gooden in his suite, hovering over his
dead body."

"Well, he'll never have to know," Sullivan said. "At
least Patricia's in there. He respected her."

Morris nodded. "How long has Sidney's wife been
dead?"

"Years. I never knew her. Monty did. He thought she
was terrific. She died in an automobile wreck in the
forties. Sidney never remarried."

"I think golf was his mistress. Only Crosby loved the
game more than Sidney. Now what golfer ever killed
himself when he could still sock the driver off the tee?"
Morris smiled. But it was a truism.

"Where's Larry Crosby? I wonder. He'll have to tell
Bing. I wouldn't want that assignment," Morris said.
Suddenly, without effort, it came to him who Aubry
Hicks was and where he'd seen him last. He'd have to
file a bulletin on the second death for the AP. Then
he'd try to find Aubry Hicks. Inspector Gooden's peo-

ple were no doubt searching the lodge and the peninsula for him. Morris wanted to speak with him first, before the sheriff's inspector put the fear of God in him.

Morris approached one of the older sheriff's deputies in the hallway. He had the friendly face of a boozer. "I'm John Morris," he introduced himself.

"Oh, yes," said the older deputy, who identified himself as Hank Waller.

"I'm betting that the bottle of scotch in the suite is clean," Morris said.

"Our guys think so," said Waller, "but we got no volunteers to taste it." He laughed, showing a mouthful of bad teeth. "Hell, I will. So long as I can sleep it off on the bed. Hell, I'd sleep it off on the couch." He had a guttural drinking man's laugh.

"Be a long nap if the wrong stuff is in it," Morris said.

The deputy again bared his bad teeth in a ghoulish smile.

"How long do you think they'll be in there?" Morris tilted his head toward the closed door.

"Not long. The ME has done his business and gone. The body snatchers are waitin'. And I ain't had dinner."

The old deputy was on the money with his prediction. The door opened, and Sheriff Whitlock stepped outside. Deputy Jordan hung back, careful to wait for instructions from Inspector Gooden, who ignored her and the other deputies in the room to make entries in his notebook, as if he alone were capable of dominating the knowledge necessary to understand the murder.

"Morris," the sheriff said, closing the door behind

him, "I'll be shocked if Sidney wasn't poisoned. But I've been shocked before. Get out your pencil and pad." He dictated: " 'Sidney Barker was found dead in his room in the Del Monte Lodge Friday night. His death is consistent with cyanide poisoning. Only an autopsy can determine if that is how he died. We are treating his death as part of the ongoing investigation into the murder of Andrew McCall.' That ought to hold you bastards."

"At least until the first subversive question. Tell me this, Tommy." Morris guided him out of the earshot of the older deputy in the hallway. "Could Sidney have killed himself? After killing McCall?"

"It's possible. He didn't leave a note. Or we didn't find one. There's no container, no evidence of cyanide in the suite, other than what was almost surely in his glass. Do you think Sidney could have been that depressed, that desperate?"

"No," Morris said. "But you can never see inside the mind of another man. He seemed his old, feisty self to me this morning. You'll know soon enough if he had some lethal disease. How about the bottle of scotch?"

"I'm betting it's drinkable. God knows how the poison got in his glass. There's no obvious evidence of anybody else having been in the suite, no second used glass. No cigarette ashes. No anything you can see with the naked eye. We'll be looking microscopically. And questioning everybody in this wing of the lodge and all the employees."

"You might as well begin by questioning Sullivan. She ran into Sidney in the lobby this afternoon, and he invited us up to his suite tonight for drinks."

Sullivan repeated her story. She remembered something else. "Sidney had a glass in his hand. It looked like scotch. He lifted it and said, 'To your health, Miz Sullivan.' He always called me that, Miz Sullivan, as if he were from Atlanta and not Los Angeles. Then he was gone into the crowd in the lobby. I went to the room and showered and put on dry things. At least five other people invited us to drop by tonight for drinks. Sidney's invitation slipped my mind."

She repeated that he seemed entirely himself and pleased with his golf. And made no mention of Andrew McCall or if a few friends were dropping by or if he was having a full-blown party. "A huge crowd in his suite would have been unusual for Sidney," Sullivan said. "Eight or ten friends would drop by and usually wind up around the piano, singing. He always had a piano in his suite."

"It's still there. But no evidence that anybody was standing around it early tonight," said the sheriff. "We'll talk to all his old friends. I know many of them. See who else he invited."

Whitlock stood a minute as if learning from the silence. "But you're right. For such a public figure Sidney was a very private guy. Somebody violated that privacy in the most lethal way. Unless . . ." He left it unsaid that Sidney might have taken his own life.

"You'd better go face journalism's savage horde," Morris said, looking at his watch.

"Yeah."

"I'll pass around your statement. And knock out a quick description of the body and the suite and pass it around too before I put it on the wire. Anything I shouldn't mention?"

"Yes. Time of death. We don't want to tip our hand, assuming we have one," the sheriff said.

"I think, come tomorrow, the sale of scotch on the Monterey Peninsula is about to hit a new low," said Morris.

The sheriff held his own in the press room. He had a way of standing in his boots and letting the more frenzied questions blow past him without visible effect. He made it absolutely clear he wouldn't stop the golf tournament. That it was Crosby's call, or nature's. Or maybe the governor of California could call it off. The sheriff knew the governor didn't have guts enough for that. The writers hit him with every nasty question, but they were enjoying the good life on the Monterey Peninsula and didn't truly want the show to stop. Not with them all on expense account.

Whitlock said, with absolute sincerity, *"Don't drink anything you didn't open and pour yourself.* That's my advice to every guest in the lodge . . . and everybody playing in and attending and covering the golf tournament." Headlines in the newspapers, and anchors on television, would scream that warning throughout the peninsula. That was just the way Whitlock wanted it.

The sheriff left the press room with questions still pouring down like rain on the roof.

Paul Shirley cornered Morris, who had called in his stuff to the AP.

"I'm scared," said the San Francisco columnist.

"Join the foursome," Morris said.

"Don't imagine the drinking will stop in the hospitality rooms or the private suites or the rental houses or the Snake Pit, now that it's open again."

"Never occurred to me that it would."

"I can hear the black humor: 'Let's have one more . . . *for the morgue.*'"

Morris laughed in spite of himself. "I'll have to use that tomorrow in my write-through."

The formal, solemn face of Larry Crosby caught Morris's eye. Larry was lighting a new cigarette off the posthumous one in his hand.

"Morris," said Larry, "I want you to go with me to the hospital. To see Bing. You can tell him how serious things are better than I can."

"Do you want to convince him to stop the tournament?"

"No. I just want him to understand the gravity of the risks before he makes his decision."

"I'll speak to him," Morris said. "I can warn you I don't believe in giving in to terrorist acts or we forfeit our lives. But then the tournament doesn't have my name on it."

Burlingame's Peninsula Hospital was nearly to San Francisco from the Del Monte Lodge. Larry Crosby managed to finish two more cigarettes before pulling in the parking lot.

The director of the hospital himself greeted Larry. Also Bing's doctor. Both of them looked at John Morris.

"He's with me. It's all right," Larry said. He did not say Morris was with the Associated Press.

The director and the doctor were not encouraging. "He's pretty doped up," the doctor said. "He's running a fever. He's not comfortable. If he doesn't respond better to antibiotics in the next few days, the only answer is surgery."

"I understand," Larry said. "Is he worse?"

"No," said the doctor. "His lungs are just not responding to treatment as we would hope. His vital signs are good. He's in no immediate danger. We've seen television reports from Pebble Beach. We know there's been another death. If you've got to tell him, do it as undramatically as possible, and get it over as quickly as possible."

"Yes," Larry said.

Crosby, when well, was a taller, more athletic man than fans realized, the opposite of many small movie stars who were larger than life only when projected on a thirty-foot screen. But Crosby was lying up in bed like a corpse. He looked terrible, his face bleached white. And he obviously felt worse. He also looked older. He never wore his hairpiece, which he despised, except when performing.

"What are you here for Morris, the obit?" Bing said, managing a smile, though it hurt him to speak.

"I want you to know exactly what's happened," Larry said. "Morris was with Sheriff Whitlock when he was called to Sidney's suite. Listen to him, then tell me what you want done."

Morris told it straight. He skipped only the intimate details of Sidney, curled on the floor of his suite, his hands grasping his burning throat. There was enough burning in the hospital room already in Crosby's lungs.

"Tommy has no idea who did this?" Bing asked.

"None," Morris said. "He assumes Sidney was

poisoned the same as McCall and that the two deaths are related."

Morris knew that Crosby loved Sidney as much as he didn't love McCall.

"The man swung a sweet golf club," Crosby said, then coughed and cursed mildly at the pain. "Are others in danger, Morris?"

"Yes."

"Tommy thinks so?"

"Yes. He's warned everybody to drink only what they open and pour."

"What I wouldn't give for a toddy," Crosby said, weakening with every word. "Do you think I should call the whole thing off, Morris?"

"No. Tommy doesn't either. He won't stop it. He says it's your call. He'll support your decision. Who's to say the killer won't be back at the same murderous stand next year? I know it's not easy. Expectations of the players, the fans, television, your charities. But the possibility of another death . . . Whatever you decide, we'll carry it on the AP wire exactly the way you state it."

"Don't carry this," Crosby said. "I think it's personal. Somebody hates my guts. You survive in this racket forty years, and you make your share of enemies. Some I'm not proud of. Some I am. But why now? I'm an old song and dance man, facing the setting sun."

Crosby rose up as much he dared. "It's an easy decision," he said. "Hell, no, we don't call it off. But I'll respect anyone who wants to pull out and go home. I wish I could stand up. I'd play again myself for the first time since 1956. We'd better live while we can. We'll hit the hereafter soon enough. I may die here lying on my back. And might feel better if I do." He coughed, doubling up in pain. Then recovered his breath. "That's it. You look out for my family, Larry."

"Not to worry. I've already doubled security."

Morris couldn't resist saying, "Phil Harris will be glad. He'll enjoy stealing your weekend time on the tube."

Crosby smiled sickly. "Harris. Tell him if he sings one note, he's fired." Crosby collapsed onto his pillows.

On the way back to the lodge Larry inhaled another cigarette. "Thanks, Morris, for your help."

"God knows if I helped or hurt the cause. But he made the right decision. Even if I'm the next to go."

"Do you think Bing is correct? That the killing is personal? That somebody hates him?"

"I don't know about that. He's a sick man. Lying there in pain and bad news, he must feel like the world does hate him. Though the world feels otherwise. Who can know what drives one person to kill another?" Morris added, "On this peninsula we'd better make it our business to find out."

Morris remembered to ask, "Larry, do you know where I might find Aubry Hicks? He's not in his room. Or wasn't when the inspector was looking for him about an hour ago."

"Maybe. Why?"

"Between us . . . Sidney had written down Aubry's phone number at the lodge. I don't know when he wrote it, I don't know why. Aubry's a friend who, as you know, fell on hard times. I'd like to talk to him before the inspector scares the wits out of him."

"Try Jim Nichols's room," said Larry. "He and Jim were always friends on the tour. And Jim kept up with him after he hurt his back . . . and had the drinking problem. I understand Aubry has a pro job at a club in San Diego and is doing better. Bing always invited him to the Pro-Am as a past champion, even when he couldn't play anymore."

"That's Bing. I hope he gets better without the surgery. But these days surgery is no big deal." Morris thought, *So long as it's not your lungs they're cutting into.*

Morris navigated through the lobby, deflecting questions like a senator under an ethics investigation. In the press room he knocked out a quick bulletin from Crosby. The tournament would continue. And "damn the torpedoes!" . . . except here he was quoting Admiral David Glasgow Farragut, who came from six strokes back to win the 1864 competition at Mobile Bay. Morris quoted Crosby saying he wished he could stand up and play himself for the first time since 1956. So much for the cowardly threat of a poisoner.

"How did he look, Morris?" asked Paul Shirley.

"Like a San Francisco columnist after a long week in the Snake Pit. He looks like he feels, lousy. Or he'd be here, believe me."

There was much relief among the ink-stained wretches that their expense accounts lived and the party would go on.

Sullivan gave Morris a huge hug in their room as if he himself had survived hospitalization.

"How's Crosby?"

"Fine. So long as he never again has to use his lungs.

Terrible, really. He's probably facing surgery. His doctor says his vital signs are good. Which usually means things are about to get worse, like after a vote of confidence for a baseball manager."

"Poor baby."

"He's tough. He says let the players play. Let the tournament continue. Crosby'll be okay. It's us guys drinking the scotch who are an endangered species. Larry told me we might find Aubry Hicks with his old tour buddy Jim Nichols. Let's give it a try."

Simple as that. Hicks was holed up with his old pal, going over videotapes of Nichols's swing, which had recently deserted him. Hicks couldn't imagine what the AP wanted with him. But Morris had always treated him fairly. He agreed to come to Morris's room.

There was a time, fifteen years ago, when Aubry Hicks had it all. Everything was an uphill two-foot tap-in for eagle. He was young and blond and strong, with a grin to sell homeowners' insurance to bedouins. He was even a nice guy. Not full of himself, even though he came out of Florida State University to win the first pro tournament he entered. His second year he won the PGA championship in a play-off with Raymond Floyd, and with it a ten-year exemption on the tour.

Seven victories and five years later, on Christmas morning, Hicks tore the rotor cuff in his left shoulder while bench-pressing two hundred pounds without warming up. "Some Santa Claus," he said to Morris at the time.

One operation didn't help. After the second operation it was hopeless. His professional golf career was finished. Very soon his marriage was on the rocks with his vodka. His old sponsors avoided him at every opportunity. The fall from grace was instant. The long way back had been a bitch.

Hicks stepped into the room with the same lopsided grin that had twice made the cover of *Sports Illustrated*. Despite everything, he looked a young thirty-seven.

Sullivan gave him a no-holds-barred hug. "Damn, it's good to see you. I hear only good things about your life."

"It's not as exciting as a five-year hangover," Hicks said, "but my life does belong to me again."

"What would you like to drink?" Sullivan asked.

"A Coke if you have it."

Sullivan retrieved a Coke from the small antique refrigerator in their room.

"No ice, thanks," said Hicks. He lifted the can: "To the simple life."

They all drank to that.

"How do you like San Diego?" Morris asked.

"The town is as good as the weather. I'm at a friendly club that takes its golf seriously. No swimming pool. No tennis courts. Just golf. I can't believe how much I've enjoyed teaching the game. And how much I've learned doing it. I swear, Morris, with what I've learned I might have been a real player."

"You weren't easy pickings. Never saw anybody, since Hogan, hit a sweeter mid-iron."

"What's up?" Hicks asked to cover his embarrassment.

"Have you heard about Sidney Barker?" Morris asked.

"No. What do you mean? I saw Sidney this afternoon. Still a nice guy with a sweet golf swing. Got me tickets a year ago when the late-night talk show came to San Diego. We sat right up front. Sidney even had Johnny recognize me on the air. My date thought I was a big shot. Maybe that's why she agreed to marry me."

Sullivan interrupted, delaying the impending bad news, to determine that he had married a schoolteacher, a Southern Cal grad, no less, with an eight-year-old daughter he was crazy about and a son on the way.

"That's wonderful," Sullivan said, dreading the facts to come.

"The news is not wonderful about Sidney," Morris said. "He died early tonight. Almost surely he was poisoned."

The grin was long gone from Hicks's face, which took on the weight of its thirty-seven years.

"I saw him in the dining room," Hicks said. "He insisted I sit down and have a cup of coffee. Remember, we won the Pro-Am here the year I lucked into the championship. He was really pleased to have broken 80 today—at his age in this weather. He couldn't ask enough about my life, my marriage, my new daughter. We didn't send out invitations. You know, the second time around for us both. But Sidney heard about it and sent a gift certificate for all new carpets in our condo. Boy, we could use them with an eight-year-old and two dogs." There were tears in Aubry Hicks's eyes.

"What happened to him, Morris?" he asked.

Morris told him, again leaving out the more intimate details.

"Do the police think it was murder?" Hicks asked.

Morris nodded. "There's nothing to suggest suicide."

"They think the same guy poisoned Andrew McCall?"

"They think," Morris said. "You knew McCall?"

"One of his big advertising clients was the first to drop me," said Hicks, "even before I had the second operation." His voice was all bitterness.

"I know those were tough times," Morris said.

"One day everybody wants to buy a piece of you. You can't pick up a check in a crowded restaurant. The next day nobody returns your phone calls. My own agent left me with a telegram." He did not have to say that booze became his best companion. And that his wife finally gave up on him in disgust.

"Tuesday night, in the Snake Pit," Morris began, "you were at the bar when McCall made a scene about getting his drink."

Hicks rubbed his forehead with the palm of his right hand, a gesture Morris remembered from the days when he was considering a critical putt. "I was there," Hicks said, "ordering a Coke."

"I know. I was standing behind McCall," Morris said. "He shoved his drink past you and the other guys at the bar."

"I started to pour it down his trousers," Hicks said, with iron resentment in his voice. "If I had, maybe the bastard would still be alive."

"Did you speak to the kid Jake Hill and to your contemporary Ed Waters, standing at the bar?"

"I saw them. I didn't speak. I recognized Hill from his photographs. Ed I hadn't seen in years. We were rookies together. But we were never close. I don't think Ed hung out with anybody. I've learned to keep a low profile, Morris. Especially in crowds. People half remember your face, rarely remember your name. I've been gone from tournament golf nearly nine years. Some pros speak. Some pros walk past me—from what I've read the way soldiers walk past the dead and dying on the battlefield. Except for pure luck they could be lying there."

"I've spoken to them both," Morris said. "Jake saw you. He didn't know you. Jake is obsessed with one golf game, his own. Ed said he was watching the bartender, and then McCall made an ass of himself, and he just didn't look to see who was standing next to him." Morris did not say that Waters had had no trouble recognizing Jake Hill.

Hicks nodded slowly. "I never caught his eye. I was careful not to. I doubted he'd remember me. I doubt he did. Probably he just caught a glimpse of my face and nothing registered. If it had, he might have remembered the time I caught him on the 71st hole at the Champions in Houston with a birdie for the title." An old bitterness crept back into his voice.

"I expect he would remember that," Morris said. "I was there. I remember it. Jackie Burke and Jimmy Demaret were standing at the 18th green to shake your hand. Did you happen to notice if McCall picked up his own glass after the bartender finally filled it to his satisfaction?"

Hicks shook his head. "The man's arrogance irritated me so much I paid no attention to the glass he picked up."

"When did you last have any dealings with McCall?"

"Oh, nearly eight years ago," Hicks said. "His client, the golf ball king, tried to back out of my contract before it was up. My agent didn't want to fight them. He didn't want to upset them. He had other clients. I phoned McCall myself and told him to kiss my ass. That was when my agent sent me the wire saying adios."

Hicks grinned his old grin. "But I'm over all that, Morris. I have my health, a job I enjoy, a beautiful wife and daughter, and a son on the way. What do I need with old regrets?"

"What, indeed?" Sullivan said.

"The reason I called you . . ." Morris said.

Hicks took on a worried expression.

"Sidney had written down your telephone number here in the lodge. Inspector Gooden found it in his suite. Can you think why Sidney would have been trying to call you?"

Hicks shook his head slowly. "No. I did have the cup of coffee with him this afternoon. Maybe he was going to invite me to dinner or up to his suite after dinner. I don't know. He sometimes, as you know, has a bunch of friends in his suite, and he loves to play the piano and sing. I was always embarrassed. I can't sing a note."

"But he didn't invite you up to his room tonight?"

"No," Hicks said, looking down into his Coke.

Morris's own voice became more businesslike. "Sidney didn't mention McCall's death to you this afternoon?"

Hicks squinted both blue eyes. "In fact . . . yes, he did. He asked if I saw the tussle in the Snake Pit. I told him I did. That I was pulling for him to flatten the bastard."

"What did he say to that?"

"He said, if you hadn't stopped it, Morris, he would have killed him before somebody beat him to it. I didn't take him seriously. You know how Sidney could get excited."

"Did he say anything else about McCall?"

"He said plenty of the old-timers had had enough of McCall. That they were going to ask Crosby not to invite him again."

"He didn't say *which* old-timers?"

"No. That was all he said. Then he was asking me about my wife, how I'd met her. That sort of thing. Morris, do you think this inspector has some idea I'm involved in these murders?" Hicks did not disguise his concern.

"He's just following up on the telephone number Sidney left in his suite. He's a bit of a bastard, this inspector. But Sheriff Whitlock has confidence in him. You know Tommy?"

Hicks grinned. "I used to. He'd just gotten elected sheriff the year I won The Crosby. A nice guy."

"You'd better check the messages on your house phone," Morris said. "Just tell the inspector what you know. Don't hold back anything. Don't let him rattle you either. Sorry to catch up with you on such a bleak night. Sullivan and I loved Sidney the way you did. Unhappily somebody felt differently about him. Or about the tournament. But Crosby isn't stopping it. They'll play tomorrow if the rain will let them—"

Morris interrupted himself. "The inspector will want to know where you were early this evening."

Hicks bit his lower lip. "I was in my room. I missed lunch. I ordered a sandwich about four-thirty. Then I took a shower. And went up to see Jim Nichols about . . . six-thirty, I guess."

Morris did not say that Sidney Barker apparently died at 5:30 P.M., not a good time to have been alone in your room.

Sullivan hugged Aubry Hicks and patted him an encouraging good-bye.

"Morris, it's unfortunate he was in his room alone. But there's no way that young man hurt Sidney or anybody."

"Let's hope not. He could put some hurt on the golf ball. And he had good reason to hate Andrew McCall. He and Sidney seemed to have stayed friends. But it's tough to lose everything, Sullivan. He admits he lost five years to booze. It's possible that Sidney, his old championship Pro-Am partner, ignored him all those years . . . here at The Crosby. And then fanned his resentment with a sudden wedding present. What would you do, Sullivan, if you lost downtown Denver?"

"I would live off my moneyed friends in journalism," she said.

"An impoverished life you could not imagine," Morris said. "It's hard for me to believe that Ed Waters stood at the bar, next to Aubry Hicks, who came on the tour the year he did, a guy he teed it up against for *seven years*, and *didn't recognize him*."

"Doesn't seem likely," Sullivan said.

"Even if he caught just a sliver of Aubry's profile,

you'd think he'd recognize him," said Morris. "You're telling me he couldn't remember having the tournament snatched away from him in Houston?"

"I'm not telling you that," Sullivan said, all smiles.

"And that was before Waters had won on the tour, as I remember. And then, of course, Ed dropped Sidney as his Pro-Am partner, after last year, when he showed up on the tee drunk on the last round and cost him a payday he could have used. I want to talk again to Ed Waters."

"You have my permission," Sullivan said.

Morris then remembered: "But first let's talk with the young pro Jerry Boyd. He was Sidney's partner in the Pro-Am. According to Sidney, they played very well today. I wonder how Sidney seemed to Boyd. And what they might have talked about after the round."

Catching up with young Boyd was not as simple. He was renting a house in the Del Monte Forest. Finally Morris snagged him on the telephone just as he got back from an early dinner. On the Monterey Peninsula, during The Crosby, anything before daylight was considered early. Boyd had heard about Sidney's death and was one part broken up and one part frightened. The sheriff's office had not yet contacted him. But he had been out, and the phone in the house he was renting had no answering machine. Boyd invited Morris and Sullivan by for a drink.

The rain had blown inland, but the streets through the forest were slick with water. Morris was supposed to navigate. He was lost in his thoughts and missed the driveway that led to the house hidden in the trees.

"I've got to get a new crew," Sullivan said, turning the Ford around. "Good help is hard to find."

"It's the captain who has the responsibility, who goes down with the ship," Morris said.

"Oh, yes, the captain. She's all-powerful. Can even perform *marriages*." She looked at Morris, while setting the hand brake in front of a massive imitation Tudor house. Morris busied himself exiting the car with his cane.

Jerry Boyd was not your picture postcard golfer. He was neither blond nor classically handsome. His dark hair grew close over his forehead, and he had the square face and jaw and deeply burned complexion of a shrimper. In fact, his daddy ran a shrimp boat in the Panhandle of Florida. Young Boyd had grown up hauling nets and culling trash fish off the working deck of the boat. Still, he'd found himself on dry land enough to earn a golf scholarship to the University of Florida, where he'd stayed only one year before turning pro.

After six years Boyd had yet to win on the tour. But he'd won enough money each year to keep his playing card. His swing was no thing of beauty, but his short game was first-rate, and he could grind out a score like a young Doug Ford.

Boyd opened the door himself. He shook hands with Morris. He'd known Sullivan to nod to. She and Morris were only four years older than Boyd, but he seemed a generation younger, circulating, as they all did, in the whippet-fast world of professional golf.

"This Inspector Gooden just called me," Boyd said. "I have to meet him at the lodge. But I have a few minutes. I'm sick about Sidney. What happened?"

Morris gave him the shorthand version of the death of Sidney Barker. "How did you two get together in the Pro-Am?" he asked.

"Mr. Crosby paired us up. I got a note in the mail. I found out Sidney asked for me. He insisted I call him Sidney. He said half the people in show business didn't know he had a last name. He'd seen me a couple of times on television. And he needed a pro partner."

Boyd did not say, or maybe know, that Ed Waters had dumped Sidney for showing up drunk on the last day of last year's Pro-Am.

"I understand Sidney was on his game today," Morris said.

"Damn if he wasn't. I wish I had his swing. Damn good tempo. And he can"—Boyd caught himself—"he could putt for an old guy. We were ten under. I liked our chances of winning the Pro-Am."

"How did you hit it?" Morris asked, knowing he was only three shots off the lead.

"I scrambled all over Cypress Point," Boyd said. "Half the time I was hanging from my spikes over the ocean. Thank God we could put our hands on the ball . . . in all that mud. I managed to get up and down for a 70. I deserved a 75. Sidney helped me several times when I was about to underclub myself. He knows—he knew—that golf course like he'd built it."

"Did he invite you up to his suite tonight?" Morris asked.

Boyd grabbed his square jaw to keep his emotions from subverting him. Finally he said, "Yep. But I didn't go. I thought I had a date. But the girl never showed."

He looked embarrassed. Hard to know if it was because the girl didn't show or because he'd stood up Sidney.

"Sidney also invited us," Sullivan said, to ease his discomfort. "We were visiting with the sheriff, an old friend, and we forgot the invitation. We remembered it only when the sheriff got word that Sidney was dead. Did he say who else was coming to his suite?"

"He just said a few friends. For after-dinner drinks. I thought I might drop by with the girl. But when she didn't show in the lobby, I decided I'd turn in early. I don't even know her last name. Her first name was Anne. She was standing around the practice putting green. Said she was from Palo Alto. A student, I think." He sounded wistful.

"What did she look like?" Sullivan asked.

"Tall. Tall as I am. Short, dark hair. She looked like an athlete."

Morris could see Sullivan polling the Annes in the Palo Alto-San Francisco phone book, to get this boy a date.

"How did Sidney seem before and during the round?" Morris asked.

"He was up. He loved golf. He didn't give a damn about the rain and mud. He was ready. He had a sweet swing. Hell of a fairway wood player. And he hummed all around the course. Different tunes. People recognized him and shouted song titles to him. Songs he'd written, I think. I rarely stay up late enough to catch the late-night show. I didn't know he was a bandleader until I asked him what he did." Boyd might have been blushing. He face was so burned from years in the sun that it was hard to tell.

"Did he mention the death of Andrew McCall?" Sullivan asked.

"Yes," Boyd said. "He said McCall was a bastard. Got what he deserved. I was surprised. Mr. Barker—Sidney—seemed such a fun guy. But he had it in for this McCall. I was glad I turned down one of McCall's advertising clients to sign with a competitor. It's tough enough out here. Who wants to do business with a bastard?"

"Did you ever meet McCall?" Morris asked.

"Sure. He put pressure on me personally. I didn't want to be just one of all those guys endorsing his client's golf ball. I thought I could make a bit of a name for myself with a lesser-known ball. It's worked out fine. They know I'm not Arnold Palmer. But I stay in contention most tournaments. Maybe everybody will fall dead some Sunday, and I'll win one." He winced at his own word, *dead*.

Boyd checked his watch. He had the appointment with the inspector. "I'd better admit to this Inspector Gooden that I was in the Snake Pit early Tuesday night. But I left alone and came back to the house before McCall fell dead. Unfortunately nobody was here but me. I ordered in a pizza."

Morris nodded that he should tell all that. "How do you get along with Jake Hill?"

"We say: 'You're up. You're away.' That's it. Not even 'Good shot.' That's Jake. He's a tough one. I wish I had his iron will. Hell, I wish I had his tee shot, short but straight. If he could hit his tee shot twenty-five yards farther, he could win one of the majors. Maybe he will anyway. Now Jake is a guy who knew this McCall. I

saw them in a nasty argument at Doral in Miami. I
don't know what they were shouting about. But Jake
was in his face."

"That was last summer?"

"Yes. Jake's not a guy you want to fool with. Not that
he's ever been anything but a tough competitor with
me."

Jerry Boyd had dragged in many a shrimp net with
his big forearms. He didn't look like a fellow who'd
back off from Jake Hill.

"You better go see the inspector," Morris said. "It's
always best to tell the cops what you know. Not hold
anything back."

"Tonight, just like Tuesday, the three other guys
staying in the house all had appointments or dates for
dinner," said Boyd. "I was supposed to meet this Anne
at five-thirty in the lobby of the Del Monte Lodge. I
got there a few minutes early. But she didn't show."

"And you—"

"Grabbed a hamburger at McDonald's. And came
here and sat down in front of the television."

Morris offered his big hand for a shake. "The inspector's a bit of a hard ass. But you've been in the press
tent. You've heard all the nasty questions."

"Haven't I?" said Boyd, smiling, his square, strong,
homely face yielding a bit more to the boy he had not so
long ago been.

Sullivan steered the Ford through the fog and mist-
ing rain toward the Del Monte Lodge.

"These athletic young guys eating dinner alone in
their rooms . . . it's against nature," Sullivan said.

"Let's hope it wasn't a crime against man," Morris said.

"I'm going to hang around the practice putting green tomorrow—isn't Boyd playing Pebble Beach?—and see what happened to this Anne. Jerry seems like a solid fellow. Sheriff's business, you understand."

"Sure," Morris said. "You have no peers as a world-class matchmaker. I still don't know how it is they did keep you out of the cast of *Hello, Dolly!*"

Morris shifted his bad leg, which was stiffening in the rain and cold. "The Sidney Barker that Boyd described on the golf course was the good-time Sidney Barker we always knew. He didn't sound like a guy looking for an exit to the next world. Or a guy afraid for his life."

Sullivan nodded her agreement. "And we have another account of Jake Hill, tough guy. If he was also eating dinner alone in his room tonight, it will be a scandal against the young women of California. Do you imagine Jake wanted out of his contract with McCall enough to kill him?"

"Say he did. What did he have against Sidney Barker? Assuming we have one killer among us."

"We don't even know if Jake knew Sidney."

"We'll ask him."

"Careful. The boys don't mess with Jake Hill."

"I'm from Georgia too, remember. Crackers don't mess with us Atlantans."

"How did the poet James Dickey celebrate growing up on your side of town: 'Looking for the Buckhead Boys.'"

"That's us," Morris said. "Now there is a poet who can spot you three verbs a side and beat you to the clubhouse. And not a shabby athlete in his time. Which was way before my time, understand."

"Is it true he's never beaten you in tennis?"

"It is—if he's not in the room," Morris said.

CHAPTER EIGHT

Sullivan parked the Ford, which definitely seemed to be taking on airs among the Mercedeses and BMWs.

"I'm starving, Morris."

"Yes. Let's hit the Pit. They'll have sandwiches."

"Do murderers poison sandwiches?"

"That would be cheating. Like rolling your ball over in a hazard."

They stepped inside the crowded but eerily quiet Snake Pit to the slow action of Jackie Melton on the piano. His clear tenor voice subdued the room with " 'You can say that I'm your friend,/You can see my life begin and end,/I'll always play for you.' " A great sadness that Sullivan could feel in the roots of her hair ran through the room. And there were other trained voices to sustain the old Sinatra standard that called back the sad/good times with Sidney Barker on the bandstand.

With the last note the room burst into random conversations, a frenzy of words called up to drown the melancholy.

Morris led the way through the revelers, who were suddenly drinking and laughing as if death had been trampled underfoot. Two deputies stood at the bar, watching every action of the new, older, much-experienced bartender. Another deputy, Patricia Jordan, watched over the table of sandwiches and hors d'oeuvres looking lost, like a girl in grammar school who had not been chosen by either side at recess.

"Sheriff's Deputy Jordan, may we have one of your sandwiches?" Morris said.

She smiled to see them.

"Excuse me if I take two for the lady, who has an outrageous appetite."

Sullivan did not deny it.

"Inspector Gooden"—Jordan's voice was all acid—"has assigned me to permanent watchdog status. I'm not to question any of the witnesses or suspects . . . if he can identify one."

"What does the sheriff say about that?" Sullivan asked.

"I don't go to the sheriff with my on-the-job problems."

"The inspector can't order you not to listen while you watch over our sandwiches," Morris said.

She pulled out her notebook.

He caught her up on his visit with Crosby. And on their conversations with the young pros Aubry Hicks and Jerry Boyd. How Hicks "wasn't surprised" that Ed Waters hadn't recognized him here at the bar Tuesday night. How unlikely that seemed, their having been rookies together on the tour. Waters had not only recognized Jake Hill, but had kept up with his glass of scotch. Why deny recognizing his old competitor Aubry Hicks, standing there asking for a Coke instead of a scotch?

Morris described how McCall had tried to renege on Hicks's endorsement contract, when he ruined his shoulder nine years ago. "Not a scene McCall was likely to forget." How Aubry himself admitted falling into a years-long alcoholic funk. And how Sidney had "not invited" Hicks, his old winning Pro-Am partner, to his suite tonight, though he had invited his current partner, Jerry Boyd.

Morris described Boyd describing a happy, even joyful Sidney Barker, humming his way around the golf course this morning, breaking 80 and he long past the age of seventy. Not the profile of a man about to kill himself.

Boyd had said he had ignored pressure from McCall to endorse the golf ball sold by one of his clients. "Another scene McCall was not likely to forgive." But apparently not as nasty as the shouting match Boyd "saw at Doral in Miami" between Jake and McCall. Boyd didn't know the source of their discontent, but it was likely Jake's attempt to lose McCall as his tour sponsor.

"Three angry, ambitious young men and one angry, greedy, powerful old man . . . a volatile combination," said Morris.

Sullivan told how both Hicks and Boyd "ate alone"

in their rooms tonight while Sidney took his lethal swallow of scotch. She described the Anne who was supposed to have met Boyd in the lobby of the lodge but never showed, leaving him there alone about the time of Sidney's death. "I'll find her myself," Sullivan said. "Might not be good for Morris's cardiovascular system to stumble on so athletic a beast alone."

Question was, Did the eligible Jake Hill also "eat alone"? Or was he in the fabled company of the very active Ms. Tana Daly?

Sullivan said, "Morris has volunteered to pursue this line of questioning with Jake, the Georgia mountains tough guy, whose daddy poisoned two Atlantans, which is a misdemeanor in Georgia. Morris will not approach Ms. Daly. A good journalist knows when he's overmatched. I'll see her myself." Sullivan ignored the threat of Morris's large balled fist.

"Tana Daly 'puts it about a bit,' " admitted Morris. "I wonder if Sidney ever fell under her formidable charms."

"Good question. I'll ask her," Sullivan said.

"The three golfers seem to have had the opportunity, and at least some sort of motive, to hate McCall," said Jordan. "But why Sidney? Of course Ed Waters dropped him as his Pro-Am partner. But the only hard feelings about that should have been Sidney's."

"I hope so," Sullivan said. "Highly paid single guys are an endangered species."

"I'll pass what you've heard along to Tommy," said Jordan, folding away her notebook in her purse. "I'm not opening my mouth to the inspector. Unless I catch someone stealing these free sandwiches."

Sullivan eased over to the piano bench, where Jackie Melton happily made room for her to sit down. His ready fingers tickled the keys into chords and hints of melodies, as if they had performing lives of their own.

"Oh, the music stopped for Sidney," said Melton, and the theme of his late-night talk show lifted into the air as if his soul were passing over the jangle of glad noise in the room. "Bet you didn't know I wrote that melody," Jackie said.

"I didn't. But who can keep up with all the tunes you've written?" Sullivan said.

"It was in 1938. My second favorite year . . . to the next year, when I met my Mary." An old love ballad of Jackie's rose from the piano, one he had written for Mary and that she used to sing here at The Crosby, which Crosby himself always requested and always joined in: " 'Listen to my heart . . . beat for you alone . . . all the reason why . . . I can still go on.' " Melton was not embarrassed by the tears in his eyes.

"Jackie Melton, every woman would hope to be loved that much."

" 'Good-bye, so long, and farewell' to my generation, Sullivan. Our song is about sung. Soon only the tunes will be left, and soon enough the tunes will be forgotten." His fingers ranged over the keys as if feeling for music already lost.

"Sidney was the sweetest man," Sullivan said.

"Oh, yes. He could be that. He was a musician who knew good music when he heard it. Let's pick it up a bit, Sullivan."

Jackie's fingers jumped to the beat of the old Olympia Brass Band, famous among New Orleans funerals:

"Hey, didn't he ramble." The crowd heard it, and knew it, and raised a loud, spontaneous cheer.

"I don't think, Sullivan, we had to stay until the last song was sung."

"But that was you singing it, Morris," Sullivan mumbled, without taking her head out from under the pillow.

"There's that," Morris said. A great glass of water barely helped. He stood in a cold shower as if in penance. A rough toweling jump-started his lapsed heart. He might even live through the entire day. Julia Sullivan had fallen from grace, all right, but only back into sleep. No possibility of raising that one in the single-digit hours of the morning.

Morris, stopping only to pick up the Saturday *Monterey Peninsula Herald*, made his way to the dining room and a cup of hot coffee that made life seem possible, if not probable. He could see Jake Hill across the room, eating breakfast alone, soon to make the walk to the first tee alone. Only at his own execution could a man be said to be more surely alone than a professional golfer stepping up, club in hand, to the first tee in a PGA tournament. No other man's knowledge, or killer instinct, or habits, or talent, or experience, or goodwill, or resolution could so much as help settle the ball on the tee. The golfer might as well be alone on an undiscovered continent. It was a sort of religious experience without benefit of God, all faith, but only in oneself.

Morris realized he had been staring directly at Jake Hill, who looked up and ducked his head back into his breakfast. Morris thought of approaching him, to find out where he had spent the early hours of the past evening. But he could catch him later. Let him enjoy these last minutes of peace at breakfast before taking on the terrors of Spyglass Hill.

Morris unfolded the *Herald* with the satisfaction that he always got from the slippery feel of fresh newsprint. Sports Editor Ted Durein, who doubled as the press director of the tournament, wrapped up Friday's rainy-day round with the efficiency of the veteran that he was.

Morris read carefully through the front-page lead on the death of Sidney Barker. Sidney's career in many ways had paralleled Crosby's. He'd played the old vaudeville circuits, and written songs and directed music for early radio, and spent many years under contract to Paramount Studios, often directing the music for movies starring Crosby and Hope.

Sidney had never missed a beat when television came along. He'd directed the music for any number of regular shows and TV specials and was most famous at the end of his career for his band and his music on America's favorite late-night talk show. Morris was amazed at the number of hit songs Sidney had written, many of them sung by Crosby. Small wonder he had been a regular invitee to the Pro-Am since its beginning. Morris was not surprised to read that Sidney had once shot a 68 at Pebble Beach in the California State Amateur.

Quoted in a front-page sidebar, Sheriff Tommy Whitlock went straight for the jugular, calling Sidney Barker's death "suspected murder." He also said he believed the same person or persons were responsible for the death by poisoning of Andrew McCall.

Down in the lead story Inspector Stanley Gooden

stated that he would "let the unfolding evidence speak for itself as the case progressed." Which meant the sheriff was out on a limb by himself with the charge of murder . . . until they turned up evidence against a murderer.

Morris skimmed through the rest of the paper. Society on the peninsula had not slowed its rounds of elaborate parties despite the deaths of two prominent revelers. He quit his skimming and came to a dead stop on the page featuring the *Herald*'s longtime much-feared gossip columnist. The headline read: THE HIGH SHERIFF AND HIS DEPUTY MAID MARION.

The opening paragraph was even more lethal: "A little murder among friends never stopped romance. What sheriff has been seen making goo-goo eyes at what sexy sheriff's deputy during the Crosby Pro-Am? My, my, all these late hours looking *vainly* for a suspect to the terrible murders at the Del Monte Lodge have not been entirely wasted! One shouldn't ask, Is that the county's job to underwrite romance? Meanwhile, as the Hollywood High Muckety-Mucks fear for their posh lives, the body count beats on."

"Splendid," Morris said to himself, "just what the tournament needs, a dash of character assassination." He was sure Tommy would not be nearly as horrified as Deputy Jordan. Not that he would be thrilled.

What the hell? Time for some golf, man's best antidote for a declining civilization.

Morris abandoned his resolve to leave Spyglass Hill to designer Robert Trent Jones and novelist Robert Louis Stevenson, whose book *Treasure Island* lent the course its name. He would catch up with Jake Hill and see how the Georgia mountain boy was surviving the terrors of the Del Monte Forest and the watery throes of the Pacific Ocean. Stevenson himself had also walked these sand dunes in the years he was courting the fair Fanny Osbourne. Individual holes carried such swashbuckling names as Billy Bones, Admiral Benbow, Long John Silver, Jim Hawkins, and Treasure Island itself. The players, since 1967, had other, less elegant titles for these infernal holes. Though as the course matured, especially the greens, the players gave the layout a certain grudging respect. Still, three to one, they preferred that other public fee course Pebble Beach.

Morris came on Jake Hill on the par-3 12th hole, which Jones had designed, drawing for inspiration on the Redan hole of North Berwick in Great Britain.

A heroic young woman, who never lowered her chin despite the rain and the falling temperature, brandished the scores of the two professionals on a short pole like an accusation. Jake stood at level par, a feat against the wind and rain and mud. The other pro, a rookie from South Carolina, had lost eight shots to par in 14 holes. He had the look of a young man whose bride had run off with the preacher.

A drizzling rain blew into Jake's face as he handed his five-iron back to his short, stout, silent caddie for a brawnier four-iron.

Jake addressed the ball and snatched his club backward and then forward in a stroke so short and so quick it would not be out of place on Saturday morning at any public links in America. Yet the ball streaked low into the wind and bit savagely into the green, knocking a long gash as if a tiny artillery shell had landed and exploded. He was left with a makable putt of fifteen feet.

Jake ignored his own lawyer–amateur partner, as well as the rookie pro from South Carolina and his tall, excitable amateur partner to stalk after his ball. His putting stroke was as much of a jab as his swing. The ball lapped the hole and died on the edge, with half its dimples hanging in midair. Jake never changed expressions as he deliberately tapped it home. His first putt might have missed by a yard. There was only iron resolution in his stare as indifferent to their putts, and indeed to their lives, he turned his back on the other players.

The 13th hole offered no relief. It ran 440 yards to a par of 4. And now the wind had shifted and was blowing left to right. Jake slashed a drive that burned low under the wind but was sucked to a premature halt by the muddy fairway. It might have bounded 100 yards ahead for the absence of expression on Jake's face.

He lifted and cleaned his ball and took out a four-wood where the mighty Nicklaus would have managed the distance with an iron. Jake picked the ball cleanly off the chosen lie, but it struck a rare firm spot on the green, skidded forward, and was lost in casual water at the bottom of a sand bunker. It might have gone in the cup for what you could read in Jake's eyes.

Morris could see that Jake did not carry the ball far enough or high enough to dominate a major championship, with the possible exception of the British Open, when played in Scotland. But he had the murderous concentration of a banker foreclosing on a widow woman.

Jake had to fish the muddy water with the teeth of a

rake to recover his ball. He dropped it, with no penalty, in a curve of the bunker not underwater and exploded sand, mud, and ball to within one foot of the hole. His lawyer-partner yelled with encouragement. Jake might have been stone deaf. He lined up the one-foot putt as if it were half the width of the green from the hole and stroked it home. Watching Jake play golf was as cheerful and engaging as watching a pathologist labor over a body two weeks lost underwater. But one could enjoy the trees bending in the wind and the distant, cold beauty of the ocean.

Jake Hill, as he stepped off the green, stopped directly in front of Morris, startling him. He lifted all the coldness in his face directly up at Morris and said in a monotone, "One day after the bastards are dead, nobody gives a damn."

Morris—breaking a career resolution not to speak to a professional golfer in the act of his profession—said to the back of his head as he brushed past, "Jerks who believe that live for visiting hours."

Hill stopped, his putter in his hand, and looked murderously at Morris, who tipped his rain hat to him, knowing full well that Jake's old man was doing perpetual time in the Georgia penitentiary for murder. Jake opened his narrow mouth, as if to reply, looked at the putter in his hand as if he might lift it in anger, looked again at the formidable bulk of John Morris, and stalked on toward the 15th tee.

Morris skipped the 15th and took up a spot on the 16th green. A tall, older man smoking a pipe was the only other spectator around the elevated green. He looked somehow separate from the golf tournament, like a man who had come to make an offer on the property.

The 16th was the best and perhaps the most frightful hole on Spyglass. It ran 465 yards and played to a par of 4, although the day's scores would average nearer 5 than 4. Morris could see the lean form of Jake Hill, standing over his ball, more than 200 yards away. The sudden slash, and the ball was on its way, never more than 20 feet in the air until it splashed off the fairway and onto the green, a feat of a shot.

Morris did not stay for the putt as a great burst of rain struck the course. It was followed by drifting sleet and chased by honest snow, to freeze the hearts of the faithful. The clutch of spectators on the course was actually gathering up snowballs out of the tall grass and throwing them at one another. Nature seemed not to have resigned itself to the winter playing of golf on the Monterey Peninsula.

Morris hitched a ride to the lodge and built a splendid Bloody Mary to carry in a plastic cup to the press room. Golfers, their hair plastered to their foreheads, staggered in like shipwreck survivors to tell of the experience.

Young Gary McCord, in his drenched plaid crapshooting trousers, sat down a long way from his 65 of the day before. But his 65–73—138 kept him in the early Saturday lead. Word from Spyglass was that Johnny Miller, in his own soaked bell-bottoms, was hanging wet and tough.

McCord told Morris, "I know the earth is three-fourths water. I didn't realize that most of it occupies the Monterey Peninsula. It could have been worse, old sport. A lot worse."

Nicklaus seethed. He didn't appreciate the contours of the 73 he had scored. He admitted, "If I was playing better, the weather wouldn't seem so bad."

He couldn't have been more serious, saying, "Everybody knows it rains in California in January. Why fight it? It's just stupid. I can't understand why they don't start the tour in Florida, where the weather is sensational in January. They could come out to California in February or March, when the rain goes away."

Jack complained, ungenerously, "The only reason The Crosby is here in early January is that it's a slow time for hotels in Monterey. Nobody wants to come down and play at any of these three courses this time of year. That sort of antiquated nonsense has to end. I'm more interested in good golf than I am in selling real estate down here."

It was an argument Nicklaus never won. And one day he was on the other side of the development equation in a major way.

Johnny Miller stepped into the press room, roughing up his shag of blond hair with a towel as if drying a friendly dog. Up close Morris could see that the days in the sun and wind were not kind to his youthful complexion. The assortment of weathers—rain, sleet, snow, sun, wind—and the resulting mud did not give him pause, being a native of Northern California who had grown up playing these Monterey Peninsula courses on fair days and foul.

Neither did it occur to Miller to dilute what he said

with false humility, a natural candor that was to serve him well one day as a golf analyst on national telecasts.

"I hate to say it," said Miller, "but with good putting, I could be waltzing away with this tournament. I could be six or seven shots in front. I'm playing the best golf of my life. I'm hitting the ball better than I ever have."

He meant it. Not like Gary Player, who *always* said, "I'm hitting it the best of my life," no matter if the ball was leaving his club sideways.

Miller had turned Spyglass in an almost casual 70 strokes—putting for birdies on nearly every hole—for a two-day total of 138, tying the rookie McCord for the second-round lead.

Young journeyman pro Grier Jones, a former NCAA champion, lingered in the wings with a superb second-day 69 and 140 total.

Jake Hill had birdied the last two holes at Spyglass for a 70—141, two shots out of the lead. Jerry Boyd outlasted the elements for a 71—142, in no way out of contention.

Paul Shirley whispered to Morris, "Our young Mr. McCord will find himself in fast company tomorrow."

"If it were Wall Street, the slick money would be shorting Mr. McCord," said Morris.

"What are you two whispering about?" asked Miller as he made his way out of the press room.

"We were just saying that young Mr. Miller might swim away with this tournament," Shirley said.

"I might," Miller said. He had the terrific grin of all youth. "Where I hit it today, you two could have putted in for a 70."

"We do our best work in the Snake Pit," Morris said.

"I believe it. Morris, what do they know about what happened to McCall and Sidney?"

"The Mormon Church is right, scotch whiskey will kill you dead. I can't believe I said that," Morris said. "In truth they don't know much more than they did four days ago. Suspects include everybody who hated McCall and everybody who loved Sidney. That includes everybody at the bloody tournament."

"How could you not like Sidney Barker?" Miller said. "I think he could have made a living on the early golf tour, his swing was that good. I expect he made a lot more money with his music."

"Indeed," Morris said. "The rights to his music are worth millions. I know this. He played one casual round with you when you were a kid amateur, and I heard him say, 'Look out for that boy. He's got a magical touch with the irons.'"

"I remember that round," Miller said. "I must have been . . . maybe fifteen. I didn't know then you could miss a putt of less than ten feet. If *that* Johnny Miller had been putting today, I would have shot about 63." Which happened to be the incredible, unequaled score that Miller had shot the year before on the last round at fearsome Oakmont Country Club to win the U.S. Open championship. The thought of that feat was likely to keep young McCord and the rest of The Crosby field awake tonight.

Miller was off with a grin and a punch in the ribs for John Morris.

Jake Hill dragged himself into the press room with

all the enthusiasm of a truant boy being delivered back to school by a hostile deputy.

The interview went like this:

"How was your round?"

"Wet."

"Were you pleased with your two under 70?"

"No."

"Did it snow on you?"

"Yes."

"Were you pleased with your score of 71 under the conditions?"

"No."

"Did your amateur partner help your team score?"

"No."

"Does your game lend itself to the rain and mud?"

"No."

"How many fairway woods did you hit?"

"Seven."

"How many greens?"

"Eleven."

"How many hours did it take you to get around the course?"

"Six."

"What was the longest putt you sank?"

"About nine feet."

"Please don't interrupt the questioning," Morris said, to an abundance of laughter, provoking hot daggers in the eyes of Jake Hill.

Morris asked, "Did you know Sidney Barker?"

Jake missed a beat before answering, "I knew him to know who he was . . . at the piano."

"Did you go up to his suite last night?"

Jake missed two beats. "I didn't bring my lawyer," he said. "This is a golf interview."

"Where did you eat dinner last night?"

No answer at all.

"Was Andrew McCall suing you for breaking your contract with him?" Morris asked.

Hill stood and kicked the chair backward he'd been sitting on. He left the press room without saying another word. If looks could kill, he'd be in Georgia in the penitentiary with his old daddy.

"Morris, I'm glad to see you Georgia boys stick together," said Paul Shirley.

"Do you believe he knew Sidney only to see him at the piano? Why not say he did or didn't go up to Sidney's suite?"

"I don't believe what he said. I don't believe what he didn't say," said Shirley. "But what beef could Jake have had with Sidney? They were born in opposite eras on opposite ends of the continent."

"Beats me," Morris said. "Maybe it's not what he did but what he knew."

"Maybe," Shirley said.

Sullivan was surprised at the warmth in Tana Daly's voice, even through the telephone. Odd. Maybe she was more curious than welcoming.

The sheriff's office had sealed off Andrew McCall's suite and found the redhead a tiny room normally reserved for emergency help.

Tana swept her upturned palm around the claustrophobic space, then invited Sullivan to sit in the only chair, which was as straight and as hard as a bishop's bench. She sat on the bed, propped against her out-spread arms, aware of the seductive quality of the pose.

Sullivan got directly to the point. "Did you know Sidney Barker?"

"Yes." Tana did not hesitate.

"How well?"

"Very well. Oh, I cried last night when I heard he was dead." Tears leaked into her eyes. "I never cried for any other man."

"Where were you when you heard?"

"In the Snake Pit. Where else? I can't sit alone in this tiny room. Jake Hill was supposed to take me to dinner. But he never showed. How about that? Stood up by a hillbilly. Everybody in the Snake Pit hushed at the news Sidney was dead. No one was playing the piano. The empty piano stool looked lost."

Sullivan was sure the redhead had rehearsed her lines, but that didn't mean they weren't genuine. And what had happened to Jake Hill, boy golfer?

Tana leaned forward, forgetting the seductive pose. "What do you know about what happened to Sidney?"

"Not much. The maids found him in his suite. Apparently poisoned. Dear Sidney." Sullivan was surprised at the tears that jumped into her own eyes. "How did you get to know him?"

"I met him when I first came to Los Angeles. Three years ago. I was just a kid. I was singing in a little neighborhood bar in Seal Beach. It seemed a thousand miles from downtown Los Angeles and from Hollywood. But I liked it. I had a room over the bar, which I helped sweep out. He used to drop in and play the piano. I didn't know who he was. He got a kick out of that. He was very sweet. But honest. He told me I had better make it as an actress. That I sang very well, but my voice wasn't original enough."

Sullivan contained her surprise. She had not imagined the connection.

"Were you lovers?"

"Sure. Sometimes. It was just friendly sex. Why does anybody give a damn about that?" Tana seemed honestly curious.

"I don't," Sullivan said. "I just wondered how well you knew him."

"Sleeping with a man doesn't necessarily mean you know him very well," Tana said. "Then sometimes it means you know him too well."

Sullivan could laugh with her at that. "Did you two fuss and split up?"

"We were never together. Not that way. We were just friends who sometimes fell into bed. Sidney never got over his wife's death all those years ago." Tana didn't seem to be faking her compassion. "He told me he lived 'little encounters' with women over the years. That he would never again take up with any one woman. That was another reason we got on so well, though he was ages older than me. But who cares about that?"

"Not me," Sullivan said. "Did Sidney help you with your career?"

"Yes. He got me an audition for the television movie. But I got the part myself." She wanted that understood. Maybe it was even true. Sullivan found herself almost respecting Tana Daly. Maybe because her name had been Dora Hudgins. Or maybe she herself was just a sucker. "Not likely," Morris would say. She almost smiled to imagine Morris saying it.

"And the same TV movie . . . that's how you met Andrew McCall?" Sullivan said. *Small world*, she thought, and in fact, the world of movies and television was small enough.

"Yes. He was no Sidney. Not a sweet man. Not much of a lover, for all his macho talk. But he was a powerful man." Tana summoned up no false remorse at his death.

"What did Sidney think about your taking up with McCall?"

"He hated it. He told me it was one thing to use him—sometimes you had to do that in this business— but it was a sin to fuck him." She laughed. "Sidney was such a gentleman. It wasn't a word he often used. And his fight with Andrew was so unlike him."

"Do you think he could have been angry that you were staying with McCall?" Sullivan said.

"Yes. Disappointed with me. Angry with him, I think. I was glad Sidney hit the bastard. If McCall hadn't died, he would have seen it in my face. He would have thrown me out. I would have been dead in television." She didn't try to hide her relief.

"Not sure I would say all that to Inspector Gooden." Aware she was overstepping a citizen's responsibility, Sullivan cautioned her. But in no way was she sorry to have said it. She would tell Morris everything. Maybe they would share it with Deputy Jordan or Tommy. Those two they could trust. Maybe. When it came to murder, she had learned, the state wouldn't trust St. Patrick himself. "The inspector hasn't called you today?"

"No." Tana lost any relief in her eyes. "Will he ask me about Sidney?"

"I have no idea," Sullivan said. "It seems logical that he would since you were so close to the first victim. Listen, just now I didn't mean that you should try to hide anything from the inspector. Answer what he asks you, but you don't have to volunteer your private life if it doesn't have anything to do with the murder. For God's sake, don't lie. Or mislead the cops. The jails are full of those who've tried it." She didn't say the streets of Los Angeles were full of those who'd gotten away with it.

"I see why that big fellow, Morris—who has never spoken a word to me, but the way he looked at me in the Snake Pit, he suspects me, I'm sure of it, of something terrible—I can see why he likes you so much," said Daly, in a convoluted nonsentence appropriate for a sexy guest actress on a late-night talk show.

"Morris never saw a beautiful, red-haired woman in his life that he hated," Sullivan said, offering a one-armed hug of encouragement she could not have imagined when she walked in the tiny room.

Morris waited outside the press room until Ed Waters had finished describing his even-par round in the cold and wet, leaving him only five shots off the lead.

"Got a minute?"

"For you, yes, Morris. But make it a minute. I want to get out of these wet things before I die of pneumonia."

"That's the operative verb these days, *die*. I know you had the falling-out with Sidney—"

"Godamighty, Morris, I hated to hear Sidney was dead. I—" Waters kicked the walkway with his spikes. "I went up to his suite early last night. And knocked on the door. Nobody answered. I wanted to square it with him. Before he went out to dinner. Or before he had his usual small gang of people in his suite. He was wrong to show up drunk last year. But I didn't need the money that badly. I overreacted. Showed my ass, to tell the truth. I hate it I didn't get to tell him that."

"I'm sorry," Morris said. "I wish he had answered the door. Maybe you two would have wound up at dinner. And maybe Sidney would still be alive."

Morris thought about that. "Then again he might have offered you a drink . . . and you might have been the one killed."

"Jesus, I never thought of that." Waters opened his mouth as if to take in more oxygen.

"What time did you go by his suite?"

"Just before five. I didn't know what I was going to say. Except . . . square it. I liked Sidney. And he could move the ball off the tee for an amateur. I heard months later—after I'd had my blowup with him—that the night before our last round someone had begun singing one of his wife's old favorite songs and Sidney had fallen drunk. I've felt like shit ever since, to tell the truth."

There was apparent concern in Ed Waters's eyes. But he made no effort to appear more pained than he felt. His words were altogether respectful. But there was an absence of honest regret in his voice that was off-putting.

"Did you run into anybody else last night, looking

for Sidney?" Morris asked, a routine question begging the routine answer, no.

"Yes, I did," Waters said. "Jake Hill was coming up the hallway. He must have seen me knocking on the door. He said, 'Sidney's not in?' "

"I said he didn't seem to be. Or maybe he was in the shower or something. He said he'd try later."

"That was just before five?"

"Yes. Maybe ten till."

"Tell me something, Ed." Morris looked straight down into his eyes. "Tuesday night. In the Snake Pit. You didn't have any hint of recognition, any sense that you were standing at the bar next to Aubry Hicks?"

Waters blinked. He said, "I knew you were going to ask me that. I don't think you believed me when I said I didn't know who was standing there. I doubt you'll believe me now. The truth is . . . I'm not sure. I mean. I know *now* Aubry was standing there. I even seem to remember a *hint* of him there . . . to use your expression. I don't know if I blocked the fact of him out of my mind. Or if I didn't know what to say to him and just denied to myself he was standing there. I swear I don't know."

"I don't remember any bad blood between the two of you," Morris said. "Not even the time in Houston when he took the tournament right out from under you on the 72nd hole."

"That hurt," Waters admitted. "I did not take it personally. Similar things happened to me before I finally won a tournament. Similar things have happened to me since. I haven't won in a long time. It's the life we lead."

"What would you say to Aubry Hicks if he were standing right here now?" Morris asked.

The question took Waters by surprise. He twisted his head in thought. "I don't know. I guess . . . I'm sure . . . I've shied away from all the guys who came up with me who failed, or suffered injuries, or dropped off the tour for whatever reason. I don't know what to say to them. I don't want to think about their problems. The tour is my life. I don't look left or right. I just wait for the next shot, the next hole, the next week, the next tournament. I don't want it ever to stop. There's nothing else out there for me . . . in some one tidy place in America."

Morris wished to hell he'd had that quote when he filed the rainy-day lead on Ed Waters.

Waters repeated Morris's question: "What would I say to Hicks: 'Where've you been all these years, Aubry?' Or, 'Congratulations, your playing career is over.' Or, 'I hear you are no longer lost in the bottle.' "

There was a cynicism in his voice that cut deeper than any fears he might have of losing his playing card.

Morris said, "You know something, Ed, I don't believe you. I think you knew Hicks was standing there. I think you hold something against him you don't want to spit out and talk about."

Waters swelled up, and said, with iron in his voice, not of a survivor, but of a predator, "I don't care what you think. You reporters only know how to ask predictable questions and copy down the names of the winners. You don't know a damn thing about what happens out there in the mud and rain."

"Maybe not," Morris said, gratified to hear at least

an echo of his true voice. "But those men who bear up under it . . . with honor . . . seem to identify themselves over the years."

Waters opened his mouth as if to lash back . . . or maybe to offer a fake apology . . . but closed it and stormed off to the locker room.

Morris couldn't guess what might be eating at him. But now he wondered if Waters had indeed seen Jake Hill outside Sidney's suite or if he was placing him there out of some unspoken malice. If so, it was a dangerous game at best.

Sullivan had left a note pinned on the bathroom door. "Come on down and help me hold the sheriff's hand. Or I might wind up a juicy item in the local *broad*-sheet—every pun intended. Selah, Sullivan."

She wasn't holding his hand. But she was sitting on the edge of the lodge manager's confiscated desk, swinging a lissome leg. Tommy Whitlock was reared back in the swivel chair, looking as if he owned the joint.

Deputy Patricia Jordan sat against the wall, her chin down, in an attitude of self-reprimand.

"Glad to know I'm among the beautiful people," Morris said, unable not to smile.

"Hey, this is Hollywood moved to the Monterey Peninsula," said the sheriff. "A little sexy ink never hurt in an election year."

"You two behave," Sullivan said. There was honest concern in her eyes for the sheriff and the deputy.

"I see the inspector's fingerprints all over that item

in the *Herald*," Morris said. "Don't say you weren't warned, Sheriff."

"The inspector denies it."

"Imagine that." Morris waved to Deputy Jordan until she looked up and smiled. "That's better," he said. "You caught the high sheriff up on what we talked about last night?"

"Oh, yes," she said. "I told him everything you two found out. He's"—she did not look at the sheriff—"passing the word along to the inspector. Me? I'm being promoted. Tonight I'm guarding the press room instead of the sandwiches." There was more humor in her voice than anger.

"The parking lot of the lodge looks like a Hollywood production unit has moved in," Morris said. "I don't think there's a television station in California that doesn't have a talking head here."

"Tell me about it," said Tommy Whitlock, trying his hardest to be unimpressed. "The state, even the feds, are calling to offer their help. For prime time, of course. We don't need help, Morris. We need evidence."

Morris told of his fiery conversations with Ed Waters and Jake Hill.

"Still at the same old stand, making friends among the professionals," Sullivan said.

"That's me, Mr. Congeniality. And I missed you in the rain and mud, kid."

Sullivan said, "We Hollywood types rarely venture out in the rawer elements." She saw his true disappointment. "I promise. I'll be out there tomorrow, come rain or typhoon."

He gave her a thumbs-up smile.

Sullivan said, "I wouldn't be surprised if Hicks and Waters did run into each other outside Sidney's suite about five P.M. Tana Daly told me Jake was supposed to take her to dinner last night but never showed up."

"He's going to show up in this office in"—the sheriff looked at his watch—"about fifteen minutes. We'll hear where he was last night. And if he ever caught up with Sidney. And why he was looking for him in the first place . . . if your man Ed Waters is telling the truth."

"Ed Waters is not 'my man.' He's an enigma," Morris said. "Don't doubt he's a plenty tough one, however benign he might appear. Ask Jake if McCall threatened to sue him if he kept trying to break his contract."

The sheriff nodded. "I'll ask him and his lawyer."

Sullivan repeated for Morris how Tana Daly had met Sidney Barker while singing in a bar at Seal Beach, when she first came to L.A. How they'd become casual May–December lovers. And how Sidney had gotten her an audition for the TV movie sponsored by an Andrew McCall client.

"Then Sidney saw them together in the Snake Pit," Morris said. "And I'm sure that's why he shouted at McCall—to embarrass him. I didn't understand it at the time. It wasn't like Sidney."

"Add Jake Hill, and you have a lovers' triangle," Sullivan said.

"Add all of Tana Daly's lovers, and you might have a geodesic dome."

"I'm impressed, Morris. Have you been reading Buckminster Fuller?"

"Yeah. Doesn't he rate the nags in the *Racing Form*?"

Morris turned serious. "Speaking of the talking heads, what are you telling those guys?"

"Very little," the sheriff said. "The late-night TV host himself is calling. He wants Tana Daly as a guest. Tonight. I can't stop her from leaving the county. If she agrees to come back."

"I can see her now . . . dressed in a black miniskirt," Morris said.

"Oh, yes," Sullivan agreed. "But I think some of her tears will be real ones. She liked Sidney . . . as much as she despised McCall. It should be an interview to remember. I can feel a television movie coming on."

"Let's hope her role doesn't carry her all the way to the state prison," Whitlock said. "Poison, like diamonds, can be 'a girl's best friend.' "

"Doesn't seem likely," Sullivan said. "Why kill the two old men who have helped jump-start your career?"

The phrase *old men* made Morris think. "Maybe we are looking in the wrong generation. Maybe the killer isn't among the young golfers and lovers. Maybe he or she comes from the victims' own generation. Maybe it's an old hatred that boiled over into murder."

"It's possible," said Sheriff Whitlock. "There must be two or three dozen amateurs who have played in The Crosby for more than twenty years. Hell, some have played in it since it started. A bunch of the old-timers run America's biggest corporations. I've talked with eight or ten today, guys I've known over the years. I can't see any of them risking their careers, their celebrity lives killing either of those fellows over some argument.

"Most admitted they were sick of Andrew Reed Mc-

Call. They loved Sidney. All of them were invited to parties all over the peninsula . . . both Tuesday night and last night. A few were in the Snake Pit on Tuesday. Dozens of people saw them last night, can account for them. But poison can be a hell of a time capsule to check up on. It can be put out many hours, even days in advance."

"In Sidney's suite, sure. But in a crowded room?" Morris said.

"That's a problem," the sheriff admitted. "We've talked to everybody we know was in the Snake Pit the night McCall died. We may have missed one or two. Probably we did. It must have been a typically wild scene. The hell of it is we can't be certain which individuals were close enough to McCall, or to his glass, to drop cyanide in it."

The sheriff stuck his hat on his head, like a cowboy star about to mount his horse and ride off into the sunset. "So finally we are back among the tight little group of logical suspects we *know* were close enough to poison McCall: the golfers Hicks, Waters, Hill, the publicist Martin, the bartender, the redhead, and Sidney himself—if we are looking at murder/suicide. Of course, if we are looking at murder for hire, it could have involved anybody, anywhere."

"Morris, I forgot to tell you," Sullivan said. "Young Jay Martin got a reprieve from ABC. He doesn't have to move to Manhattan. The wedding is on again."

"Every man to his own annihilation. Give my regards to the lovely Trudy Standridge. You'd have to say the death of Andrew McCall made somebody happy." Morris suddenly remembered. "Did you talk with the movie producer Jacob Hyche? I ran into him Tuesday night in the Snake Pit. Not far from McCall and the redhead. He said he was looking for his wife. He didn't look too happy about it."

Whitlock glanced at Deputy Jordan.

She opened her notebook. "Yes. The inspector talked with Mr. Hyche. He admitted being in the Snake Pit, looking for his wife. He said he enjoyed the fight. He wished you hadn't stopped it. He said McCall's death 'was a bloody good scene in a bad movie.' Hyche said he was not invited to Sidney's suite Friday night and didn't see him."

The sheriff said, "I wonder if Jacob's wife was actually in the Snake Pit Tuesday night?"

"No, she wasn't," Jordan said, looking again in her notebook.

"Odd that," Morris said. "But come to think of it, the Snake Pit seems the last place his aristocratic, highly educated, outdoors-loving wife was likely to be—especially without her 'genius' husband."

"I'm the only person in America who loves Hyche's bleak movies," Sullivan admitted. "Elizabeth is a sport to bankroll them. But I don't know why she puts up with Jacob's depressing cynicism, not to mention his legion of domestic and foreign girlfriends."

"Charm," Morris said, "some of us have it."

Sullivan couldn't breathe for laughing. Even the beleaguered sheriff had to chuckle. And the smiling deputy forgot for a moment that she was no longer in the loop of the investigation.

"Isn't she a good bit older than Jacob?" the sheriff

asked, looking over forlornly at the very young Patricia Jordan.

"Yes, and she's a hell of a lot sexier," Sullivan was quick to say.

Morris thought, *Hyche is not as old as Sidney or McCall. But he's known them for twenty years. Plenty of time to hone a grudge. Any failed producer in Hollywood can get up a friendly hatred over lunch about music or television rights.*

Morris said, "I think poison might be an acceptable alternative to sitting through one of Jacob Hyche's God-abandoned movies."

"You just want to put him safely in jail, so he can't produce another one," Sullivan said.

Morris grinned his blessing on the idea.

Sheriff Tommy Whitlock took his hat off his head and dropped it on the desk in exasperation. "We've got a deputy or a security guard standing by every bottle and glass in this bloody lodge. Not to mention every room key. Anybody lifting a drink in Pebble Beach he didn't pour himself knows he's a total fool. Tell me why I'm still sweating through this uniform."

"Sidney Barker probably poured his own drink in his own suite," Morris said. "Who can protect against that?"

"You know it too, Morris. It's not over."

Morris sat there, not speaking, sure the sheriff was absolutely right to be afraid.

CHAPTER NINE

Morris checked his watch, then the radio alarm clock by the bed. Julia Sullivan had been under the shower for thirty minutes. There were fish in the ocean who were not as wet. Finally she shut it down. And stumbled through the door and collapsed on the bed wrapped in a towel like Cleopatra run out of oxygen.

"My God, the Monterey Peninsula has seen the last of the hot water," Morris said. "Saturday night dinner among the the Hollywood set will be a mite gamy."

"That's the word, Morris: *dinner.* Take me somewhere romantic, with soft music and quiet, intimate conversation and the ocean washing on the beach, and where they serve extra-large portions of everything. Only after the last bite of dessert can either of us mention either of those favored human diversions: golf or murder."

"You've got it," Morris said. "With you in that towel, I like our chances for a first-rate table."

Sullivan guided the rental Ford through the omnipresent mist and traffic into the heart of Carmel. She had to make three passes up Ocean Avenue to luck into a parking place. Good old Morris had made reservations a month ago in the small French restaurant.

"Dare we order a scotch?" asked Sullivan.

" 'Two for the morgue,' " quoted Morris.

The menu was the real killer. "No wonder France has the same fifty million people it had fifty years ago," Morris said. "They can't afford to eat enough to reproduce."

"Hush. You're spoiling my appetite."

"Some chance."

The scotch was only grand. The food, even priced by the bite, was even better.

"Saturday, January fifth, 1974. What do you imagine we will be doing twenty years from now, Morris?"

"I think we will be having dessert. Probably here at this table if our waiter doesn't get back in the next two decades."

"It's not good for you to eat too fast."

"Then we should be healthy enough to live forever."

"I think we will be living on my mountain in Denver," Sullivan said.

"You own the entire mountain?" Morris asked, but he already knew the answer.

"It's not a big mountain."

"Of course, you own only half of the downtown. That must be discouraging."

"Why don't you come out to see me more often?"

"Because nobody has invented mountain golf. I'd hate to read anything I wrote on snow skiing."

Sullivan began to giggle.

"What's so funny?"

"I was thinking of you, Morris, skiing. It would be like the mountain itself coming down the slope."

Morris was not laughing. "I might surprise you."

"Promise you will." Sullivan touched her glass to his. "I remember the first time I ever saw you, John Morris."

"I'm sure I was going about my work in an honest and sober manner."

"You were standing at the piano with Monty, arms around each other because neither of you could stand alone, singing some auld Scottish ballad at The Masters in Augusta."

"Scandalous. But the man had a tenor voice. If he'd had the same touch with the putter, not even Hogan could have beaten him. And what were you doing?"

"I was the one laughing," Sullivan said.

"How did you meet Monty?" Morris had always thought of them together, Monty Sullivan, twice her age, living the life of eternal youth on the golf tour until the automobile accident that killed him dead and ruined his own knee and, thank God, spared Julia Sullivan's life. If the wreck had to happen, Morris was glad that he had been there, hitching a ride, to pull them both out of the carnage. Too late for Monty, golf's blithe spirit. Somehow being there had helped bury the guilt, which they never practiced, for the good life they continued to lead—when they weren't occupying separate states.

Sullivan knew what he was thinking. "I was waiting tables, working my way through college, in San Francisco—"

"I never knew that," Morris interrupted. "I thought you'd always lived in Colorado. Did you go to Berkeley?"

"Yes."

"For how long?"

"For three days. Monty played this exhibition at the Olympia Club. His crowd came by the Russian restaurant where I was waiting tables. Up on Nob Hill. I didn't know him. I didn't know from golf. I thought clubs were something you went to after dark."

"What were you studying?"

"International politics. I was going to join the Foreign Service."

Morris couldn't close his mouth. "That would have been the end of the Cold War all right. The Russians would have given up the ghost. It's not how much vodka you can drink; it's how much you can keep down."

He then asked, seriously, "Do you ever regret dropping out of school?"

"No. I've tried to never stop learning. I even read the Associated Press," Sullivan said. "In truth I've gotten to see my share of the world. Have come to understand something about life and/or death . . . and some of the things can make men and women desperate enough to kill one another. We've seen it happen a few times,

Morris—not to speak of this week. I've even come to know that fourteen clubs are allowed in a bag."

Sullivan paused only to take a breath. "He was terribly handsome, Monty."

"By God he was," Morris said.

"He kept calling me back to his table, asking for another 'Mother Russia vodka.' "

"That had to be Monty."

"He wanted another napkin. A cheese blintz. A glass of water."

"It had to be serious if Monty Sullivan wanted a glass of water."

"I thought he was terribly funny."

"God knows he was," Morris said.

"He wouldn't leave until the restaurant closed."

"If he'd owned the keys to every joint he closed, Monty would have been the biggest landlord in North America. Maybe he did. He damn near was."

"I lived in this one-room walk-up on the cheap side of San Francisco . . . when there was a cheap side."

"I don't think I want to hear the rest of this story."

"Jealous, are we?" Sullivan lowered the lip of his glass with her trigger finger.

Morris waved to the waitress for a refill, and his glass was only half empty.

"Well, I never went back to class. And that's the name of that story. You know the ending." Her smile was sweeter than it was bitter.

"I never thought I would run across you again after the funeral," Morris said. "Luckily tournaments kept having ceremonies in Monty's honor. And how can you have a ceremony without the comely widow?"

"How can you indeed?" Sullivan could not contain the laughter.

"You've only had the one scotch. What's so funny?"

"The first couple of ceremonies for Monty were legit," she said. "Golf honored him, and I was truly the bereaved widow."

"You were quite smashing in black," Morris said.

"I meant to be . . . by the next year's ceremonies." Her hand couldn't contain her laughter.

"What do you mean?"

"Who do you think got up the memorial service to Monty Sullivan at the Quad Cities Open? Monty never changed planes there, much less played in the bloody tournament."

"*You?* Why did you do that? You always donated the checks to charity."

"Who do you think wrote the checks in the first place?" Sullivan had to bury her laughter in both hands.

"I don't get it." Morris was too sober to figure it out.

"I know, I know. I had to keep coming back to the tour, you lout, to get your attention. I nearly bankrupted myself on black miniskirts."

Now he got it. Now he was too embarrassed to be pleased. Or too pleased to be embarrassed.

"What the hell did you see in me?" Morris, to this moment, continued to be amazed but had never before risked the question. "Nobody would confuse me with the blond-haired Joe College flat bellies who play golf for a living. I can't even begin to carry a tune like Monty."

"No. I wouldn't be caught dead with Joe College. And I like all the ways you are different from Monty.

You don't fear dying, Morris. I believe Monty lived from one town, one tournament, one party to the next to keep from hearing the years blow past. If he didn't stop, they'd never catch him. Thank God time caught him in an instant, and he never had to fear it coming."

Sullivan raised a toast to Monty.

Morris smiled to remember him, and what she said about his fear of oblivion—where no music played, no songs were sung—was very likely true.

She said, "But I especially enjoy all the ways you *are* like him. You are so damn serious about your work you never take seriously. And I wouldn't give up all the crazy enthusiasms you two have shared."

"And especially for you," Morris said, and quickly took a drink to drown the words.

"John Morris, I believe you almost said . . . at least thought . . . the *L* word."

"Impossible," he said.

"It's close enough to count," she said, touching his glass again with her own.

"Twenty years from today we will have a drink right here in this restaurant," Morris promised, tapping the table to make it official.

Sullivan opened her daybook and recorded the promise like a legal document.

"Okay, kid," she said. "Let's talk a little death and dying. Why would a young professional golfer kill one old man, not to say two old men?"

"Money," Morris said. "A broken contract, which is the same as money. We know McCall had his hand in Jake Hill's pocket. He pressured Jerry Boyd to endorse his client's golf ball. Another of his clients tried to drop

Aubry Hicks when he was injured. Ed Waters has been ignored by all the advertisers, including McCall's clients. It's possible Ed hates all their guts. I got an earful of the nasty side of Mr. Waters."

Morris said, "Sidney Barker was a rich, generous guy. Maybe he put up a loan on a deal that went sour. Maybe he wanted his money back. We know Andrew McCall and Jake Hill got on the wrong side of Sidney when they took his once-'casual' lover Tana Daly to bed. Let me tell you something about lovers: They are never *casual*."

"Is that a promise, Morris?"

He ignored her question. "And maybe that drink Tuesday night was meant for Jake and not McCall. I'm running out of maybes. Help me. Why would any of them kill Sidney, God bless him?"

"You said it once before, Morris. Maybe it's something the victims *knew* and not something they *did*."

"Possibly. That would leave the door ajar for motives we can't begin to fathom until we know who the killer is. Which puts us back to square one."

"Morris, I forgot to tell you. Patricia Jordan sneaked out of her sandwich detail, and we hung around the practice putting green and the practice range, looking for this mysterious Anne who stood up Aubry Hicks. We checked out some cute California girls—sexy even in their rain gear. But we didn't see a tall, dark, short-haired athlete who seemed to fit Aubry's description."

"Maybe she's his fantasy alibi."

"I don't think so," Sullivan said. "He looked so . . . wistful . . . describing her."

"If she's alive and on the peninsula, you'll find her.

And God help her if she isn't already attached . . . or maybe even if she is."

"I'll find her," Sullivan said. "I talked to Jackie Melton again this afternoon. He was all by himself, noodling on the piano in the Snake Pit. I asked him who could hate his old friend Sidney. He said Sidney was a hard man to hate. That whoever killed him would have to work at hating him. It's ironic, Jackie and Sidney both outliving the wives they loved so desperately. I want to be missed like that, Morris."

"Good Lord, you'll outlive me into the second half of the next century."

"You forget. The human physiognomy can only stand so much. *I* have to put up with *you*."

"There's that," Morris said. *"Physiognomy?* You're sure you were at Berkeley only three days?"

Sullivan lifted her chin as if that were higher education enough for the thoughtful.

Morris said, "Of course, the clever money is on Hyche. Jacob Hyche."

"You're serious."

"He's old enough to have known both men well . . . for a hell of a long time. He's played in The Crosby since just after the big war. He married rich. But he's broke enough to have to beg to produce his wretched movies."

"Watch that."

"I don't think Andrew McCall was a guy you would want to owe money. Or a favor. Sidney was truly talented. What if you screwed Sidney? Worse than that, what if you screwed up his music? Didn't pay for the rights. Worse than that, didn't give him proper credit? I

don't know what I'm saying. But Jacob Hyche was in
the Snake Pit. He was standing in the death zone. How
did he describe it? 'A good scene in a bad movie.' This
man is all heart. I'll say this. The death scene would
beat the shit out of any movie he ever made."

"Morris, I believe you are serious."

"Maybe."

"I don't know. Jacob thinks too much," Sullivan said.

"No. His characters talk too much. They don't know
from think."

"I love you, Morris. I always knew I'd fall for an
existentialist."

"Don't tell me. You discovered them on the second
day at Berkeley."

Dessert came with their brandy.

Morris grew contemplative. "Speaking of time passing, I love to look at the old black-and-white photographs of The Crosby when it was played at Rancho
Santa Fe. Porky Oliver, his trousers riding up under his
chin on his follow-through. Hogan loved to be paired
with him; Porky's game was so consistent, he struck the
ball so squarely Hogan could handicap off his distances.
Why can't we have players anymore named Porky Oliver? All the players today are named Tom, or Ben, or
Johnny, or Jack. What the hell happened to Porky? And
the old photographs of Sam Snead, when he had his
widow's peak. And Hogan in his cap, hard in the eyes,
with a cigarette in his hand. By God, what happened to
cigarettes? The young Palmer was known to throw
them down with great élan and drive the ball to eter-
nity. Now he hides his cigarettes from his wife."

" 'Élan.' Now there's a word we also learned my second day at Berkeley."

Morris ignored her. "Crosby, with his pipe, and Hope, on the first tee squaring off against each other, *mano a mano*, with golf clubs. Why couldn't I have been there?"

"You would be old as hell, Morris. And I would be eating here alone in this restaurant twenty years from now."

"There's that," Morris said again. He was still young. But it seemed he belonged to an earlier time. Maybe 1938. And it always would seem that way.

Morris said, "Jackie Melton, like Sidney and McCall, played in all those Crosbys, including the first one, until this year. Jackie's had plenty of years to work up a killing grudge against the victims. But it's hard to pin a Snake Pit murder on a man with both hands on the piano keys. I hope Jackie keeps coming back forever. We need his piano, his tenor voice, his bawdy lyrics."

"He reminds you of Monty," Sullivan said. "Never been a tune or a set of lyrics Jackie didn't know . . . or write."

"Yes," Morris said. "I know this, Sullivan."

She paused, her glass touching her lips.

"The first one of these murders was horrifically imprecise. That glass Ms. Daly held could have killed her or any number of people. We don't know much about Sidney's death. We don't know who poured the drink or even, for certain, if it was for Sidney. We only know the young pros who say they *weren't* in his room when he drank it. It's the imprecision that frightens me. The killer may have had these two victims in mind. But he or she was willing to let the poison flow where it might."

"Why don't you write that?"

"I already did. I hope to hell the people on this peninsula will read it and believe it."

Sullivan looked at her brandy and peered over the glass at Morris apprehensively.

"We're safe," Morris said. "Who was ever poisoned in a French restaurant? Here they kill you the old-fashioned way . . . with the check." He rose up out of his chair and leaned across the table and kissed Sullivan squarely on the mouth.

She sat unprepared to say a damn word.

CHAPTER TEN

S unday morning. Late.
    Her feet dry in her boots, her sweater and jacket
snug around her, and the rain ticking off her golf umbrella, Sullivan was as comfortable as possible in an
alien element. Were the rain a drifting snow and she
standing at five thousand feet altitude instead of sea
level, the pleasure of it all would be sinful.

Only a clutch of friends and wives hung around the
practice putting green. The golfers themselves squinted
under their rain hats as their putts sent up little rooster
tails of water, skittering over the wet grass toward the
cups, some of which were half drowned.

Jerry Boyd was all concentration, a lock of dark hair
curling over his forehead. But he was pushing every putt
to the right to his caddie's unspoken disgust. Sullivan
was sure that he had his putter blade open at address,

and if he had been a living Monty Sullivan, she would have told him so. And if Monty were indeed living, he would have handed her the bloody putter with a bow to have a bloody go at it . . . and she would have, and had in the past, to his delight. Her mind wandered until her eyes fell on a tall, wide-shouldered form in a colorful rain suit and hat. She was young and very careful to keep a small gathering of fans between herself and the players putting on the green.

Sullivan eased over her way. She could see a damp wisp of the girl's short hair, and it was dark as a crow's wing. Sullivan stopped near enough to the girl to say, without taking her eyes off the golfers, "Anne, who are you picking to win?"

The girl made a small sound in her throat, as if she'd stepped on a rock.

Now Sullivan turned toward her, and the girl's face was one handsome puzzle.

"Whoever beats Johnny Miller has a hell of a chance," Sullivan said.

The girl was biting her lip in curiosity.

What the hell, thought Sullivan. She said, "Anne, why did you stand up Jerry Boyd?"

The girl touched her mouth with a smooth, athletic fist. "How do you know my name? How do you know—" She had a husky contralto voice that went exceedingly well with her tall, strong physique.

"I guessed," Sullivan said. "How many tall, dark, beautiful"—she threw in the honest *beautiful* on her own—"athletic young women are going to be hanging out in the rain around the practice putting green? My name is Julia Sullivan."

The girl took her slim hand in her own firm one.

"And you are Anne . . ."

"Robinson. How do you know—"

"I wormed it out of Jerry. He doesn't know your last name. He was disappointed you didn't show up at the lodge last night."

"I couldn't. . . . I can't believe I said I'd meet him. God knows I've never been a groupie. But I felt bad about it. I thought I'd come over and apologize. But I haven't the nerve."

So Jerry Boyd had not been lying. He did have a living reason to be at the Del Monte Lodge at 5:00 P.M. Friday.

"I'll introduce you," Sullivan said, nodding toward young Mr. Boyd.

"Wait!" Anne was not so sure about that.

"Not to worry. I know him fairly well. My friend John Morris, the AP writer, knows him very well. He's a solid guy, Jerry Boyd. And you look fit enough to take care of yourself. Are you a basketball player?"

"No. Volleyball," she said, smiling. "Does it show that much?"

"We'd all kill a songbird for your height," Sullivan said. "Where do you go to school?"

"Stanford. I'm a senior. My last year of volleyball. I've played something all my life. I just discovered golf. I love it. But I'm terrible. I'm trying to learn how to play. I'd never seen professionals before. They hit it so far . . . it's terrifying."

"I have a hunch you are about to get some professional instruction. Where are you staying?"

"In a Bonnie and Clyde motel in Monterey. I

sneaked away up here with a teammate for the weekend. She's lying in bed with a virus. She has enough energy to ridicule me for backing out of the date. Guys don't frighten her. Half the boys at Stanford have asked her out."

Sullivan thought, *Boys, you've been hitting on the wrong roommate.* She said, "Come on. Bite the bullet. Boyd won't fuss at you. It'll do him good. Take his mind off his putting. He has a frightfully real chance of winning this tournament."

Anne took a deep breath and allowed Sullivan to lead her to the edge of the putting green.

"Hey, Jerry. I ran into a pal of yours," Sullivan said.

He looked up. He was no eight-by-ten glossy. But he had a good, strong smile. He took Sullivan's hand, then dropped his mallet head putter on the green as his eyes shifted to the tall presence of Anne Robinson.

Sullivan introduced them.

Anne opened her mouth but couldn't think how to begin.

"It's okay. Spit it out." Sullivan took her arm, feeling the tense, strong muscles under her sleeve.

"I'm sorry," Anne said. "I couldn't believe I said . . . I would . . ." She faltered.

"Sullivan's right. It's okay," said Boyd. Her embarrassment gave him confidence. "I'm no matinee idol. No empty-headed girls trail across the country after me. I'm still surprised I had the nerve to ask you to dinner. But we have a neutral witness here now. How about tonight? Assuming I don't drown or hit it badly and jump off one of these cliffs."

Anne Robinson had a world-class smile. "Okay," she said.

"See you in the bar at the lodge," Boyd said, picking up his putter from the green. "About six."

"I'll be there," Anne said, crossing her arms, waiting to watch him putt.

"Morris and I will treat the two of you to a drink. Then you're on your own," Sullivan said. She was sure Anne had no idea how attractive she was. All her adult life she had been five-eleven and feeling seven feet tall. Jerry Boyd in his spikes was almost her height. And he was strong enough to bench-press the volleyball team.

"Shoot a lot of threes," Sullivan shouted over her shoulder, setting out to find the lost John Morris.

She found him just off the first tee.

The rain had lifted for the moment, and Morris leaned on his cane, which sank in the soft earth. He said, "Pebble Beach Golf Links." He might have been announcing the mighty course to the nation. "I think we are standing on the right ground, Sullivan."

She said, "Old Samuel F. B. Morse would be proud of us. We could be taking it intravenously, by tube, in the bar."

"Not us. The course would be worth the walk if no golfers were playing on it," Morris said.

Sam Morse, captain of the 1906 Yale football team, had loved the out-of-doors, and the Monterey Peninsula was the out-of-doors in its most godlike expression. The century was still in its teens when he handed Neville and Grant this piece of ocean real estate unequaled in North America for the design of a golf course. How could two amateurs have reached into their collective imagination and drawn out plans for so great a layout? It did not hurt the enterprise that Grant had played the ancient links courses of Scotland and England and made sketches of the most enduring holes.

Jack Nicklaus, the greatest player of the age and of all time, calls Pebble Beach his favorite course in the world. Nicklaus has never been a man easily satisfied, not even with the twenty major championships he ultimately won.

The U.S. Amateur was first played at Pebble Beach in 1929. The immortal Bobby Jones of Atlanta, in a first-round upset that moved California like an earthquake, lost to Johnny Goodman of Omaha. It was the only time in his last seven U.S. Amateurs that Jones failed to reach the final round, and he won five of those seven tournaments.

Goodman, who had hitched a ride to Pebble Beach in a cattle car, was no country bumpkin golfer. In 1933 he became the last amateur to win the U.S. Open, which Jones of course won four times as an amateur. One Harrison R. Johnston defeated O. F. Willing for that 1929 U.S. Amateur championship.

The 1947 U.S. Amateur at Pebble Beach was won by a golfer with the delicious name Skee Riegel. Of course The Crosby moved to the Monterey Peninsula that same year.

Nicklaus began his personal assault on Pebble Beach and the U.S. Amateur in 1961, defeating H. Dudley Wysong in the finals. It wasn't a defeat. It was a dismantling, Nicklaus settling the matter, being eight holes ahead with six to play.

In 1972, finally, inevitably, the U.S. Open came to

the Pebble Beach Golf Links. Nicklaus had already won The Crosby that winter. The last Sunday of the Open he led Lee Trevino by one shot. Arnold Palmer hung in there three shots back.

A gale blew in off Carmel Bay, causing small-craft warnings that canceled the scheduled yacht races and played mortal hell with airborne golf balls. The ghost of the January Crosby was howling over the June Open.

Trevino was an early casualty that Sunday. But the deciding moment came with Nicklaus staring down an eight-foot putt for a bogey on the 12th hole. Ahead, on the 14th, Palmer stood over an eight-footer for birdie. Should he sink and Nicklaus miss, Palmer would be leading the Open. History shows the opposite result, and Nicklaus went on to stab a one-iron within inches of the par-3 17th hole and post a winning total of 290.

He shot 74 that Sunday, and it was a heroic 74. How tough were conditions? To find a winning Open score over 290, you have to go back to 1935, when Sam Parks won at monstrous Oakmont in 299 strokes.

National championship golf had come to Pebble Beach and was to return over the years and decades, adding history to the art of the course.

Morris and Sullivan set out in the now-drifting rain to walk the eighteen holes of Pebble Beach, which are laid out in an approximate figure eight design. The first three holes move inland and seduce the unwary player with three deceptively modest challenges.

The 1st hole of 373 yards bends gradually to the right, and two well-placed shots present a legitimate putt for birdie.

The par-5 2nd hole of 502 yards has always played

the easiest of the eighteen. It can be reached in two shots if the bold player risks a large tree overhanging the green and perilous shrubs just beyond it. In years to come, the bold, if not reckless, Lanny Wadkins was to smash a fairway wood onto the 2nd green and sink the eagle putt that helped him win the first PGA championship to come to Pebble Beach.

The 3rd hole makes an abrupt dogleg swing to the left for 388 yards to a modest green that rises between two bunkers.

Now the course makes its fated turn toward the cliffs and Carmel Bay, where it will wander for six of the next seven holes, unequaled in golf for beauty and peril. The two architects, especially Neville, preferred small greens to test the nerve and accuracy of the golfer, and the 4th green is the smallest on the course. At 327 yards, the 4th hole is also the shortest of the par 4s. The cliff tumbling into the bay threatens the drive and the approach shot.

Suddenly the Del Monte Forest encroaches on the par-3 5th hole of 166 yards as if the trees themselves were jealous of the attention the ocean was getting. Best that your attention not wander here as professionals have scored as high as a 9 on this straightforward hole.

Now, again, to the sea. Here is where the Pebble Beach Golf Links truly begins. The par-5 516-yard 6th hole runs terrifyingly down past a fifty-foot-long bunker on the left and a fifty-foot-high cliff on the right, dropping down to Stillwater Cove, with its yachts anchored among the sea lions and otters. A gale-force wind can add a hundred yards to the playing of the hole. The pitch shot, sharply uphill to a small green on a narrow peninsula, the highest point along the shoreline, will test the mettle of any living player. And No. 6 is the least fearful of this stretch of five oceanside holes.

The 7th hole, like the 16th at Cypress Point, is among the most photographed holes in golf. On a calm day the par 3 is a 107-yard tease, a soft wedge onto a tiny hint of a green, as narrow as 16 feet wide and so near the ocean that waves have been known to shatter over the grass. It is the shortest hole in championship golf. Yet, when the winds rage off the ocean at fifty knots, world-class golfers have been known to hit full three-irons off the tee. Sam Snead, in the face of such a wind, once took his putter to the ball and sent it rolling down the hill toward the hole.

There is no stretch of three holes in all golf to rival the 8th, 9th, and 10th for brute difficulty and beauty to die for. The volatile U.S. Open champion Tommy Bolt once paused in front of Crosby's house on the 13th hole and shouted, "I'm gonna get that crooner out on this golf course and make him play the 8th, 9th, and 10th holes over and over until he pars them all." Formidable as they surely are, Crosby had already been known to play the three of them in even par 4s. But rare is the professional who does it regularly in tournament competition.

Standing on the 8th tee, the golfer faces a blind, uphill carry to a plateau that it shares—very much like certain holes at St. Andrews—with the 6th hole. From the plateau the 8th fairway bends for an excruciating 190 yards, over a 100-foot-deep chasm, with the sea pounding on the rocks below, to a small, lightning-fast green that slopes toward the Pacific. This is the second shot that Nicklaus calls the greatest in golf. Golfers who push their drives have been photographed hanging on to the side of the cliff by their spikes, risking their lives to pitch the ball back into play. It is not a hole for the faint of heart.

Yet the 9th plays clearly tougher than the 8th. And is in fact the most treacherous hole at Pebble Beach, consistently playing to the highest scores. Dale Douglas in 1963 made a score of 19 on the 9th hole in The Crosby.

Just for starters, the 9th plays 464 yards to a par of 4. The fairway slopes more than mildly from left to right to the cliffs and the sea. Bunkers and deep rough on the left penalize the overly conservative tee shot. Should your second shot reach it, the slick 9th green lies at the very edge of the cliff. Players have been known to putt their balls off the green and over the cliff and into the sea. A bogey 5 is an honorable score among even the artists of the game.

If the front nine holes start benignly, the back nine holes begin sadistically. The 10th hole plays 426 yards to a par of 4. The fairway falls everlastingly from left to right. Even a tee shot struck exactly down the middle will very likely spill over the cliff and onto the rocks. Nicklaus sliced a drive over the cliff in 1972 and very nearly lost the Open championship. If possible, the 10th green clings even nearer the cliff's edge than the 9th green, presenting an approach shot to freeze the blood in the veins.

If there is a commonplace hole on the back nine, it is the 384-yard uphill par-4 11th, which heads back inland. Curtis Strange, in future years, made a $360,000 memory of the hole. His eight-iron second shot went into the cup to help him win the Nabisco Championships, played that year at Pebble Beach.

The long iron is the weapon of choice to confront the 202-yard par-3 12th hole, on which the green runs as thin as mercy on the back nine.

If it weren't in the record book, it could not be believed, but in the 1956 California Amateur, Ken Venturi, a native son, and ultimate U.S. Open champion, played holes 5 through 12 at Pebble Beach in *eight consecutive 3s*, to win the finals of the match play tournament, 2 and 1. *Threes* on the 8th, 9th, and 10th? Who can believe even the record book?

The 392-yard par-4 13th is most feared for its sliver of a green, which falls precipitously from left to right. This green, and the tiny 8th green, were redesigned by the Scotsman Alister MacKenzie when he was creating the companion Cypress Point course. Charity on the greens was not a part of the MacKenzie mystique.

Prepare three shots to play the 565-yard par-5 14th. The hole bends consecutively to the right to the most seriously tilted green on the course. The green was once protected by a huge cypress tree along the fairway's right side. In 1967 Arnold Palmer, in heated pursuit of Jack Nicklaus in the final round of The Crosby, went for the green with a three-wood. Hesitation to take a chance never defined Mr. Palmer. In fact, he went for the green twice. And twice his three-wood shots hit the tree, and twice his ball kicked out of bounds. He took a 9 on the hole and finished third to Jack's championship. Funny thing. The next day a huge storm blew over the course, and lightning struck the cypress tree and knocked it down dead. So much for the natural landscape that got in the way of Arnie's Army, some of whom apparently enlisted from above.

A right to left draw is needed on the 397-yard 15th to keep your drive in bounds. Then it's a short iron to the green. A bit of a fade off the tee is required on the 402-yard 16th. You are left with a short iron shot over a ravine to a green tucked into the trees.

Then, 218 yards away, comes the hourglass 17th green, with all of the Pacific Ocean waiting for the overly ambitious tee shot. It is one of the storied par 3s in all golf.

Memories of the 17th hole wash onto the shore with the tide. Palmer absorbing his 6 over par 9. Nicklaus nailing his tee shot within inches of the cup to win the 1972 U.S. Open. On the lighter side, Phil Harris in 1951 sank a birdie putt on the 17th green that won him and Dutch Harrison the Pro-Am title. A lot of stories have been told as to the length of that putt. Phil Harris claimed it was a modest ninety feet. Dutch Harrison said that night at The Clambake, "Hell, it broke that much." Years and years after this 1974 Crosby, Tom Watson lifted a chip shot out of the high grass and directly, impossibly, into the 17th cup to snatch the U.S. Open championship from—who else?—Jack Nicklaus.

The 18th is simply the most famous, most photographed, best-loved finishing hole in championship golf. The 18th began as a par 4 of some 379 yards. Chandler Egan, hired to modify the course in the late 1920s, moved the 18th tee back onto a scenic spit of land extending over the Pacific behind the 17th green, changing the identity of the finishing hole into a nerve-rattling 548-yard par 5. The hole curves away to the

right, with the Pacific Ocean following it the length of
the fairway to the green. Two enormous pine trees
guard the right side of the fairway. Years ahead, in the
windblown 1982 U.S. Open, two players scored 9s on
the hole, and five others would suffer 8s. Fifteen years
after that a rookie professional phenom, Tiger Woods,
became one of the few players ever to reach the 18th
green in two strokes but fell one stroke short of winning
The Crosby, which by then had been reinvented under
a depressing corporate name and sponsorship. But that
is a subject of another story and later regret.

Morris leaned under Sullivan's umbrella, enjoying
the rattling of the rain and the moment in time.

But the golf course was filling up with water, which
rose above the level of the greens on many holes and
covered the bottoms of most of the bunkers.

Morris and Sullivan, with every instinct for the sadis-
tic, wandered over to the cliffs that imperiled Nos. 6, 7,
8, and 9.

Jerry Boyd, his square jaw set against the wind and
rain, slogged through the four ocean holes like a man
escaping from his own nightmare. On the tiny par-3
7th, he twice backed away from his tee shot to test the
wind and rain blowing in from the ocean. He switched
from a wedge to a nine-iron and then sent his tee shot
bounding over the green onto the spray-drenched
rocks.

"Take your penalty, and drop it back into play," Sullivan said to herself as through her binoculars she
watched a familiar catastrophe about to develop.

Boyd ignored the advice. With the ocean washing at

his heels and over them, he played a sand wedge off the dark rocks onto the green.

"*Olé!*" Sullivan shouted into the stillness, as if she were at a bullfight.

Boyd took aim on the twenty-foot putt and rolled it through the casual water directly into the hole for an improbable par.

A tall figure in a bright rain suit let out a collegiate yell to rival Sullivan's as the putt dropped.

"I'm thinking his life on a shrimp boat was not wasted," Morris said. "If he had been any nearer the ocean, he would have been under sail."

"Looks like he has a volunteer for his crew if he does go to sea," Sullivan said, looking toward young Anne Robinson, her long legs sending her easily after young Mr. Boyd to the eighth tee.

Paired with Boyd was Ed Waters, aptly named for the conditions. Ed was his anonymous self, taking no chances, playing well away from the cliffs, conceding any hope for birdie putts, seeking only the high ground in the fairways and the center of the greens. Still, he lost two shots to par when the wind and the slope of the 9th fairway sent his tee shot bouncing, splashing over the cliff into the bay.

Jerry Boyd played the four ocean holes in even par, gaining a couple of strokes on the field.

Jake Hill came striding down the 6th fairway. He might have been plowing wet ground back in Georgia for the relentless expression on his face. His short, short backswing and sharply descending stroke dug up huge quantities of mud but sent his ball flying low and straight. He missed all four greens at Nos. 6, 7, 8, and 9 but saved par three times with surgical chips from the muddy fringe. He never smiled. Never raised his hand in triumph. In fact, he never looked up from the wet earth upon which he would take the next step.

Should Miller and McCord slip on the muddy track, Boyd, Waters, or Hill might find enough high ground on the back side to steal the lead in this, the third round. The way the rain was continuing to fall, it would take a dry miracle to get the fourth round in on Monday.

Gary McCord did not just slip. He lost all footing and drowned on the first nine holes, which took him forty-one strokes to finish. Twice McCord, in his checkered trousers, sent his tee shots fading over the cliffs and into the sea. He had the familiar "thousand-yard stare" that comes to the traumatized in golf when all sense of feel and direction is lost. It was not a pretty sight.

"Hang tough," Morris whispered to McCord as he stepped toward the 9th tee.

"Too late," McCord said out of the side of his mouth, "I'm hanging . . . period. But not out to dry."

Johnny Miller, lean in his sweater and flowing bell-bottom trousers, swept his iron shots off the soaked turf as if they were sitting on tees. Still, he could not putt, settling for pars where birdies were begging to be had.

Sullivan set out after him on No. 9, with Morris struggling to keep up, his cane sinking in the mud with every step. Miller's second shot found a greenside bunker in which the water rose to the top of the ball. Not bothering to ask for a free drop, for there was no dry sand on which to drop it, Miller splashed the ball out with his sand wedge, stopping it near the hole with the confidence of a skilled plumber attacking a leaking sink. He holed the putt to turn the front side in even-par 36.

Only the journeyman Grier Jones, playing up ahead, had any faint hope of catching him.

Miller kept his drive on the high side of the 10th hole's tilted fairway and found the green and his par 4. At the 11th Pebble Beach offered its one easy moment on the back nine, and Miller quickly took advantage. He sent a seven-iron as high as the low clouds, the ball spinning to a stop for a short putt that he drained with the water pouring in the cup.

Miller's three-iron on the 202-yard 12th was true to the thin green. And he took another par to the 13th tee.

The long-deceased Scotsman Alister MacKenzie was unsuccessful in hiding the minute 13th green from Miller's precision iron. He sank another putt and was two strokes under par for the day and clear of the field, barring some calamity of nerves or nature.

"Let's skip the inland holes and cut over to the 17th," Morris said.

Sullivan led the way.

They reached the frightful par 3 just in time to see young Lanny Wadkins take the tee, 1 under par for the day and only three shots off Miller's lead.

Wadkins took his quick, quick, quick cut at the ball and sent a low, hard screech of a shot just over the narrow green 218 yards away. Morris borrowed his own binoculars from Sullivan and watched as Wadkins made a sensible chip to within six feet of the hole. Never a man to tarry, Lanny bent over the ball and applied a firm putt. Too firm. Now the ball was nearly the same distance from the cup on the opposite side of the hole. Wadkins, as if mesmerized, sent the ball rolling back past the hole in the same direction. Now he bent to his work more deliberately. Too deliberately. And left his fourth putt short of the hole. He tapped in his *fifth* putt on the green and staggered to the 18th tee with a quadruple bogey 7 to break the heart of a thirty handicapper, not to say one of the great players in the world.

The number 7 seemed branded into his thought processes, and Wadkins repeated the score on the par-5 18th. Years later fate returned the favor by allowing Wadkins to sink a slippery twenty-foot putt at Pebble Beach to keep his sudden-death hopes alive as he won the PGA championship in a play-off.

Jerry Boyd, Ed Waters, and Jake Hill all put their tee shots on the green at the 17th, and each took three putts less than Wadkins to make his par.

"How's he playing?" Sullivan asked Anne Robinson, who seemed to be holding her breath at every shot. Sullivan did not have to identify the "he" as Jerry Boyd.

"He's one under par for the day," Anne said, wiping the rain from her eyes as it blew under her rain hat. "He's the bravest thing I've ever seen. He's missed almost every green but chipped the ball so close and made so many terrifying putts."

Sullivan said, "I think someone has inspired him."

Anne was off to the 18th tee.

Boyd waved in their direction. Waters seemed to be playing alone. And Hill dared the world so much as to whisper to him.

"Get 'em, Jake," Morris yelled, just to see if he was conscious, but Hill never lifted his eyes.

Boyd and Waters, and then Hill, all parred No. 18. Sullivan could pick up the scoreboard behind the 18th green with the binoculars. The three of them were tied at 1 under par 215 for the tournament, seven shots off the pace set by Johnny Miller.

Gary McCord, his sideburns almost touching the ground in despair, dragged himself through the last two holes with a ghastly score of 80 trailing after him. Morris did not have the heart to offer false encouragement.

Afterward, in the press tent, McCord said, "I played terribly. I just hoped it would be washed out." But the round was to stand on the scoreboard and in his recollection forever.

Miller stepped up to the 17th tee as if it were his private property. His look-alike amateur partner, Locke de Bretteville, breathed the air as if running short of oxygen. The two of them held the Pro-Am lead by one thin stroke over B. R. ("Mac") McLendon of Birmingham, Alabama, and David Kirkland.

Miller, with his smooth, very upright swing, sent his long-iron to the 17th green with the touch of a man playing a pitching wedge. He made the par and moved to the 18th tee, a tiny spit of land suspended over the sea. In his bell-bottoms he seemed to be standing on the deck of a ship with the ocean under him.

Miller's second shot on the finishing par 5 tumbled into the long bunker that ran along the seawall protecting the fairway and green. He tested the sand with his feet and stood over the shot for a long time before sending it onto the green, where he two-putted for a par 5 and a 2 under par 70 for the day. His three-day performance of 68-68-70—208 was good for a four-shot lead over Grier Jones, alone in second place.

"My third shot on 18 was my best shot of the tournament," Miller said in the press room. "I was in an area [in the bunker] that had been washed out . . . no sand at all. I took a nine-iron and hit it one hundred yards, and it ended up ten feet from the pin. I missed the putt, but the greens are so tough. I haven't been putting well this tournament. But I don't think anyone has. If I had putted well, I would be way, way ahead."

He putted well enough to suit young Gary McCord, who saw Miller pick up *seventeen* strokes on him over only *ten* holes.

Grier Jones was more unhappy with the rain and the muddy condition of the course than with his own even-par 72 for the day and his three-day total of 212. "They play here until it's almost ridiculous," Jones said.

"No," Morris whispered to his old pal Paul Shirley, "until it's totally, wonderfully ridiculous."

No one realized it at the moment, but the 33rd Bing Crosby National Pro-Am was history. Drowned in water . . . and murder. With Johnny Miller to be declared the winner of the professional tournament, and he and his amateur partner, Locke de Bretteville, winners of the Pro-Am. But that decision did not come until the next day, when the rains failed to yield.

Neither did anyone realize that the rain of murder was not yet over.

CHAPTER ELEVEN

John Morris, without looking up, knocked out his seven hundred words on Sunday's third round of The Crosby.

Paul Shirley leaned over his shoulder to see what Morris had written that he could steal for the *San Francisco Chronicle*.

"Morris, what are the chances they'll get the final round in tomorrow?"

"Faint . . . and none."

"Pebble Beach is the highest of the three courses, and it's drowned," said Shirley.

"I know. I swam over it."

"Morris, did you hear what Phil Harris, working the broadcast for Crosby, said today on national television? On Sunday afternoon, for God's sake—if God will forgive the expression."

"No." Morris was already laughing.

"Johnny Miller hit the great bunker shot out of the sand and water. Chris Schenkel, the last gentleman, praised his 'smooth touch.' Harris said, 'Yeah . . . as smooth as a man lifting a breast out of an evening gown.' "

Morris laughed so hard he was afraid he'd fractured something.

"Not long after that," Shirley said, hardly able to speak, "Schenkel identified Gay Brewer, who was walking up the fairway to the eighteenth green. Harris said, 'Gay Brewer? I always thought he was a little fag winemaker from Modesto.' "

It was impossible for either man to speak for laughing.

Finally Morris was able to say, "I bet they had to anesthetize Bing up in the Peninsula Hospital."

"Yeah, Larry almost had a heart attack. The phones are flooding ABC worse than the rain is flooding the Monterey Peninsula. Schenkel had to keep a straight face. But the truth is he loved it. A little something to wake the bastards up on a Sunday afternoon. Speaking of bastards, what's up with the murder investigation?"

"Ask me in an hour," Morris said. "I've got to find the high sheriff."

Morris dropped by lodge manager Jack Houghton's office, but it was locked. The sheriff was curiously missing. Deputy Patricia Jordan was nowhere to be found. None of the other deputies were talking or looking him in the eye. Inspector Gooden could not be found in the lodge.

"What the hell's going on?" Morris said to himself.

He checked by his room to find Julia Sullivan showered and dressed and looking nothing like the drowned sea otter of two hours ago.

"Get a move on, Morris. We've got a date for a drink in the bar."

"Where's the sheriff? Where's Deputy Jordan? I couldn't even find bloody Inspector Gooden. What's going on?"

"Get a move on, and we'll find out," Sullivan said, pushing him toward the bathroom like a small boy condemned to a bath.

"That's what I need . . . a shower," protested Morris. "I've been rained on for five hours standing in water up to my . . . you don't even want to know."

Sullivan shut the door on his protests.

Morris had to admit he felt better in dry clothes. It was time to get wetter on the inside.

Anne Robinson had been watching for them. She returned Sullivan's hug as if they were sorority sisters. Jerry Boyd's muscular hand disappeared inside Morris's larger one. Boyd had a huge smile on his face, not altogether accountable by his three-round 1-under-par standing at 215.

"Gutsy work today. You're in for a Top Ten finish and a good check," Morris said.

"You think tomorrow's final round is a washout?"

"Unless the rain gods lose their touch overnight," Morris said. "Who was the tall, dark-haired beast cheering you on out there?"

"Me," said Anne, introducing herself with a bow, which would have done justice to volleyball royalty.

"So, you're Stanford," Morris said. "I heard about you."

"Yep. I've heard about you," said Anne, unintimidated by his size and reputation since he definitely wasn't a blind date. "Why don't you put women's volleyball on your AP wire?"

"Touché," Morris said.

"Oh, no," Sullivan said. "All those young athletes in their outfits? Morris has a congenital heart condition. It's true it only has a weakness for young women with two arms, two legs, and two eyes."

"Tell you what, Stanford, I'll buy you a drink. And one for the shrimp boat captain too," said Morris.

Boyd made a passable salute.

"When you're not playing golf, do you captain a shrimp boat?" asked Anne, much impressed.

"My old man does," Boyd said. "That's how I grew up. Pulling nets on the Gulf of Mexico. That's why a little rainwater on the Monterey Peninsula doesn't frighten me. *Much*," he added. "Morris, did you hear that Wadkins *five-putted* 17?"

"We heard it all right. It didn't make a sound . . . like sinking in quicksand. We also saw it . . . all five putts. None of them a tough one. It was like he was trapped in a Kafka novel. I swear Lanny could breathe in, but he couldn't breathe out when he got to the 18th tee. It's a miracle he finished at all. He's a tough guy. It's a good thing. A lesser man could never get it out of his brain."

"So you think Johnny has won The Crosby," Boyd said.

"No question. God knows he deserves it. Two years

ago he lost the sudden-death play-off to Nicklaus. That's a known hazard of the game. Jack has drowned a generation of golfers." Morris raised his glass to the bartender for a refill. "But that year Johnny was walking up the 16th fairway. Three holes to play. He led Jack by a stroke. He said, 'I can't say I've played very well, Jack. It's taken me sixty-nine holes to figure out my problem. But I've got it corrected now.' The golf gods were listening. Johnny pulled out a seven-iron for his second shot. He cold-shanked the ball. And lost in the play-off."

"Please don't use the *S* word, not even in the bar," Boyd said.

"What's a sh—" began Anne.

"SSSHHhhhhh," Boyd said. "Don't even ask. Some things it's best never to know."

The figure in the door to the bar belonged to Sheriff's Deputy Patricia Jordan.

"Stanford, don't keep this young man out too late," Morris said. "It's possible, it ain't likely, but it's possible, the rains will stop falling, and he will have to earn his money tomorrow at Pebble Beach."

"I can't stay late. I have to get back to school tomorrow," said Anne. She didn't seem thrilled by the prospect.

Jordan led Morris and Sullivan to her broom closet–office, closing the door after them.

"Here's what's happened," she said. "Jacob Hyche's wife, Elizabeth, was murdered. This afternoon. Hyche admits mixing and handing his wife the drink that killed her. He swears he didn't know there was cyanide in the scotch and soda. He admits he lied to the inspector, that he *was* in Sidney Barker's suite just before Sidney died. One of the maids at the lodge, who's been out sick, saw Hyche leaving the suite not thirty minutes before Sidney's body was discovered. Hyche admitted he 'was scared and lied.' But he swears he and Sidney had a friendly drink. He said they talked about a musical score for Hyche's next movie. Hyche swears he didn't see Sidney die. He swears he didn't kill Barker, or Andrew McCall, or his wife. Of course you saw Hyche in the Snake Pit just before McCall died."

"It doesn't look good for our boy," Morris said.

"It looks worse than that. It's not likely the two men were having a 'friendly drink.' Sidney had filed a lawsuit a month ago, claiming unauthorized and uncompensated use of his music in Hyche's last movie."

"I'm surprised there was only cyanide in his drink," Morris said.

"It also turns out that Hyche owed Andrew McCall money. A lot of money . . . not guaranteed by his wife's millions," said Jordan. "McCall also was taking legal action. And Hyche admits he stands to inherit his wife's huge estate. The man was upset at her death. But you'd have to say he was dry-eyed. Inspector Gooden got a warrant for his arrest and charged him with murder two hours ago."

"That much evidence? Enough to convince Sheriff Whitlock, and the district attorney, and a magistrate?"

"Tommy didn't know about Elizabeth Hyche's murder or the arrest. He was in court this afternoon on another case. The inspector never consulted him. He took the evidence to the district attorney, then on to a superior court judge for a warrant, and made the arrest himself. Tommy is hot about it."

"The DA's office didn't *talk* with the sheriff *personally* . . . on a high-profile arrest like this one?" said Morris.

"The DA does not love the sheriff," Jordan said. "He's a Republican. Tommy of course is a Democrat."

"A Republican—that's grounds for a citizen's arrest right there," Sullivan said.

"Believe me," said Jordan, "the district attorney would enjoy seeing the sheriff's office arrest the wrong man. Especially a famous man. But if it's the right man, the DA's office will want to share in the credit . . . with *the inspector*, not the sheriff. It's an open secret. Inspector Gooden is very likely to run as a Republican against Tommy in the next election."

"What's murder compared to a little political assassination?" Morris said.

"Tommy agrees the circumstantial evidence against Hyche is powerful," Jordan said. "But he sees no reason to have rushed into an arrest. Jacob Hyche is not likely to skip the country. Tommy feels we should have kept digging and taken the evidence—if it held up—to a grand jury for an indictment. That way there would be no chance of a false arrest. I agree with Tommy. But who am I, a lowly sheriff's deputy?"

"What will Tommy say to the press?"

"Very little. He's letting Inspector Gooden speak for his own arrest. The sheriff's caught between a rock and a hard place. His own homicide inspector has come up with evidence strong enough to sustain a warrant. And he's already made the arrest. And maybe he has the right man."

"Maybe," Morris said. "Hyche's team made the cut in the Pro-Am. Did he play this morning?"

"Yes," Jordan said. "He was still wearing his wet golf clothes when he and his wife drank the scotch."

"A man plays golf for nearly five hours in the rain and mud," Morris recited, "he comes to his room cold and soaking wet, and the first thing that comes to mind is to kill his beautiful wife, who gives him everything he ever wanted. Makes a lot of sense," he said with every skepticism.

"Hyche thinks too much," Sullivan said for a second time. "If you think too much, the act of murder looks entirely too stupid for an intelligent man to commit."

"Plenty of bright men have killed their wives," Morris said.

"Yes. There's a difference between 'bright' and 'thinking' men," Sullivan said.

"Tell you who they should have killed in his damn boring movies," Morris said, angry that Elizabeth was dead. "They should have killed the director."

"How about life without parole?" Sullivan said, laughing in spite of herself. She suddenly remembered. "I have to give you credit, Morris. You did speculate how Sidney might react to improper use of his music. Or how tough it would be to owe money to Andrew McCall. Reasons you just pulled out of the air Jacob Hyche, or anyone else, might have for killing the two men. You were the first guy singing the executioner's song for Mr. Hyche."

"Yeah, but like Tommy, I wasn't ready to arrest the

bastard. How does Jacob explain the drink he handed his wife?" Morris asked Jordan.

"He said he poured himself a scotch and his wife a scotch . . . out of the same bottle. He took water. She took soda. He poured them both. They drank. And she fell dead." Jordan added, "There was no evidence of cyanide in the bottle of soda water."

"Maybe the goddamn air in the goddamn lodge is poison," Morris said in frustration.

"I'm not supposed to know this," said Jordan. "And even Tommy doesn't want it out. And it's the main reason he isn't firing Inspector Gooden for insubordination. A solid stain of cyanide was found on the kitchen floor of the Hyches' suite. As if it had been spilled there and smeared by foot traffic."

"Oh, shit," Morris said, "ring down the curtain on the director."

"There was no other evidence of poison in the suite or in Hyche's clothes or luggage or in his car. The Los Angeles police are already searching the Hyche estate in Beverly Hills."

"I don't like the man's movies," Morris said, "and he was a fool to run around on Elizabeth with a bunch of bimbos, but to be honest, he is in many ways an okay guy. He can be very funny. Something his movies never are. He's a solid amateur golfer with an honest handicap. Honest handicaps can be thin on the ground at The Crosby. And if everybody in Hollywood killed everybody suing them, it would be civil war."

"He's got to be sick," Sullivan said. "McCall? Give him that homicide. But sweet Sidney? And his beautiful, generous wife? No way a sane man does that. As long as

I'm talking, I don't believe Jacob Hyche killed the three of them for a minute, but as soon as I shut up, I'll be inclined to believe the verdict: 'guilty as charged.' "

The press conference was only slightly less chaotic than the Spanish-American War. Golf writers and police reporters, contemptuous of one another, struggled to see who could ask the next nasty question. Sheriff Tommy Whitlock sat on his handcuffs while Inspector Stanley Gooden preened and answered the questions with the arrogance of an overweight diva.

Bond had been set at a "modest" one million dollars. Hyche had posted it and was "resting" at a private residence on the peninsula, with orders not to leave the area.

Morris waited for the inevitable lull and asked one question. "Inspector, do you believe Hyche killed McCall and Barker so that he could kill his wife, inherit her money, and blame it on an unknown murderer?"

"Yes," Gooden said with great satisfaction, as if he'd won a debate on the Senate floor. "But he also chose two victims to kill first who were suing him. Pretty convenient, wouldn't you say?"

Morris did not say that the drink in the Snake Pit might have killed one of many people, not just Andrew McCall. Did that make Jacob Hyche merely a killer for money or a monster? Or all of the above.

Morris took careful pains to compose his lead on the murder of Elizabeth Hyche and the arrest of Jacob Hyche with absolute dispassion. He left out only the evidence of spilled cyanide on the Hyches' kitchen floor. He made it clear that the arrest of Jacob Hyche and the ensuing charge of murder had been at the instigation of Inspector Stanley Gooden, acting on his own belief.

If the murder charge stuck, Gooden's campaign for sheriff would get a hell of a lift. If the charge fell apart, the inspector might be looking for another line of work. Morris hated the ambiguity for Tommy. But there was nothing to be done.

Tommy read Morris's lead and dropped it on his desk. "Gooden's got enough evidence to put the poor bastard away forever," Whitlock said. "It's all circumstantial. But what do you need, other than motive, opportunity, and cyanide on your kitchen floor? I'm sure Deputy Jordan told you about that."

Jordan raised her chin defiantly rather than blush. "You would have told him yourself, Tommy."

He nodded that it was true. "Thanks for not writing it, my friend. If the case goes to trial, we'll have to disclose the fact to the defense, of course. Can you believe in Jacob as a triple murderer, Morris?"

"I've been trying to since the Snake Pit. Jacob had been around long enough to have serious differences with McCall and Sidney. I had no idea if in fact he was feuding with either of them. I just guessed they might have fallen out over money or music. The two things McCall and Sidney cared about . . . and controlled a lot of. And Jacob, making his movies, had great need of both commodities."

Morris swung his scotch in his glass. "Yet I can't see him as a killer. He's too damn *thin*. Too gentlemanly. He plays to an honest fourteen handicap. He must believe in his goddamn movies. Nobody would make them who didn't . . . since nobody bothers to see them. He runs around with a bunch of dames, but his wife stuck with him. Why? I wonder. Then he up and kills Elizabeth and my theory of his innocence with her—if we believe the evidence. It's powerful evidence."

Into the long silence Sullivan said, "If not Jacob, who?"

"That's the name of that game," Tommy said.

"Are you going to keep the investigation alive?" Morris asked.

"I want to," Tommy said. "But how can I? The damn golf tournament leaves town tomorrow, whether the fourth round is rained out or not. I can't hold golfers and celebrities hostage, with a man out on bail for a million dollars charged with the murders."

"You might be able to," Morris said.

"Tell me how . . . quickly."

"If the real killer offs somebody else," Morris said.

"Jesus, I can't hope for that."

"Hope won't have anything to do with it."

"You think it's not over? Hell, I'd rather be wrong and out of office. I don't have to be sheriff of Monterey County."

Morris said, "The evidence, hard evidence, says it's over. But did you find any kind of delivery system, something as simple as a match box, that would have let Hyche quickly dump the cyanide in a glass?"

"Nothing."

Morris said, "I keep finding myself agreeing with Crosby. There's something about these killings that goes beyond money. In the very *public act* of them. The choosing of the forum itself: The Crosby National Pro-Am. It's somehow *personal*. In some way a *vendetta*. Even if Crosby is out of bounds thinking the acts were against him personally and his tournament. If Crosby is basically right, and the murders are somehow personal, how do we know the vendetta is over?"

"You frighten me," Sullivan said, folding her arms to keep away the chill in the room. Rain again beat against the tall window.

"The thought makes me sick to my stomach," said the sheriff. "I'm keeping security as tight as ever, until after tomorrow."

Morris thought of Crosby, lying up in the hospital, hearing the terrible news. "I don't envy Larry having to tell Bing. Bing loved Elizabeth Hyche. But who didn't? And Jacob was a twenty-year competitor in the Pro-Am, come 'hail' or high water."

"With an accused killer in jail, at least Bing is off the hook," Sullivan said. "He doesn't have to think about canceling the last round tomorrow. If by some miracle the rains stop and there is a last round."

"At least all the 'unarrested' suspects hang around for one more day," Morris said. "Maybe the discomfort the four of us feel is not misplaced. Maybe the inspector has caught the wrong man. Maybe the true killer will get careless, make a mistake. Wars have been lost in twenty-four hours."

"Not to mention elections," the sheriff said. "I don't give a damn. Just so we have the right man. Just so it's over."

* * *

Dinner for two seemed a solitary happening, as Morris and Sullivan occupied separate worlds of thought.

"Hey, over there," Sullivan said, suddenly aware of the silence.

"Sorry. I was looking at the ocean, at the dark place it's supposed to be," Morris said. The steady rain obscured the view from the nineteenth-century inn. Rain falling on an ocean seemed an absurd excess.

"I'll show you my thoughts if you'll show me yours," Sullivan said.

"I had become convinced that potassium cyanide was a colorless, odorless, invisible element that could be invented in a glass in plain view and not be seen. Like voodoo magic. Until it showed up on Jacob Hyche's kitchen floor. Finally. At last. A solid piece of incriminating evidence. Why didn't Jacob realize he had spilled it and stepped in it? He'd been damned careful to slip it into drinks twice without spilling so much as a gram, and once in a crowded room. I still can't picture exactly where Jacob was standing in the Snake Pit just before the fight. I swear I was closer to McCall and to Tana Daly, who was holding his glass, than Jacob was. I'm just talking to hear myself think," Morris said.

"Don't stop."

"Maybe the cyanide wasn't meant for Elizabeth. Maybe it was meant for Jacob. And his wife drew the wrong glass. But how could that be? Just the two of them there. No poison in the scotch. No poison in the soda water. I go back to the odd possibility there was poison dusted on the side or on the rim of the glass. Remember, it doesn't take but fifteen four-hundredths of an ounce to kill you. But that brings us back to who got which glass in the Snake Pit and to the golfers at the bar and the bartender. And the random nature of such an act. But if the cyanide was meant for Jacob and killed Elizabeth, that's as random as murder gets . . . and as heartless. What were you thinking, Sullivan?"

"The fourth most terrible thing that could happen, after the three murders . . . if the murderer has finished and they convict the wrong man."

"Would it be less terrible if he killed again, and we caught the right man?" Morris said. "It's a question for a philosopher, not a failed sportswriter."

The food at the inn was passably good. But they had little appetite for dinner.

CHAPTER TWELVE

All that missing hunger built up in the night hours, and Julia Sullivan, who could sleep away the seasons of the year, pulled John Morris out of bed, pushed him into the shower, and dragged him into the dining room.

"I feel like I've been drafted into the army," Morris grumbled, but he himself was ready to lay waste to a stack of pancakes.

"Look who's having breakfast," Sullivan said, "but don't stare."

"How do I look when I look and don't stare?" Morris said, smiling to see Anne Robinson and Jerry Boyd sitting across from each other.

Anne didn't mind if he was staring. She waved and stood up and came over and patted Sullivan on the shoulder as if she'd been an especially good girl.

"I owe you," Anne said, "whatever comes of it or nothing. He's an intense—no, he's a strong young man . . . rather quiet. Even though he's pretty famous, I don't feel awkward around him at all. My roommate, who is honestly sick, is calling me in sick too. But I feel wonderful. I'm going back to school tonight."

"You're looking good, Stanford," Morris said. "I'll be watching for you in the new world of beach volley-ball."

"Oh, no. I've seen those outfits," Sullivan said.

Anne shook Morris's big hand and kissed Sullivan and stepped back to her table, where Jerry Boyd was giving them his shrimp captain's salute.

"I don't think a little murder has put a damper on their tournament," Morris said.

"I'm betting they haven't been watching television or maybe even heard about Elizabeth Hyche's murder," said Sullivan. "The young don't have time for the dead. Nor should they."

Larry Crosby stopped by their table. "It's official. It's over," he said. "We couldn't play today in water wings."

"Johnny Miller will be a popular champion," Morris said, "and a deserving one."

"It never hurts the history of our tournament to have a defending U.S. Open champion win it," said Larry. "Bing is pleased. Johnny is a terrific young man and, as you know, grew up playing here on the peninsula."

"How did Bing take Elizabeth's murder?" Sullivan asked, the conversation taking the appropriate turn, golf always having more immediacy than mortality.

"Hard. They'd been friends forever. Even fishing buddies. Elizabeth was a lady, but she was also a pal you could hang out with. Who could imagine Jacob with a fishing pole in his hand?"

"What do you and Bing make of him as the killer?" Morris asked. He couldn't hide the growing skepticism in his voice.

Larry hesitated. "It's insane. Jacob must be insane. Elizabeth financed his movies. Hell, she would have paid any debt he owed to McCall. She ignored his philandering. She was crazy about Jacob."

"She had to be to sit through his goddamn movies," Morris could not resist saying.

Larry was glad to be able to laugh. "I didn't say she sat through them, she just financed them. Jacob is a gentleman golfer. He is fun to play with, has a quick wit. The pros like to be paired with him. You just can't imagine Jacob Hyche killing anybody—least of all Elizabeth. Maybe himself," Larry said, after some thought. "He could fall into a black depression. But I never saw him as suicidal, even in a suicidal town, and certainly I never imagined him as murderous."

"No," Morris said.

"Do you have serious doubts that Jacob *is* the murderer?" Larry asked.

"I do. But the evidence against him is potent. He lied to the cops. He's going to be a very rich man. And as you know, McCall and Sidney were suing him."

"So, who isn't being sued? They'd have to get in line at the courthouse in L.A.," Larry said. "It bothers me the sheriff's people finding no evidence of cyanide in his suite."

Morris and Sullivan were careful to keep any knowledge of the cyanide on the kitchen floor out of their eyes and faces.

Larry Crosby might have read their minds. "Inspector Gooden assured me that all the evidence against Jacob had not been made public. I hope not. I mean, if he's guilty. I hope to God there is no question they have the right man . . . if Jacob did it. I've never been so glad to see a tournament end in my life, Morris. We'll have a brief ceremony honoring Johnny in about an hour. It'll have to be in the press room. It's never going to stop raining."

Morris nodded that he would be there.

Miller was all legs and blond hair and smiles and generosity to his competitors. But you could not miss the hard flint of his own confidence.

"If I had putted well," he told Morris, "the tournament would have been over halfway through the second round."

"Were you glad Jack was not wading along behind you?" Morris kidded him.

"Nobody wants to look over his shoulder and see the big shadow of Nicklaus in the fairway. But when I hit the ball that well, I'm not worried about who's behind me," Johnny said, unable to keep a smile of great satisfaction off his lips. The sudden-death loss to Nicklaus two years ago at Pebble Beach was history gone out with the tide.

"Congratulations. It's not a shabby cup to have your name on," Morris said.

"I think not." Miller kissed the trophy. "Morris, I hate it for the Hyche family and all the families of the victims. I've played with Jacob several times. He had a dry humor . . . even in the rain. And his wife might not have loved golf, but she treated us all like part of her family. I'll just have to block everything out of my memory—except the way it felt to win the tournament before the home folks."

Morris had his wrap-up lead for the tournament.

Sullivan waited for him in the lobby of the lodge. Players, pros and amateurs, were checking out, their bags and clubs packed up and ready to go as if they had their own schedules to keep. The amateurs were headed, reluctantly or fearfully or gleefully, back to their corporate lives. The pros were folding their checks into their coat pockets, and the PGA Tour was moving to the Arizona desert, an appropriate place to dry out from the rains of Monterey County. Agents and advertising executives and broadcast heavyweights hustled one another among the luggage in a timeless dance of shared greed. Caddies were gathered outside in the parking lot, many of them sharing rides to the next tournament, all of them complaining about the rain and the goddamn mud and the easy uphill putts their men had blown that meant another two thousand dollars for sure.

Sullivan smiled and raised her Bloody Mary to friends trooping past or standing in the checkout lines. She smiled and said gay things, but the final days of tournaments always left her with a private sadness, knowing that these moments could not come again. The tour would surely lap back to The Crosby come next January. But not *this* Crosby in *this* January with *these exact same friends and strangers* waving to one another. She should have been all happiness to see the week's tragedies recede into time. But time was a promiscuous fellow who might whisper your own name into the last silence.

Sullivan smiled even wider and shouted to Aubry Hicks, who shouted back, not words, just a friendly shout from a former champion, going back to his new life. Jake Hill, his sizable check sticking carelessly out of his back pocket, kicked his luggage forward with one foot, while slinging his heavy golf bag over his shoulder, too intent to get to the next tournament to wait for his caddie. Jake did not look up, or wave, or shout to her or anyone but struggled on to his solitary destiny. Ed Waters stuck his head in the lodge door, calling to someone who wanted a lift to the airport. He did smile toward Sullivan, but it was more careful than friendly.

A familiar cut of red hair bobbed through the crowd, followed by a bellcap under an avalanche of luggage. Tana Daly pointed her chin toward the lodge door as if she'd never met or heard of any of the mob of commoners in the lobby. Sullivan liked this tough broad's chances in a tough business.

Jerry Boyd and Anne Robinson came from the dining room and picked their way through the lobby, which was as crowded with people and luggage as a staging area for a serious battleground. But the two of them were aware only of each other. Sullivan eased discreetly behind them and stepped outside the door to see the strong young man bend down into her car for a serious kiss. Sullivan gloated as if one of them belonged to her.

Back in the lobby she waved to Larry Crosby, who

seemed to be everywhere, speaking to everybody, taking condolences for Bing, regretting the horrendous murders of old friends, not to say the weather, congratulating the players, the PGA officials, the television crew on surviving the monsoon season, promising the tournament "would never again, *ever*, be played in the first week of January."

Morris, looking for Sullivan in the chaotic lobby, bumped into Phil Harris, hiding his night before behind dark shades.

"See you next year, AP," Harris said. "Bing'll be back stronger than rye whiskey."

"Have you seen him?" Morris asked.

"Yeah. Just got back from the hospital."

"Did Bing catch your description of Miller's sand shot? 'Smooth as a man lifting a breast out of an evening gown?' You didn't really say that on national television?"

"Pardner, it just slipped out." Harris made his famous evil leer. "Bing said they had him doped up to his eyeballs, but that line got his head up off the pillow."

"That I believe."

"He loves Johnny as the winner. Great kid. Great player. One of the home boys."

"His name fits nicely on the trophy alongside Snead, Mangrum, Nelson, Hogan, Middlecoff, Venturi, Nicklaus. He belongs among them. How is Bing, truly?"

"Our boy is facin' the long knives," Harris said. "He's tough. But he's weak and scared too. Wants to see a couple of the old hackers. Just in case he dudn't wake up. Hell, Morris, what's this fool stuff about Jacob confessin'? He couldn't kill a bedbug," said Harris.

"It's bizarre," Morris said. "And hard to believe."

"The cops can shout all they want . . . I ain't believin' it," Harris said. "Oops, there's Alice. Got to go."

Morris lifted a trigger finger in a good-bye salute. And there was Sullivan, finishing off her Bloody Mary.

"Get your car keys, kid," Morris said, taking her empty glass and setting it on a table, safe among all the traffic. "We're off."

"Where to?" Sullivan's hand was already reaching inside her shoulder bag. "We're off" was among her favorite expressions.

"To see Jacob. He's expecting us."

"How on earth did you find him?"

"I have extraterrestrial friends. You do realize that I am a reporter. We have our ways."

"Most of which would not bear the light of day."

"True." He put a powerful arm around her shoulders.

She said, "Of course there is very little wrong with the dark of night."

The everlasting rain beat down on the Ford until the windshield wipers were overwhelmed. Sullivan squinted through the torrent of water and slowed the car to a crawl. This time Morris did not miss the turnoff in the Del Monte Forest.

Jacob Hyche himself opened the tall front door.

"John Morris . . . with my favorite sex symbol." Jacob welcomed them with a handshake gone weak for Morris and a hint of a kiss on Sullivan's cheek. His thatch of gray hair seemed to have turned grayer and his thinness given way to gauntness.

"Well, Morris, it's me who's drowning in 'this dark drama in the Pacific.' "

Morris remembered the exchange from his conversation with Jacob that first night in the Snake Pit. Sullivan had no idea what he was talking about . . . except that Jacob was in deep trouble, as deep as trouble gets.

Sullivan and Morris accepted scotch in a glass. As they lifted their drinks, all three of them looked questioningly at their glasses, then smiled all the way into laughter in spite of themselves.

"Some things you take on faith, old friends," said Jacob, taking the first swallow.

Sullivan was pleased to see that she was still alive after her own first sip.

"Jacob, did you kill Elizabeth?" Morris asked, with no opening small talk.

"No! Great God, no!" Jacob said, more in surprise at the question than in anger. "Nobody ever tolerated me like Elizabeth."

"Why? Why did she tolerate you?" Sullivan asked.

"We were friends. I would like to say we were equals, but Elizabeth was far smarter than me, better educated. God knows she was richer. She loved art. Had a strange fascination for the out-of-doors I found obscene. I love the dark sides of sex she found obscene. We worked it out."

"She wasn't leaving you?" Morris said.

"No. Not so far as I have any idea. She was talking of building a new house. Something less grand. I didn't encourage it. I love the great decadence of her family estate."

"Surely you didn't kill her over the house?" Sullivan

said. She could see fear in the slight trembling of Jacob's hands, which his laid-back voice could not disguise.

"I think I might only ever be able to kill myself," Hyche said. It was startlingly close to Larry Crosby's words, speaking of Jacob's sometimes dark depressions.

"Why did you lie to the inspector about not being in Sidney's room? Before he was killed?" asked Morris.

"When I heard what time he died, I was frightened. I knew I'd been in his room just minutes before he was murdered."

"For a 'friendly talk' about the music for your next movie?"

"Sidney was screaming at me. He thought I had stolen his music in my last film."

"Had you?"

"Well, yes. In a way. His music inspired the theme for the film."

"So you stole it?"

"I'm afraid the courts will say so. You know the courts?"

"Why didn't you pay the man? It couldn't have been a huge expense in a film budget?" Morris said.

"All the expenses, small and large, kept piling up. I overpaid for my lead actress. It's a sin what they demand these days. It's all out of reason. I dreaded going back to Elizabeth for more money. And Sidney wrote the damn music thirty years ago, and it never became popular. But it had an eerie, unnerving quality to it. Exactly what I needed. And I knew he never went to my films."

Morris did not say, "Sidney was standing at the end of a long line." He did say, "So someone told him?"

"No doubt. I was ready to settle. Elizabeth was bailing me out again."

"Can you prove that?"

"No. I only confessed to her this week."

"What was her reaction?"

"Amusement. Everything I did amused her. Sometimes it was annoying how she tolerated me," Jacob admitted.

"Annoying enough to want to stop it forever?" Sullivan said.

"No, if it had come to that, I would have simply left her. I didn't want to leave her. Who would I have gone to? Who would have put up with me, with my work? And I miss her. I did care about her, no matter how imprudent my behavior."

"I guess you have to sell that to the inspector," Sullivan said coldly, feeling sympathy for the man but none for his longtime promiscuous behavior.

"That I can't do," he said. "My only hope is to convince a jury of my peers."

" 'A good scene in a bad movie.' " Morris sent his quote back to him, his own description of McCall's death.

Morris said, "Where were you standing, exactly, on Tuesday night when McCall turned from the bar with his drink in his hand and Sidney first shouted at him?"

"I was nearer the door than the bar," Jacob said. "I was going to my room. I'd left my reading glasses. I'd need them for the restaurant menu. Elizabeth and I were having a late dinner in Carmel."

"Can you prove that? Did you have a reservation for dinner?" Morris asked.

"Yes. We had a reservation. I don't know if I can prove it."

"They might still have Tuesday's reservation list at the restaurant," Sullivan said. "We can find out easily enough. Where was it?"

Jacob identified the same small French restaurant where the two of them had eaten later in the week.

Morris already had the telephone number. "May I use the phone?" he asked.

"Certainly." Jacob was speaking for his very wealthy host, who obviously was not making an appearance.

Morris raised the maître d' and in a surprisingly quick time he confirmed that Jacob Hyche had made a reservation for two for 10:00 P.M. Tuesday, a reservation that he had not kept. There was much indignation in the last of his response.

Morris advised him not to destroy the Tuesday night reservation list as it might be important to a sheriff's investigation. The maître d' showed little interest and did not recognize Jacob's name as the accused felon in the Pebble Beach murders.

"The reservation doesn't prove anything," Morris said, having hung up the phone. "It does lend some credibility to your story. Nothing that a tough-ass prosecuting attorney couldn't rip apart in a few seconds. But it helps me believe in you, Jacob."

"Do you really?" He said it with genuine surprise.

"How near did you get to the red-haired girl, Tana Daly, during the fight?" Morris asked.

"I moved nearer to get a better look. I was amused."

"Could you have touched her?"

"Yes," he said. "I was looking over her shoulder."

Morris winced. "Not a happy proximity."

"My unfortunate luck. But that's where I was standing," Hyche said, running his hand through his thatch of gray hair. "I shouldn't be surprised if they convict me, Morris. For my past sins. I will have to admit to unpaid debts and to many adulterous relationships. And this is powerful Republican country. They won't be tolerant."

"Good for them," Sullivan said, "when it comes to your financial and sexual behavior—not the murder you didn't commit."

Hyche looked at her with more genuine surprise. "You also believe me, Sullivan?"

"Yes. I don't think you loved Elizabeth enough to kill her. You love yourself, Jacob. Your movies prove it. I think that's why I like them so much. They have a seductive passion, even if it's all selfishness and corruption."

"I like that," Jacob said. "I'll steal that . . . should I ever make another film."

Morris made the decision to violate his word to Deputy Jordan and to Sheriff Whitlock. Well, the defense would have to be told sooner or later in discovery, but still, he was going back on his word. What the hell, one man's life was worth one man's word.

"Jacob, when did you spill cyanide on the kitchen floor?" Morris asked.

Jacob looked at him as startled as if he'd been told he'd grown a second nose. "Cyanide? In the lodge suite?"

Morris nodded.

"I never spilled cyanide there. Or anywhere. I never had it in my possession in my life."

"The same as you were not in Sidney's suite just before he died?" Sullivan said.

"No. Not the same as that," Jacob said. "Who found cyanide in our kitchen?"

"Trust me. It was there. On the floor," Morris said. "It may keep you in the state penitentiary for the rest of your unnatural life."

"I didn't spill anything on the kitchen floor," Hyche said. He thought about that for a good two minutes. "There were old friends in and out of our suite every night. Even in the daytime. Some of them went into the kitchen when our bar ran low on tonic water or liquor or ice. Someone almost surely spilled something." He did not have the will to say "cyanide."

"Can you make a list of who came by your suite?" said Morris.

"The police asked me that. I did the best I could. I couldn't begin to remember them all. You know The Crosby, people in and out all week. Old friends, golfers, people I never saw before in my life, Elizabeth's friends on the peninsula who have nothing to do with golf. The only thing I can remember ever being spilled on the kitchen floor was maybe a patch of water."

"When?" Morris asked.

"I have no idea. Surely more than once. You know how it is with people in and out every night, making their own drinks. Getting their own ice."

Morris forgot where he was standing. His thoughts turned back through the three murders. He stabbed his cane on the hardwood floor. *Ice.* The perfectly innocent, portable commodity that could be dropped into any refrigerator or ice bucket, that could find its way into any glass.

"Oh, shit!" Morris said. For a minute so many considerations ran through his head that he was paralyzed to act or even speak.

"What, Morris? What are you thinking?"

Sullivan's voice and touch broke the spell.

"*Ice*, Sullivan. The goddamned ice in McCall's suite, in Sidney's suite, in Jacob's suite. Someone could have come to The Crosby with ice loaded with cyanide. And left it to do its random work in the victims' own refrigerators."

"Is that possible? To freeze it in ice?"

"Why not? A dry powder."

"But it might have killed anybody?"

"It did. It killed Jacob's wife. And not Jacob."

Jacob Hyche looked down at the ice in his drink and shakily set the glass on the table.

Morris nodded, taking Sullivan's own glass from her hand. "It wouldn't be lethal until the ice melted enough to release the cyanide," he said.

"But McCall was poisoned in the Snake Pit. You don't think the bartender killed him?" said Sullivan.

"He had his glass in his hand when he came in the room. Remember? He must have downed his first drink in his suite in an instant. Before the ice had a chance to melt. He even took a quick, safe sip after the bartender refilled the glass. By the end of the fight with Sidney the drink was murderous."

"What other poison ice might be out there, Morris?"

"God knows. Most of the golf pros, amateurs, officials are checking out or have checked out of the lodge. But we better call the manager, Jack Houghton, and warn him. Other people will be checking in. Of course I could be crazier than the killer."

"And who is the killer?" asked Sullivan.

"God knows. Or maybe the devil knows."

Morris got Houghton on the line with the first ring of the phone. The sheriff had vacated Jack's office.

"The ice?" Houghton repeated.

"I know it sounds lunatic," Morris said, "but I swear I think it's possible. It's worth rounding up the ice in every room and suite in the lodge. Any contaminated ice might well be a different size . . . frozen somewhere else."

Houghton hesitated and then said, "I'll put a hold on the ice in the bar and the dining room too. Might as well look like a complete idiot. Better than a fourth dead guest."

"I'll call the sheriff. Ask him for a technician to test the ice," Morris said. "I might as well sound like an idiot to the Monterey County Sheriff's Department."

"Morris, who would do such a thing?"

"Not a question I can answer."

The sheriff was brooding in his office when the phone rang. Quickly Morris explained his fears.

"Morris, are you sober?"

"Unfortunately I am. Or I would be thinking clearer. Tommy, it might save a lot of time testing ice, if your technician looks first for odd-shaped or odd-sized cubes."

"You think our man froze the cyanide in ice cubes and brought it to the lodge?"

"Or our woman," Morris said.

"Where did you get this crazy idea?"

"Something Jacob Hyche just said to me. About drop-in visitors going in the kitchen for their own ice and spilling patches of water on the kitchen floor, where they found the cyanide."

"Jesus Christ, you're asking the man accused of a triple murder to solve it for you."

"Takes one to catch one," Morris said, laughing, not altogether sanely.

"Morris, goddammit, you've broken your word. Disclosed critical evidence in a murder investigation."

"I know. It seemed the thing to do. You don't want a fourth death."

"Morris, if you make me look like God's last fool . . ."

"Join the club," Morris said.

Hanging up the phone, he had the sinking feeling of the boy who cried wolf when the wolf wasn't there.

"Morris, who else might be a logical target?" asked Sullivan.

He thought about it. "Damn. Johnny Miller, for sure. If you want to destroy a tournament, kill the man who won it. And this is so close to his home, I doubt Johnny's left the peninsula. Sullivan, call Houghton. Or his secretary. Find where Miller is staying. Get word to him not to drink or serve anything with ice in it."

"Done," she said.

Morris said to Jacob, "Look, bastard, don't tell me it's you who has been custom-freezing the ice?"

He shook his head no. He opened his mouth as if he needed more oxygen. "I had a scotch on the rocks in Sidney's room. I lived. How do you explain that?"

"The randomness of one or more cubes of ice," Morris said. "The killer had a macabre sense of humor. Playing Russian roulette with ice cubes." When he heard himself say it aloud, it sounded indeed like a lunatic idea. Morris had the sinking feeling he was losing it. Crosby, the great sportsman, would hunt him like a quail in the air if he stirred up the population for nothing after all that Pebble Beach had suffered.

"Crosby! Godamighty!" Morris said. If you wanted to destroy a golf tournament totally, *kill the man it was named after*.

"Is there another phone line?" Morris asked Hyche, who was standing watching his drink, now untasted on the table, the ice rapidly melting into the scotch.

Morris snatched up the telephone in the library, dialed the operator, and put in a call for the Peninsula Hospital in Burlingame. It only took forever. The hospital director was not in and could not be reached. Crosby's doctor was in surgery, wouldn't be available for a couple of hours. Morris was finally connected with the chief nurse, who had a dozen crises on her hands and could not grasp what he was saying about poisoned ice, perhaps killing three people at The Crosby Pro-Am.

"We've had no cases of it," she said, as if he were taking a survey of local hospitals.

Morris gritted his teeth. "No, no," he said. "I'm concerned about your patient Mr. Bing Crosby."

"Mr. Crosby does not suffer from poisoning of any

kind." The chief nurse was indignant and certain that Morris was some form of kook.

"Wait, wait," Morris said as she slammed down the receiver.

"Shit!" It seemed the only word to fit the occasion.

Sullivan came out of the library. "I spoke with Johnny. You could hear the victory party going on in the background. Everything but the clink of ice. But he understood what we fear might have happened. And he's locking up the ice. Just in case. Of course, Johnny, the serious Mormon, will be serving Cokes."

"Good work. For God's sake, try your charm on the Peninsula Hospital." He handed her the number. "The director's out. Crosby's doctor is in surgery. The chief nurse thinks I am certifiably insane. And maybe I am. I'm going to jump in the car and beat it over there. You try to make somebody understand not to let Crosby drink anything with ice in it. Especially if he's had any recent visitors."

Sullivan picked up the phone and began dialing.

Morris pointed to Hyche. "Take her where she wants to go, old man. Most likely to the lodge. Whoever you might have killed, it wouldn't do to lay a hand on Julia Sullivan. Not in this life or the next one."

Odd, Morris felt little discomfort in leaving Sullivan in the house with an accused triple murderer. "Careful," he told himself, "don't let your instincts overwhelm logic." But what about his life, or Sullivan's, had ever been logical?

Morris gunned the rental Ford through the rain. It would be a miracle if the sheriff's boys didn't stop him, the fierce time he was making over the slick pavement. Jesus, he should have thought to call the sheriff. Tommy could rush somebody to the hospital. With any luck, Sullivan would think of it if the chief nurse continued to stonewall.

Morris's stiff left leg was on fire by the time he pulled into Burlingame and the Peninsula Hospital. And the rain had begun to fall again with a vengeance.

A sheriff's car was parked at an acute angle to the entrance to the hospital, its headlights on in the rain, as if it had been abandoned in an emergency. Steam still rose off the hood. The car could not have been left there longer than a few minutes.

Oh, Lord, thought Morris. He poled his way up the steps, careless of the rain smashing into his hair and face. He did not stop at the receptionist's desk. Visiting hours be damned. He knew where Crosby lay on the second floor and ignored the voice calling after him as the elevator door closed behind him.

Two sheriff's deputies were standing at the door to Crosby's room, their hands and arms awkwardly at their sides. A large woman, swathed in white, who had to be the chief nurse, stood defiantly before them.

Morris did not slow his pace but poled himself around the two stymied deputies and the bulldog nurse into the room he knew to be Crosby's. Crosby in fact had propped himself up against two pillows and was lifting a water glass off the small bedside table. Morris left his feet, making a gargantuan belly flop against the bed that would have done justice to a drunken sea lion, sending the bed and patient screeching against the near wall. With his cane, Morris knocked the glass out of

Crosby's hand as smoothly as Johnny Miller exploding a golf ball from a sand bunker. Glass, water, and ice smashed into the same near wall. Crosby, forgetting his illness, sat straight up in the bed, grabbed Morris by the vast label of his jacket, and drew back his own sizable fist to let him have one between the eyes.

"Good Lord, John Morris! What the hell are you doing?" Crosby, reared back in his bed, looked at Morris as if he had chosen him as his fourth murder victim.

The two deputies scrambled into the room, the short one drawing his revolver. The tall, heavy one dragged Morris to his feet, his cane clattering onto the tile floor.

The chief nurse swarmed after them, as stout as a pulling guard for the 49ers, pointing a hefty finger more serious than the deputy's handgun in Morris's face.

"I'm John Morris of the Associated Press—"

"You're a crazy son of a bitch," said the tall, heavy deputy, tightening his grip on Morris's two arms.

The large nurse opened her mouth as if she might bite him.

"Did Julia Sullivan call you?" Morris asked the deputies between heavy breaths, only now realizing how winded he was.

"Some nutty dame called the sheriff's office. What's it to you?" said the short deputy, reluctant to holster his weapon.

"I know Sheriff Tommy Whitlock, an old friend," said Morris.

The deputies were not convinced.

"The three victims at the Del Monte Lodge," Morris said, recovering his breath, "there's a chance the killer salted their ice cubes with cyanide. And the victims dropped the ice in their drinks, suspecting nothing. I feared the ice in Crosby's water pitcher."

Crosby, his energy exhausted, sank back onto his bed, pale and thin and fevered and aged without his hairpiece. He looked like a man who would gladly take any poison offered to him. He turned his watery eyes on the overturned pitcher as if it might open its mouth and confess.

"I could be nuts," Morris admitted. Now the tall, heavy deputy loosened his grip on his arms, and the short deputy grudgingly holstered his gun. "It occurred to me if the scotch wasn't poisoned, and the tonic wasn't poisoned, and the water wasn't poisoned, maybe it was the ice in the glass of the victims that held the cyanide."

"That's a reach, old man." Crosby's voice sounded worse than he looked.

"You may be right," Morris said, looking at the banks of flowers in the room with get well cards from all over the world. "Who's been to see you today?"

"My boy Phil Harris. He's only trying to kill the telecast." Crosby, a shadow of his old roll-with-the-punches self, tried to laugh and wound up coughing. He recovered his breath. "Larry dropped by, of course. My wife. I'm not supposed to have visitors."

"I know," Morris apologized.

"A couple of old friends. My agent. He owes me money." Coughs again, instead of laughs, racked his lungs.

"Gentlemen, out, out!" The nurse's battering-ram voice let it be known that she wasn't buying the lunatic "ice story" and considered them all to be anything but gentlemen.

"Any other visitors?" Morris asked Crosby, with the nurse's strong hand in his unyielding back.

"Only my old piano pal Jackie Melton. Good for laughs . . . even from a dying man," said Crosby, effecting an honest smile.

Morris stood like a stone wall, the nurse's strong hand helpless against his solid back. *Jackie Melton.*

"Did he have—was he carrying anything?" Morris asked.

"Sure. Flowers." Crosby waved his hand at the mass of them in the room.

"Anything else?"

Crosby, weakly but determinedly, propped himself up again. He said, "Only a briefcase. Still scared to let his music . . . out of his sight."

"Did he drink any water?" Morris asked.

Crosby ran his hand over his hot forehead. "Yep. He did. Asked if he could 'borrow some water . . . not enough was falling on the peninsula.' Same old Jackie. You don't—"

"I don't know," Morris said, but sick with fright that he did. "How long has he been gone?"

"Not twenty minutes," said Crosby, looking at the clock on the table. "He must have . . . passed you on the road."

Morris picked up the pitcher, still rattling with half-melted ice. He tilted the wide-mouthed pitcher this way and that. Most of the ice had been frozen in perfectly symmetrical cubes. Floating among them, less melted, were a couple of cubes that were actually crescents, like quarter moons melting into the bottom of the pitcher.

Morris said to the tall deputy, "Don't let this pitcher out of your sight, no matter what. Don't let anybody touch it or, for God's sake, drink out of it."

The tall deputy nodded, taking the pitcher in his own wide hands.

The chief nurse stood, still defiant but altogether confused.

Crosby said, "Morris . . . don't . . . let it be Jackie. An old . . . song and dance pal . . . since vaudeville."

"Whoever—it's not the man you remember," said Morris, turning for the door. He grabbed the phone at the nurses' station without asking. He guessed Sullivan would be at the lodge. The front desk paged her until she came to the phone, oddly enough in the dining room kitchen.

Morris explained what he thought had happened in Crosby's hospital room and described what was left of the two half-moon cubes of ice in the pitcher.

"Thank God he hadn't drunk the water," she said.

"While you're thanking Him, also thank the two deputies for not shooting me. Was it you who called the sheriff's office?"

"Yes. But not at first. The chief nurse was not friendly but did say she would double-check Mr. Crosby's room, empty any ice or ice water in it, and call me back. I kept waiting. I didn't trust her, the way she blew me off. I tried to call her back. She wouldn't come to the phone. I finally decided to call Tommy. But he wasn't in. I did catch Deputy Jordan. And she called the deputies near Burlingame.

"You're sure you're okay?" Sullivan said.

"Oh, yeah. The old pump must be good for another twenty minutes."

"They've collected most of the ice in the lodge," Sullivan said. "But, Morris, tell me it's not Jackie"—she was near to crying—"my old piano buddy."

"You sound like Crosby," Morris said. "A man who kills three people is nobody's buddy. He's very likely headed to the lodge. He doesn't know we're looking for him. You stay away from him, Sullivan, until I get there. But keep trying to reach our friend the sheriff. He deserves to be the man who confronts Jackie. Not the goddamn inspector. Remember, this is a dangerous man. Don't doubt that. I'm leaving right now."

Morris hung up before she could answer.

The short deputy, somewhat embarrassed at having pulled his gun, offered to drive him back to Pebble Beach and the Del Monte Lodge and have the rental car sent over. Morris gladly took him up on it, fitting himself in the front seat of the patrol car, which howled through the rain as if searching for its mate.

Julia Sullivan hung up the phone. She was standing in the kitchen, watching the deputies store ice in the walk-in freezer. Each batch of it was marked as to the room or suite from which it came. She dialed the sheriff's office again and then his home, but he was neither place. She left emergency word at both locations for him to call her. She rang Patricia Jordan at her office thirty miles away and told her what had happened at the hospital.

Sullivan explained that she and Morris wanted the sheriff to confront Jackie Melton and not Inspector Gooden, who was taking bows from the press for having closed the case.

"I'll round up Tommy if I have to ring every phone on the Monterey Peninsula. You be careful. You do nothing until we get there," said Patricia.

Sullivan promised exactly that: nothing. And hung up the phone.

She immediately tried Jackie Melton's suite. No one answered. She checked her watch. If Jackie had been headed for the lodge, he should be here by now.

She left the dining room kitchen and walked through the main lodge toward the annex, seeking, perhaps, happier times. She heard the piano before she opened the door to the Snake Pit. The Pit was strangely empty except for the short, plump man sitting at the piano, with his hair spilling in blond waves of artificial youth above his round blue eyes and pudge of a nose and pouting mouth of a cherub, his hands moving over the keys drawing out notes like old memories. A full glass of scotch on the rocks rested on top of the piano.

She was well into the room before he saw her. Words joined with the music, and Jackie sang in his flawless tenor, " 'Tonight while the lights are shining/And the microphone is on/I'll play for you,/So many will be the blessings/And so short will be the time/I'll stay with you.' " He sang as if to some unseen beauty, surely "my Mary," as he always called her.

Sullivan walked directly to the piano bench and sat

down beside him. She was not afraid. She could not help the tears in her eyes.

His plump fingers led the way for the words. " 'You can say that I'm your friend,/You can see my life begin and end,/I'll always play for you.' "

"Oh, God, Jackie, why?" Sullivan said, the tears slipping down her cheeks.

His fingers wandered more quietly among the music, as if feeling for the answer.

"Nobody," he said softly, as though whispering to a small clutch of regulars in a long-vanished piano bar, "was ever going to step on Jackie again." Notes without melodies clashed in the air and receded into a soft murmur.

"You hated them all that much?" Sullivan did not wipe away the tears.

"Not Elizabeth. But she took her chances living with Jacob, who stole my music." The dark theme from Hyche's last movie insinuated itself into the air, all power and corruption, and then fell away.

"Sidney loved you, the way Morris and I love you, the way everybody loves you."

Dancing up from the piano was the theme to America's favorite late-night talk show, as if the famous host himself were about to step into the Snake Pit and bow and start his celebrated monologue.

Sullivan suddenly remembered. She said, over the music, "You told me *you* wrote the music for the talk show. I wasn't listening. Not even when Sidney said it was his. None of us was listening. And McCall killing your music for his ads. Not even the bastard McCall deserved to die." Tears were splashing on her collar.

Fingers summoned up the sprightly GE television ad that McCall had canceled.

"McCall! A liar. A cheat. A bully. A coward. A seducer of young girls. Dead. And good riddance. 'Hear the band/Hear the band,/Won't you let the music take you.'" Jackie sang with every cynicism.

Sullivan wiped the tears from her cheeks with both hands, her voice equally unforgiving. "Your oldest friend Crosby? Helpless in his bed?"

Jackie's sad, perfect tenor led his fingers into the old Irish ballad Crosby lifted into popularity. His clear voice was amazingly without regret.

The music sank, and Jackie said, "I was already the Man in vaudeville when the Rhythm Boys failed in New York. Radio found me first. He took away all my sponsors. I made the first movie . . . three movies . . . before he shut me out at Paramount. He threw me bones in bad *Road* movies." His words were as dark as the notes drowning the Pit. "I got rich in spite of him. But now I play dull music every night for a stand-up comedian. And I lost my Mary. Then he took away my golf tournament. The one thing I loved that lasted since 1937. Damn him to hell." There was no doubting the black fury of the music Sullivan did not know.

When it receded, she said, herself without mercy, "Crosby is alive and knows what you've done. Morris got to him in time. Now the sheriff is coming for you, Jackie. I wish I could say I'm sorry."

As he sat right beside her, their shoulders still touching, his faultless tenor lifted into his own song that Crosby always requested and joined in: "'Listen to my heart . . . beat for you alone . . . all the reason why

. . . I can still go on. . . .' " The words gave way only to the notes, and the notes to silence. "Except I can't," he said.

Jackie lifted the glass of scotch and melted ice from the top of the piano.

Sullivan made no effort to stop him.

He tipped the glass toward her and said, "Good-bye, so long, and farewell," and took a large swallow and instantly choked. He dropped the glass and fell forward off the bench, collapsing into the piano, making a last, ghastly clash of notes, before slumping onto the floor.

Sullivan stood, listening for his ragged breaths until they mercifully had stopped.

Epilogue

Julia Sullivan sat facing the Pacific Ocean, dark as the void. Everlasting rain beat against the window as if the three-fourths of the earth that lay in water were pounding to be let inside. She sat so quietly John Morris touched her hand to be sure she was still among them. Lovers Tommy Whitlock and Patricia Jordan would not have missed her if she had changed forms and whirled away into smoke. The ruins of their dinner lay before them, proof that tragedy did not alter time, not so much as to dampen mankind's appetite for clams.

Into the silence Morris said, "Sullivan, I know you pretty well. I've never known you to back away from a challenge. But I still can't believe you sat down on the piano bench beside a triple murderer." He said it quietly. The couple at the next table might have imagined he was commenting on the blue sweater that went very well with her eyes.

"Excuse me, Morris, but didn't you leave me on the telephone, standing next to a man *charged* with triple murder?" Sullivan said it quietly, as if recalling the shop where she bought the sweater.

"We both knew Jacob Hyche didn't kill his wife, couldn't kill anything except an innocent movie audience."

"*We* did not include the Monterey County Sheriff's Department," Sullivan said, pointing her napkin at the two lovers holding hands under the table.

Whitlock looked up at the word *sheriff's*, as if he suddenly realized that he and Deputy Jordan were not sitting alone on a rock in Point Lobo State Reserve.

Whitlock said, "Now, Sullivan, you can't hold the entire sheriff's department accountable for the action of one *ex*-employee."

"You mean Inspector Stanley Gooden has resigned his job?"

"Oh, no. I kicked his ass off the payroll. We'll be lucky if Jacob Hyche doesn't sue us for false arrest for enough to pay for his next motion picture."

"That's a depressing thought," Morris said. "But I've spoken with Jacob. He isn't suing anybody. Whatever he might need in this world, it isn't money. Not anymore. He couldn't believe Jackie would try to kill him and end up killing Elizabeth, over unwanted music Jackie wrote thirty years ago."

"Steal a man's music, you might as well steal his soul," Sullivan said. "Jacob can't excuse himself entirely for what happened. Neither could Andrew McCall, or even Sidney Barker, if they were alive."

"And Crosby?" Morris said.

"America loves him. It always has, since he left the Rhythm Boys and vaudeville, for radio and then the movies and TV. You can't hold Crosby responsible for that. However much his career might have hurt Jackie's."

"I spoke with Crosby," Morris said. "In truth he hated it. I don't think Jackie had any idea how much Crosby cared for him . . . and their old golfing days together. Crosby can be a tough cookie. You don't survive all those decades in show business as some kind of happy soufflé. But he wept over Jackie."

The entire restaurant fell curiously silent, as if it understood what had been said at the table.

"What did you find in Jackie's suite?" Morris asked the sheriff.

"Half the ice cubes in his refrigerator were poisoned. He brought them from his house in L.A. in a portable freezer. We found the freezer in the trunk of his car. He had a half-empty bottle of cyanide in the kitchen of his house. We have no idea when or where he got it. He must have been planning it for some time. He left a new will with his lawyers a month ago. We haven't read it yet. Apparently he didn't expect to survive the week."

Tommy continued, "He added the cyanide through a simple soda straw as the ice cubes hardened. He made no effort to hide the cyanide, the straw, the poisoned cubes. Of course, when the ice melted in a glass . . ."

"Swallow, you're dead!" Morris said.

"We found poisoned cubes in two of the players' refrigerators," said Patricia. "Thank God neither they nor their wives ever used them. Best they never know how close they came to tragedy."

"Tell us again, Sullivan, exactly what Jackie said before he killed himself." Morris looked at her with every expectation, as if he could *see* the words that she remembered. The two lovers, still holding hands, also watched for what she said.

Sullivan folded her own hands and re-created the entire incident in the Snake Pit, as if it were a drama that she had seen on the stage, rather than been cast in—with a speaking part. She would never forget the look of Jackie Melton at the piano and the exact words he sang to the music his hands played of their own volition. She recited it all, to the glass of scotch and melting ice on top of the piano.

" 'Nobody was ever going to step on Jackie again,' " she repeated, whispering the words that now lay on the table with the ruins of their dinner.

Sullivan concluded the scene, saying, "He sat there, in some ways the same old Jackie, my piano buddy these past few years in the Snake Pit . . . his short, plump body, his wavy blond hair. But his eyes and his hands were somewhere else. He looked *through* me. His hands *drove* the music out of the piano; even the old melodies seemed possessed.

"His money meant nothing to him. He'd lost Mary long ago. McCall he'd hated all those years, and now McCall was stabbing him in the back one more time, killing his television ad. His old friend Jacob, robbing his music for his movie. Even Sidney, whom he loved, copyrighting in his own name the theme song of 'America's favorite TV talk show,' which he lifted from Jackie. All the old grievances against Crosby rose up inside him. Losing out to him on radio, and at Paramount, on television. . . ."

Morris said, "And then Crosby asked him to give up playing in his golf tournament. Crosby meant no harm by it. He himself gave up playing in the Pro-Am in 1957, the old guys giving way to the new generation. To him it was a natural thing."

Morris shifted the unclean plates in front of him, as if he could read them like tea leaves. "I should have known how much not playing hurt Jackie when I saw him before the tournament started . . . out on the practice tee . . . in the rain . . . with one club . . . to strike his last ball at The Crosby. I remember he watched the ball in the air as if seeing his own youth falling from the wet sky, and he kept watching long after the ball was on the ground. Later, over Bloody Marys, he loved telling about the old days at The Crosby before World War Two. Those days seemed more alive to him than the Bloody Marys in our glasses. All that affection turned to hatred. How could that be?" Morris said.

None of them, not even the high sheriff, offered an answer.

Morris said, "He wanted to destroy them individually, and if some innocent person drank from the wrong glass, so be it. No worse than blind fate had treated him. Crosby was right all along: Jackie meant to destroy him and, with him, his tournament."

"I didn't know who he was at the last," Sullivan said.

"I sat next to him, touching shoulders, and he wasn't Jackie Melton."

Morris did not say, "Did you consider knocking over his glass?"

Sullivan answered his unspoken question. "I knew what was in the glass when he picked it up. I'd seen it when I first stepped in the room, but the fact of it didn't hit me. It did, when he lifted the glass. 'Good-bye, so long, and farewell,' " she repeated. "Only at that moment was there a vestige of the Jackie Melton we all knew. I didn't try to rob him of it. Although God knows it couldn't undo what he had done."

Brandy came in place of dessert.

"Enough of death," Sullivan said. "To the high sheriff and the deputy. May you rule over the peninsula."

They all drank to that.

"Watch your speed when you drive through Monterey," Patricia said. "I'm applying for a job with the police department."

"Why not here in Carmel?" Morris said.

"I don't need a designer police job," she said. "I prefer the old, faded criminal ways."

"She's also moving in with the sheriff," said Whitlock. "Anybody who wants to run against that in the next election has my blessing."

"Morris, are you game for the challenge?" Sullivan asked.

"No. I could never give up the golfing wars for mere public misbehavior."

"To next year's Crosby," Sullivan said, lifing her glass.

It was a popular toast.

* * *

Sullivan stopped the rental Ford at an overlook in Big Sur. "I didn't get you so near to heaven as I had hoped."

"No," Morris said.

"I think it's a sin. But I'll miss Jackie the most of them all."

"He was gone before he was dead."

"Could it ever happen to us that we wake up one day murderous?"

"I don't think so," Morris said, "but when it's time for drinks, I'll get the ice."

Sullivan laughed and sounded the horn into the silence, as if it were laughing too at fate.

"What about next year?" she said. "Will the tournament play on?"

"Sure. But the old guard grows older. It can't go on forever." They could not know how soon forever would come.

Still, the rain beat against the windshield, and the mountains rolled down to the fog and the Pacific Ocean as if they'd come on an earthquake.

Match wits with the best-selling

MYSTERY WRITERS

in the business!

SUSAN DUNLAP

"Dunlap's police procedurals have the authenticity of telling detail."
—*The Washington Post Book World*

☐	AS A FAVOR	20999-4	$4.99
☐	ROGUE WAVE	21197-2	$4.99
☐	DEATH AND TAXES	21406-8	$4.99
☐	HIGHFALL	21560-9	$5.50

SARA PARETSKY

"Paretsky's name always makes the top of the list when people talk about the new female operatives." —*The New York Times Book Review*

☐	BLOOD SHOT	20420-8	$6.99
☐	BURN MARKS	20845-9	$6.99
☐	INDEMNITY ONLY	21069-0	$6.99
☐	GUARDIAN ANGEL	21399-1	$6.99
☐	KILLING ORDERS	21528-5	$6.99
☐	DEADLOCK	21332-0	$6.99
☐	TUNNEL VISION	21752-0	$6.99

SISTER CAROL ANNE O'MARIE

"Move over Miss Marple..." —*San Francisco Sunday Examiner & Chronicle*

☐	ADVENT OF DYING	10052-6	$4.99
☐	THE MISSING MADONNA	20473-9	$4.99
☐	A NOVENA FOR MURDER	16469-9	$4.99
☐	MURDER IN ORDINARY TIME	21353-3	$4.99
☐	MURDER MAKES A PILGRIMAGE	21613-3	$4.99

LINDA BARNES

☐	COYOTE	21089-5	$4.99
☐	STEEL GUITAR	21268-5	$4.99
☐	BITTER FINISH	21606-0	$4.99
☐	SNAPSHOT	21220-0	$5.99

Dell

At your local bookstore or use this handy page for ordering:

DELL READERS SERVICE, DEPT. DIS
2451 South Wolf Road, Des Plaines, IL . 60018
Please send me the above title(s). I am enclosing $_____
(Please add $2.50 per order to cover shipping and handling.) Send
check or money order—no cash or C.O.D.s please.

Ms./Mrs./Mr. _____

Address _____

City/State _____ Zip _____

DGM-8/96

Prices and availability subject to change without notice. Please allow four to six weeks for delivery.